Lyn Andrews

EVERY MOTHER'S SON

headline

First published in Great Britain in 2005 by
HEADLINE PUBLISHING GROUP

First published in this paperback edition in 2016 by
HEADLINE PUBLISHING GROUP

1

Cataloguing in Publication Data is available from the British Library

ISBN 978 1 4722 3776 7

Typeset in Janson by Avon DataSet Ltd, Bidford-on-Avon, Warwickshire

Printed and bound by CPI Group (UK) Ltd, Croydon, CR0 4YY

FSC www.fsc.org
MIX
Paper from responsible sources
FSC® C104740

Headline's policy is to use papers that are natural, renewable and recyclable products and made from wood grown in well-managed forests and other controlled sources. The logging and manufacturing processes are expected to conform to the environmental regulations of the country of origin.

HEADLINE PUBLISHING GROUP
An Hachette UK Company
Carmelite House
50 Victoria Embankment
London EC4Y 0DZ

www.headline.co.uk
www.hachette.co.uk

2017

Lyn Andrews was born in Liverpool in September 1943. Her father was killed on D-Day when Lyn was just nine months old. When Lyn was three her mother Monica married Frank Moore, who became 'Dad' to the little girl. Lyn was brought up in Liverpool and became a secretary before marrying policeman Bob Andrews. In 1970 Lyn gave birth to triplets – two sons and a daughter – who kept her busy for the next few years. Once they'd gone to school Lyn began writing, and her first novel was quickly accepted for publication. She has since written a further thirty-six novels.

Lyn lived for eleven years in Ireland and is now resident on the Isle of Man, but spends as much time as possible back on Merseyside, seeing her children and four grandchildren.

Praise for Lyn Andrews' compelling sagas:

'An outstanding storyteller' *Woman's Weekly*

'A vivid portrayal of life' *Best*

'A compelling read' *Woman's Own*

'The Catherine Cookson of Liverpool' *Northern Echo*

'Gutsy . . . A vivid picture of a hard-up hard-working community . . . will keep the pages turning' *Daily Express*

By Lyn Andrews

Maggie May
The Leaving Of Liverpool
Liverpool Lou
The Sisters O'Donnell
The White Empress
Ellan Vannin
Mist Over The Mersey
Mersey Blues
Liverpool Songbird
Liverpool Lamplight
Where The Mersey Flows
From This Day Forth
When Tomorrow Dawns
Angels Of Mercy
The Ties That Bind
Take These Broken Wings
My Sister's Child
The House On Lonely Street
Love And A Promise
A Wing And A Prayer
When Daylight Comes
Across A Summer Sea
A Mother's Love
Friends Forever
Every Mother's Son
Far From Home
Days Of Hope
A Daughter's Journey
A Secret In The Family
To Love And To Cherish
Beyond A Misty Shore
Sunlight On The Mersey
Liverpool Angels
Heart And Home

For my dear Aunt and Uncle, Celia and Denise Ormesher, thank you for always being there for me.

Lyn Andrews
Tullamore, 2005

PART I

Chapter One

Liverpool, 1935

'NO! THAT WILL NOT do at all! The colours are all wrong; they make the room look so cold and uninviting! Take them down!' Vera Hesketh's aggrieved and imperious tone caused Molly to turn and stare at her in astonishment.

'But, Mrs Hesketh, they are the colours you insisted on having for the curtains. *And* the pelmet and the cushion covers . . .' Astonishment was now giving way to mild exasperation, obvious in Molly Keegan's eyes as she looked at the older woman's face, which was set in lines of discontent.

At twenty-four Molly was an attractive young woman: tall and slim with short wavy auburn hair – which she likened in moments of despair to a 'furze bush' – grey-green eyes and a pale, almost milky-white complexion. Now her forehead was creased in a puzzled frown. She had spent hours and hours making the soft furnishings for this room. She had only recently given up her full-time job in Frisby Dyke's, the large department store on Lord Street, where she had been Assistant Manageress of the soft furnishing department, and started up her own soft furnishing business. She had been so glad of this 'commission', as she called it. Vera Hesketh was a wealthy, if difficult and demanding, woman with a large Victorian house in an affluent part of Southport. Molly's very first commission had been to make curtains for Vera's sister Maud, but that had been years ago when going into business for herself had been little more than a pipe dream.

'But I had no idea at all that *this* would be the result! I couldn't live with all this depressing *coldness*!' Vera declared adamantly.

'I did point out that using blue in a north-facing room that gets very little sunlight was not a good idea, especially with that white embossed wallpaper,' Molly reminded her. She had brought swatches of material for the woman to choose from, for heaven's sake, she thought.

'I suppose you did but the material looked so nice, so rich in a smaller piece. You'll have to take them back and I'll choose something else. Oh, it's all going to take so long and I really did want this room finished for November. It's Richard's fiftieth birthday and we're having a very grand dinner party,' Vera replied petulantly.

'Mrs Hesketh, just what am I supposed to do with it all? The curtains were made to measure; they won't fit other windows,' Molly pleaded. She could hardly afford to bear the cost of the yards and yards of pale blue corded marocain, to say nothing of the lining or the fringe.

'Oh, I'm sure that someone as talented as yourself can alter them to fit someone else's windows, and I have paid you part of your fee, as a gesture of good faith. So you can take them back and bring me some more swatches so I can choose something with more warmth to it.' Vera moved towards the door of the room as an indication that the matter was closed. There would be no further discussion or argument.

Molly bit her lip; she needed the work. If she flatly refused to take back the soft furnishings there would be a huge row and she certainly wouldn't be recommended to any of Vera Hesketh's friends and acquaintances. She relied heavily on such recommendations.

She sighed as she took down the scalloped pelmet and heavy curtains, stripped off the matching cushion covers, folded them all and then wrapped them up in the thick brown paper in which she'd brought them. They were heavy and she was glad that Joe had said he'd come and meet her.

She shrugged on her dark green three-quarter-length jacket and crossed to the ornate mirror above the fireplace to put on the black velour hat with its two bottle-green feathers. She adjusted it and then sighed again at her reflection. She looked tired, she thought. Tired and 'as cross as a bag of cats' as her mother, Ita, would have said. Her expression became wistful as she remembered the farmhouse in rural Ireland where she'd been brought up. Her mam would have told her to 'count her blessings' and not let the likes of Vera Hesketh upset her so.

Molly had come to Liverpool when she'd been just seventeen years old with Bernie O'Sullivan. They had been friends since childhood and were nigh on inseparable. Neither of them had had jobs to go to and if they hadn't been promised lodgings by a cousin of Bernie's da, Ita would never have let her come at all. She'd been fortunate to get the job at Frisby Dyke's, one of Liverpool's larger department stores, and had worked her way up. Now she had her own business. Yes, she should count her blessings. She gave the hat a final pat and picked up the heavy parcel.

Vera Hesketh's maid of all work was waiting in the hall.

'Will you tell Herself I'll bring up some more swatches at the weekend?' Molly asked as the girl opened the heavy front door for her.

'Doesn't she like the new curtains?' the girl asked in a whisper.

'She does not!' Molly replied.

The girl raised her eyes to the ceiling. 'Sure, there's no pleasing some people!' she hissed, sympathetic to her countrywoman, as she came originally from County Cavan herself.

As she reached the end of the gravelled drive Molly was relieved to see the tall, well-built figure of Joe Jackson leaning against the lamppost on the opposite side of the road. He crossed to meet her and she managed a smile.

'Have you been there long? What time did you finish work?'

He smiled back and took the parcel from her. 'Not long and I finished my shift at seven. What's the matter? Why are you bringing this lot home? I thought they were finished?'

Molly fell into step beside him and slipped her arm through his. They had been walking out for five years now but she had known him since she was eighteen. 'They are finished but she doesn't like them. It's the colour; she said it makes the room look cold.'

'But she chose that colour; you told me she was insistent.'

'She was but now she hates it. It *does* look awful but I did warn her. I can't afford to lose her custom or any recommendations but God alone knows what I'm going to do with that lot! Hours and hours of work to say nothing of the expense and now I have to do it all again!'

'You don't have to, Moll. You can tell her to go to hell or get them made in one of the shops and pay a small fortune.'

Molly nodded slowly, understanding what he meant. Twice he'd asked her to marry him and twice she'd put him off. She did love him, she'd told herself, but did she love him enough to spend the rest of her life with him?

Oh, he was steady and reliable; he was a constable in the Liverpool City Police. He was kind and generous and quite good-looking with his dark brown hair and eyes and open features.

'You need never be at the beck and call of anyone. You wouldn't want for anything, Moll.'

'I know that, Joe, but I'm so tired and a little cross and I don't want to start arguing with you and saying things I'll regret.'

They had reached the station and as there wasn't a train due for another ten minutes they walked in silence along the platform and Molly sat down on one of the wooden benches. Joe put the parcel down and sat beside her. She did look tired and she was obviously upset by Vera Hesketh's behaviour. He put his arm around her comfortingly. There had really never been anyone else for him; he'd been fond of her from the moment he'd set eyes on her all those years ago. All he wanted was to make her happy, give her a life free of worry and hardship, yet he admired her ambition and her independence. He wondered if it was right to ask her to give it all up.

'Will you be very much out of pocket, Moll?'

'Not really. I suppose I can remake the curtains to fit someone else's window. It's just the time it takes.'

Joe nodded. 'Have you the time to come to a dance with me on Sunday night? There's a social at the Police Club. A dance with a bit of supper thrown in.'

Molly tried to shrug off her mood. 'I'd like that.

It's ages since I've been to a dance of any kind.'

'Good. I'll pick you up at about half past seven. It's about time you enjoyed yourself; you've been working too hard lately.'

Molly smiled up at him. 'I have to warn you that I might not be all sweetness and light. I promised I'd take Herself back there some more swatches at the weekend.'

'Then you'll definitely need taking out of yourself.' He pulled her to her feet as they heard the unmistakable sound of a train approaching.

A bitterly cold wind had got up by the time they got off the train and Molly pulled her coat collar up around her neck. Joe put his arm around her shoulders again and drew her closer to him as they walked towards Arnot Street in Walton where Molly and Bernie lived. The houses there were of the Edwardian terrace type and all were kept neat and tidy.

'Are you coming in?' Molly asked as they reached number three.

'If I do I won't get out for hours and I'm on an early shift tomorrow, so I'll see you on Sunday evening.'

Molly nodded and reached up and kissed him on the cheek.

'Is that all I get after dragging this lot all the way from Southport?' Joe laughed.

'Sure, I'm not fit company for anyone tonight! Thank you.' She apologised and kissed him properly.

'That's better. I love you, Molly.'

She stroked his cheek gently. 'And I love you, Joe Jackson. Now, off home with you and I'll see you on Sunday evening at half past seven.'

She struggled up the narrow lobby with the parcel and finally managed to open the kitchen door and dump the offending furnishings down on the kitchen table.

Bernie looked up in surprise. She was sitting at the table, where she had spent most of the evening trying to master the intricacies of crocheting. She was the same age as Molly but much shorter. She always used to be plumper than her friend but had lost the chubbiness she'd had in her late teens. Now she called herself 'petite': a description she'd read in a women's magazine and which she thought sounded much better than 'small', which was how Tess, her mother, described her. Her dark brown hair was thick and shiny and cut in a neat bob just below her ears. It was she who'd originally pushed for them to leave Ireland and come to Liverpool in search of a better future – which they had found, but not without heartbreak along the way.

'Did you not go out to Southport after all?' she enquired, her blue eyes questioning as she looked from Molly to the brown paper parcel.

'I did so.'

Bernie put down the wool and the crochet hook. 'And?'

'And she doesn't like them. "The colours are all wrong; they make the room look so cold and uninviting! Take them down!"' Molly mimicked Vera's tones.

'Ah, Moll, no!' Bernie exclaimed.

There was a sudden snort from the other occupant of the room: a small lady well into her seventies, with silver-grey hair confined in a neat bun at the nape of her neck. 'I'd say that is a very good imitation of my daughter's la-di-da tone!' Augusta Hayes put in acerbically.

The girls had lodged with Mrs Hayes for seven years and had grown fond of her; so fond that they now called her 'Aunt'. Vera and Maud Hesketh were the old lady's estranged daughters. 'And I don't suppose she paid you?'

Molly took off her coat and hat. 'No, she didn't. She did point out that she had already paid me part of my fee and, well, I need the work and isn't the customer always right?'

Augusta busied herself with the kettle and teapot. 'The customer in this case is a spoiled, snobbish eejit, as you girls would say! The choice of colour was hers and if she doesn't like the finished result she has no one but herself to blame.'

'I did warn her. The room is north facing.'

'She has no taste, that's her trouble. And for all her airs and graces you can't make a silk purse out of a sow's ear! You should have refused to take them back.'

Molly sat down opposite Bernie and shook her head. 'Aunt, haven't I just told you I really do need the work? If I'd refused she'd never recommend me to anyone.'

Augusta gave another snort of annoyance. She might be elderly and stooped, wearing a rather old-fashioned black wool dress with, over it, one of the many black cardigans she had knitted for herself because, she declared, she always felt cold, but she was nobody's fool. A pair of spectacles was balanced somewhat precariously on the bridge of her nose but, as both girls knew, very little escaped those sharp grey eyes.

'At least Joe came to meet me so I didn't have to carry them all home again myself,' Molly went on.

Augusta poured the tea. 'Have this now; you look cold and tired. I don't suppose *she* offered you anything?'

'She did not but then I didn't expect her to.'

'No manners for all she plays the "lady"!' Both Augusta's daughters had married well above their station and had hurt and humiliated her by their obvious embarrassment at both their mother and their humble background.

Bernie consigned the crocheting to her workbasket. 'I'll never get the hang of it, sure I won't!'

The old lady handed her a cup of tea. 'If you insist on going at it like a bull at a gate you won't. I'll go over it again with you tomorrow night. Now let's have this tea and then I'm off to my bed.'

When the old lady had departed Bernie began to stack the dishes in the sink.

Molly picked up the tea towel, ready to dry them.

'And what did Joe have to say about Madam High and Mighty?' Bernie asked. She had no time for either Maud or Vera Hesketh.

'That I could tell her to go to hell if I wanted to. That I wouldn't need to work if I married him.'

Bernie looked questioningly at her friend. 'He asked you to marry him again?'

'Not outright but it's what he was implying.'

Bernie handed her a soapy saucer. She couldn't see what the problem was at all. Joe Jackson was just the kind of man she wanted her friend to marry. She wanted the best for Molly and in her opinion Joe was the best: trustworthy, reliable, thoughtful; and he had a good job with prospects, but he wasn't deadly serious or dull – he had a great sense of humour.

'I don't know why you can't make up your mind about him, Moll.'

'Bernie, you do know why! You know how hard I've worked to build up my business and as a policeman's wife I wouldn't be able to carry on. The powers that be don't like you going out to work, never mind running your own business. Sure, there are all kinds of rules and regulations about what you can do and where you can live. Seeing as they pay a rent allowance, you have to live within the city boundaries. You're supposed to be able to walk to work if there's no public transport available to get you there . . . and then there's this feeling that I should be *madly in love* with him. I do love him, but . . . Oh, I just don't know!'

Bernie nodded but said nothing. She did know how hard Molly had worked to build up her business and she well remembered Molly's first love affair and how unhappily it had ended but she felt her friend shouldn't let either of those things influence her decision. She thought Molly should grasp the opportunity of a life of happiness with Joe. 'You can't keep putting him off, Molly. You'll have to make up your mind sooner or later.'

'I know.' Molly sighed then decided to lighten the mood. 'He's asked me to a social evening at the Police Club on Sunday and I certainly need a bit of cheering up.'

'It will do you good to get out.' Bernie wondered if Joe would take the opportunity to ask Molly to marry him – for the third time.

'What are you going to do at the weekend? Anything special?'

Bernie grinned. 'I'm hoping to buy myself something a bit stylish to wear for when Bertie comes home next, and I might go to the cinema with Jean.'

Molly smiled at her. Albert 'Bertie' Hayes was Aunt Augusta's youngest son. He went away to sea and was based in Southampton, but over the past year he had taken to visiting his mother more frequently and had taken Bernie out on more than one occasion.

'And that will do you good too. Right, that's the dishes finished. We'd better go up ourselves or we'll have her down here wanting to know are we going to stay up all night.'

Chapter Two

NEXT MORNING BERNIE WALKED slowly to the tram stop. It wasn't that she disliked her job, it was because she was early. She always left the house fifteen minutes before her tram was due at the stop on Walton Road; it gave her time to think and if she needed to buy a newspaper or some fruit for her lunch all the little shops that lined both sides of the road were just opening. When she and Molly first came to Liverpool, she had been in service, but now she worked on the haberdashery counter at Frisby Dyke's – a job Molly had been instrumental in obtaining for her.

It was a lovely crisp October morning with a clear blue sky and a sprinkling of frost. Bernie pulled her scarf a little higher around her neck and thrust her hands deeply into the pockets of her grey and white tweed coat. The cherry-red scarf and matching mittens had been knitted for her by Augusta and the colour always made her feel warm and cheerful. She had a lot to feel cheerful about, she reminded herself, especially on cold mornings like this. When she'd been growing up in Ireland her mam and da had been so poor that she'd never had a decent coat nor stockings nor shoes and she'd often gone hungry. Her da was a labourer who took whatever work he could, but it was often scarce. The O'Sullivans and the Keegans were neighbours, and Molly's da sometimes helped out, providing what work he could, he being a farmer and therefore better off, but times were hard for everyone. All Bernie's older brothers and sisters had taken the emigrant ship; there simply was no work for them. Still, things at home weren't quite so bad now, she reminded herself. She sent a little money to her mam regularly and owing to the fact that she wrote to her siblings in New York to prompt them, money and parcels arrived frequently at the little cabin on the banks of the Grand Canal at Cappaloughlan where she and her eleven brothers and sisters had been born.

As she reached the top of Arnot Street and rounded the corner on to the main road her thoughts turned to Molly. She could understand some of her friend's concerns about marrying Joe but she hoped that next time he proposed Molly would accept him. Molly had been badly hurt by that ill-fated love affair and it was only natural that she would be a bit wary of men, but Joe wasn't *men*, Joe was . . . well, he was *Joe*. The nicest man she'd ever met, apart from Jimmy.

Her forehead creased in a deep frown and she concentrated briefly on the worn flagstones beneath her feet that were slippery with frost. After her husband Jimmy McCauley had drowned she had thought her life was over; she couldn't envisage any kind of life without him. In her deep grief for her young husband she had wondered how people could be so stupid as to believe that 'time would heal', which was what her mam, Aunt Augusta and so many others had repeatedly told her. Gradually however, she'd come to realise that it was indeed true and that her life wasn't over. It was six years ago now and she was only twenty-four and she had to admit that she found Bertie attractive.

'Gerra move on, Bernie girl! Yer're goin' ter be late fer work iffen yer don't!'

Bernie was jerked out of her reverie by the conductor's shout as the tram rattled to a halt a little ahead of her, sparks shooting out of the overhead trolley as it came into contact with the icy points. She quickened her steps, looking a little annoyed.

'You've got to be early. Sure, I left the house dead on time.'

The man grinned. 'We are. We left the depot early, seein' as how there's a bit of ice around this mornin'. Give ourselves more time, like. Don't want ter have the customers complainin' that with the first bit o' frost Liverpool Corporation Trams go completely off the rails! Birra of a joke, that!' He chuckled at his own wit.

Bernie grimaced and cast her eyes skywards. 'Haven't you a desperate sense of humour, Tommy Banks!' She handed him her money and took the ticket he offered. She knew him well enough now; she caught the same tram every morning.

'Go right down ter the front, Bernie, it's a bit warmer. Yer'd catch yer death of cold 'ere by the door,' he advised.

She nodded and took his advice and settled herself two seats behind the driver. The familiar streets passed by and as the tram made its way along Walton and County Roads towards Everton Valley and the city centre, Bernie's thoughts again turned to Bertie Hayes.

Augusta too was thinking about her son and Bernie and about the decision Molly would have to make one day with regard to Joe Jackson. She cleared away the breakfast dishes and filled the sink with hot water. These days the household chores seemed to take her so long, even though the girls did the heavy tasks like sweeping and scrubbing and washing. It didn't seem so very long ago that she'd had so much more energy. The whole of Monday had always been taken up with the weekly wash: the strenuous work of filling the copper boiler, rubbing the clothes vigorously against the washboard, rinsing endlessly and finally folding and mangling and pegging out to dry. Time was taking its toll on her; these days she didn't have the strength to fill the boiler. Molly and Bernie did it between them and if Joe was around at all he would make light work of turning the handle of the big, heavy mangle and joke about it too.

She sighed as she began to wash the plates. She fervently hoped Molly would marry him. He loved Molly; it was plain for everyone to see. Joe would always take care of her, and he was a good lad. One of the best.

She was interrupted by the sound of the yard door opening and peering through the kitchen window she saw the figure of the coalman coming up the yard. She wiped her hands on her apron and went to the door.

The man was bent double under the weight of the sack of coal he was carrying and his face was liberally smeared with black coal dust but he grinned cheerfully at her. 'Mornin', Mrs H. Two hundredweight of the best. You'll be needing it now; there was a good dusting of frost on the cobbles this morning. I'll be having to put sacks on old Ben's hooves soon, so he won't be slipping and sliding getting up Breeze Hill.'

'I hope there's not too much slack in those sacks this time! A right load of rubbish you left me last time, Mr Gorry! Couldn't get the fire to light for love nor money,' Augusta informed him. She'd had the same coal merchant for years, Gorry's on the corner of Parkinson Road.

'You sure, Mrs H.? I always pride myself on good quality coal; you should know that. There's no rubbish in this lot. Best stuff from the Welsh valleys.'

Augusta walked across to the coal bunker and peered in

while the man adjusted his spectacles and wiped his forehead with the back of his hand.

'Seems satisfactory. Come on in while I get my purse. There's tea in the pot if you've time.'

'Just a quick one then. I've a heavy day today now the weather's turned cold.'

Augusta paid him and then poured him a mug of tea. He stood in the doorway, not wishing to dirty the kitchen floor. Augusta smiled to herself. His wife Leila had him well trained. In all the years she'd known him he'd never agreed to sit in her kitchen.

'Those two girls of yours keeping well?' he asked.

Augusta smiled at his description. 'Fine. Molly's off to a house in the south end of the city with a pair of curtains and Bernie's gone to her work.'

'Leila often says those curtains Molly made for our parlour are the best she's ever had.'

'She's good at her work but she may have to give it up if she decides to marry Joe Jackson.'

'And will she?'

'She'll be a fool if she doesn't.'

'Aye, he's a good lad and with a decent-enough job.' He drained the mug and handed it to her. 'Well, I'd best be off now. See you next month. Take care of yourself, Mrs H.'

Augusta went back to drying the dishes and wondered if her son's intentions towards Bernie were serious. She'd ask him next time he was home. She sighed. Ah, only time will tell.

*

Molly had put the brown paper parcel that contained the pair of curtains on the long bench seat beside her. The seat was near the door of the tram and it was chilly but she wouldn't risk leaving the parcel on the shelf on the half-open platform, even though the conductor had said he'd keep an eye on it: she'd spent too many hours sewing the heavy fringe on those curtains.

She'd lost count of the number of pairs she'd made: some plain; some very fancy with heavy pleating and matching pelmets and cushion covers, like those for Vera Hesketh. She'd come a long way from her first commission.

As the tram trundled its way through the city centre and on towards Upper Parliament Street, Molly's thoughts turned to Joe. Yes, she did love him. He was always there for her, he had been for six years, and there were no secrets between them. She was now older and wiser than she'd been at eighteen. True, what she felt for Joe wasn't the same wild, impetuous rapture on falling in love as a teenager, but how could it be? When she looked back she realised how young, naive, blind and utterly trusting she'd been then. She'd only just left rural Ireland and the strict confines of both family and Church. It had been such a heady time. Free to do what she wanted, earn her own living, spend her own money, and go where she pleased with whomever she wished. There had been no mam or da asking questions. She smiled wryly. Aunt Augusta had laid down some pretty strict rules when she and Bernie had first rented rooms in her house, soon after they'd arrived from County Offaly, but they'd found ways around them. Yes, she was older and wiser now and she did love Joe and wanted to settle down and in time have a family.

The tram had reached its destination and Molly picked up her parcel and got off, heading for Weybridge Street. The houses here were nice: not too big but substantially built, with a small garden at the front. They were good Victorian family terraces, kept in excellent repair. They were a far cry from the appalling streets of terraced slums in the dock area where Nellie and Matty O'Sullivan lived. Matty was Bernie's da's cousin; Nellie his long-suffering wife. Poor Nellie, Molly thought, she still fought her losing battle with dirt and poverty in the slum that should have been pulled down years ago. Yet Nellie had given them a roof over their heads and the blanket from her own bed when they'd first come to Liverpool seven years ago, before they'd moved to Walton.

She'd made Nellie a pair of curtains for her parlour out of a remnant of moss-green brocade. She'd lined them and trimmed them with pale green braid. She would never forget the look on Bernie's cousin's face when she'd realised they were for her. And then she'd broken down in tears; she'd never had a decent pair of curtains in all her married life. Molly smiled to herself at the memory. Her mam probably wouldn't approve of Nellie but she was fond of her. Nellie was rough and ready but her heart was in the right place.

Eventually she stopped in front of number fourteen. The front door was painted dark chocolate brown and the brasses were shining. The little garden was planted with late asters and Michaelmas daisies. If she owned a house like this, Molly thought, she would paint the door in a nice forest green and have smart urns planted with evergreen shrubs either side of it.

The curtains in the parcel were dusky rose brocade, which didn't go well with the dark brown furnishings of the room. If it were her house she would have heavy cream-patterned brocade curtains, edged in forest green. They would look good and tone in nicely. Suddenly, she wanted a home of her own: a home and a family and a loving, caring husband – but close on the heels of this realisation came the thought that she might have completed her last commission. The business she had built up over the last six years would have to be sacrificed. Would it be worth it? Yes, she told herself firmly. She loved Joe and next time he asked her she would give him a direct answer. She smiled to herself. She knew her mother Ita would be delighted. Ita had never met Joe but Molly had told her so much about him that Ita said it was as if she knew him herself. She wondered if they would come over for the wedding or would she go home and be married in the church at Killina, like Bernie had been. She shook herself mentally. Let's take one thing at a time, she told herself as she went up the path and knocked on the brown-painted door.

*

When she returned home with the small white envelope containing the money for the curtains, Augusta was mashing potatoes to top the cottage pie that was for supper that evening.

'Well, was *she* satisfied with her curtains? Did *she* pay you?'

Molly smiled. 'She was and she did so. Even though I often disagree with the colours people choose, at the end of the day I have to remember it is *their* choice, *their* homes.'

'Not everyone has your talent for matching colours, child. My front parlour is a credit to you.'

Molly filled the kettle. 'I'll make the tea and then I'm going to write to Mam.'

The old lady nodded. Both girls were very good at keeping in touch with their families and she knew they both sent money home. 'They'll be glad they have a shed full of turf now winter is on its way although I must say I prefer to have my fuel delivered regularly to the door, so to speak.'

'I admit there's a lot of work involved in cutting and turning and drawing the turf down to the yard, but it smells much better than coal. In cold weather you can smell the turf smoke in the frosty air outside, let alone inside, and it's lovely.' Molly's grey-green eyes misted a little as memories of her childhood came flooding back.

'Mr Gorry brought the coal today and he said his wife is always commenting on how good those curtains are you made.'

'I'm glad Herself is pleased with them.'

'She has two daughters engaged; there might be more work for you.'

Molly sighed. 'If I'm allowed to do it.'

Augusta shot her a thoughtful glance before concentrating on putting the pie in the oven. Then she took off her apron and sat down at the table opposite Molly. She had always spoken her mind and had no intention of changing now. 'So, you've decided to accept him?'

Molly nodded. 'I have so. I'd be an eejit not to. Next time he mentions it I'll say yes. I'm going to write to Mam now and tell her.'

The old lady smiled and reached for her hand. 'She'll be as delighted as I am, Molly. I know you'll be happy and that you'll be well looked after for the rest of your life. That will be a big relief to your mother and to me. I won't be here for ever.'

Molly squeezed her hand. 'I hope you'll be around for a long while yet.'

Chapter Three

'Better get those reports done, Jackson, I see it's your rest day tomorrow.' The middle-aged sergeant was scanning the duty roster without much pleasure.

'It is, Sarge, and I'm looking forward to it. I'm taking Molly to the social evening at St Anne Street,' Joe answered affably. There were only a few hours left of his shift. The room was warm and there was a fug of tobacco smoke and damp serge uniforms as one by one the members of the early shift arrived back at the Station House. It wasn't an overly large room, and two old-fashioned desks and a bookcase in which bound copies of such tomes as the Chief Constable's *Annual Report* and Moriarty's *Police Law* took up most of the space. Joe had positioned himself at one corner of the desk nearest the open fire that burned in a small cast-iron grate. It was cold and damp outside and his fingers, even though encased in thick cream woollen gloves, were half frozen.

'Mind you, don't go making it too much of a "social evening": you're back on duty at seven on Monday morning,' came the terse reply.

Joe took out his notebook and laid it on the portion of the desk he was sharing with Tom Foley, a constable with a few more years' experience than himself.

'Much to write up?' Foley asked conversationally.

'No. It was pretty quiet out there. Old Furzy Rooney was up to his old tricks though. Drunk as a lord and insisting on lying down to sleep it off in the middle of the road. If I carted him back on to the pavement once, I did it three times. In the end I threatened to either bring him in or leave him there and let him take his chances with the buses, trams and carts!'

'Sounds very much like a "drunk and disorderly" to me!' Sergeant Hopkins stated.

'Drunk he certainly was, but you wouldn't call his behaviour "disorderly",' Joe replied. The old fool wasn't causing trouble or offending anyone, he thought.

'You could still have arrested him for being "drunk and incapable".'

'Why make work, Sarge, and persecute the poor old devil? Hasn't he enough to put up with being married to Mary Ellen?'

'The last time I saw old Furzy he was being belted all the way down Athol Street by Mary Ellen. God knows what he'd done to upset her!' Foley laughed.

Sergeant Hopkins shrugged. 'It's just their way of going on. They've been at each other's throats for as long as I can remember – but that's marriage for you.'

'I'd hope for something a bit better than that carry on,' Joe answered, thinking of Molly and the fact that he intended to propose again either during or after the social.

'It's a lottery, that's what marriage is. A bloody lottery!' Hopkins muttered darkly.

Joe and Foley exchanged glances. It was well known that Sergeant Hopkins's own marriage was far from perfect.

'Isn't it about time you made an honest woman of that girl?' Foley joked, winking at Joe.

'I intend to. It's pinning her down to a definite yes that's the trouble.'

'Well, treat her to a really good night out,' Foley advised.

'Let's have less of the chat and more of the writing or we'll all be here until midnight!' Sergeant Hopkins instructed curtly, putting an end to further conversation.

Molly had decided to wear her newest dress purchased from Blackler's the previous month.

'That colour really suits you, Moll,' Bernie said admiringly. She was perched on the edge of the bed watching Molly get ready.

'I wasn't too sure about it at first but now . . .' Molly twisted and turned in front of the mirror. The royal-blue wool crêpe did look good on her. It had long sleeves with a white cuff, a fitted bodice and a box-pleated skirt. 'You don't think the style is a bit severe for a dance?'

'Not at all! It looks classy.' Bernie had been admiring a short jacket in the same colour that she'd seen in T. J. Hughes but had decided it wasn't a shade that would suit her colouring. She'd opted for a twin-set in pale blue instead.

'I don't want to appear frivolous or giddy. Some of the higher-ranking officers will be there with their wives, so Joe says, and I want to look like an asset to him.'

'Sure, you'll take the sight from the eyes of all those frumpy old wives!' Bernie enthused.

Molly grimaced. 'It's important I make a good impression.'

Bernie looked at her speculatively. 'What are you not telling me, Molly Keegan? Haven't I known you long enough to know that you're up to something?'

Molly smiled at her. 'I'm almost certain Joe will propose to me again tonight and . . . and this time I'm going to accept. I've made up my mind!'

Bernie jumped up and threw her arms around her friend. 'Oh, Moll! I'm so glad! You'll not regret it.'

'I know that. Joe will always take care of me. Aunt Augusta guessed. You know what she's like: never minces her words – she came right out with it. I've written to Mam too.'

Bernie laughed. 'It seems to me that all the world and

his wife know and the only one who doesn't is Joe himself!'

Molly looked perturbed. 'I didn't mean for it all to come out like this. You won't say anything to him when he calls?'

'I will not! Sure, I wouldn't spoil the surprise, but I'd better go and tell Aunt to keep her mouth shut!'

'Oh, yes, please do. I'll be down in a few minutes,' Molly called as Bernie ran quickly downstairs.

Neither Bernie nor the old lady were to be seen when Molly opened the door to Joe a few minutes later.

'You look lovely, Molly, and I brought you these.' Joe held out a bunch of yellow and white chrysanthemums.

'Oh, you know how I love flowers, especially at this time of year when everything is sort of dying down. I'll just put them in water and then we'll go.' With a quick peck on his cheek as a 'thank you' Molly hastened into the kitchen where Bernie and Augusta Hayes were having a cup of tea.

Bernie grinned at her. 'Nice flowers, Moll!'

'Will you put them in a vase for me?'

Bernie nodded and took the flowers, then gave her friend a gentle push in the direction of the door. 'Get off with you and put him out of his misery!'

Molly felt a little apprehensive as they arrived at the club, which was situated in St Anne Street police station. She hadn't met many of Joe's friends or colleagues. She patted her auburn hair nervously.

'You look just perfect, Moll,' Joe said, smiling. He knew she was anxious. 'Now, come on and let's find a table before it gets too crowded. We'll go over there. There's Tom

Foley and his wife.' He guided her to a table on the far side of the room, which had been decorated with coloured bunting for the occasion.

'Hello, Molly. This is Evelyn, my wife,' Tom Foley informed her with a friendly smile.

Molly relaxed. At least she had met Tom once or twice and Evelyn looked nice enough.

'Right, what are we all having to drink?' Joe asked as Molly sat down beside Tom's wife. 'I'll fight my way to the bar.' Now that they were in company he would have to wait until he took Molly home to ask her to be his wife but he didn't mind. She seemed to have relaxed and to be fitting in well and that was important.

To his surprise the opportunity to propose presented itself much earlier. There was a ladies' excuse-me waltz and after Molly had danced with quite a few of his colleagues, including his inspector, she came and got him to his feet.

'I was just thinking that I'd lost you for good! Inspector Jarvis seems to have taken quite a shine to you, although having seen Mrs Jarvis I can understand why.'

Molly giggled. 'Oh, Joe Jackson, that's a desperate thing to say! He's actually very nice.'

'Really? I wish he was "very nice" to us lowly constables.'

'She does look a bit of a dragon, though. And you know I wouldn't desert you. I always come back to you.'

He squeezed her hand. 'Will you stay with me for ever, Moll?'

Her face became serious as she gazed up at him. 'Are you asking me to marry you?'

'I've already asked you twice, but, yes, I am. Will you marry me, Molly Keegan?' He held his breath, praying there would be no evasive answer this time.

Molly took a deep breath. 'I will, Joe. I really will!'

Totally ignoring everyone else on the dance floor Joe took her in his arms and kissed her. She was the most beautiful girl he'd ever met. He admired her determination, her ambition, her generosity of spirit, her kind and loving nature. She had faced heartbreak and humiliation and coped with dignity. He knew all the details of her first disastrous love affair; there were no secrets between them.

When he finally released her he gazed down at her, his eyes shining. 'You'll never regret it, Molly, I promise. You'll have everything you want, everything I can give you.'

She reached up and stroked the soft brown hair at the nape of his neck. She'd never felt so happy, so utterly *loved*. 'I only need you, Joe!'

'You won't mind giving up your business?' He knew how important it was to her but the Police Authority would never countenance a working wife, let alone a business-woman. He didn't agree with them; he was proud of her, but they were strict about such things. In their opinion it demeaned a serving police officer.

'It will be hard, but I'll be content with making things for my own home – our home!'

'Will we set a date?' He was eager to get things finalised.

She smiled. 'I think I'd like a May wedding. The winter months are so cold and dreary.'

'Then May it is!'

'What the hell are you two up to? You're getting looks fit to kill from the inspector and superintendent!' Tom Foley hissed, nudging Joe in the ribs.

Joe laughed. 'We've something to announce! We're getting married next May!'

Molly smiled up at Joe and Tom whooped with laughter, before propelling them both bodily towards the stage.

'Let's really make this official! Let's announce it properly, from the stage!'

Molly began to blush furiously but Evelyn smiled at her reassuringly. 'This will wipe the looks of outrage off all their faces! You've a very good reason for standing in the middle of the dance floor kissing!'

Molly laughed. 'I can't think of a better reason!'

It was well after midnight when Joe walked her down Arnot Street. After being soundly congratulated by everyone they had decided to go and tell Effie and Fred Jackson, Joe's parents. Effie had dragged her husband in from the pigeon loft in the yard where he spent so many hours and told him to open the bottle of good port she'd been saving for Christmas, and she'd also insisted that two of the neighbours come in to celebrate the occasion.

Molly's head was buzzing with all the questions her

future mother-in-law had fired at her and almost before she'd realised it she had agreed to be married in Liverpool, in her parish church of St Francis de Salles. Now she wondered how her parents would take the news.

'I hope Bernie hasn't posted that letter I wrote to Mam. I'll have to inform her that she's to bring the family over here,' she said as they reached the front door.

Joe looked a little concerned. 'They will come, Moll? They will understand that this is your home now?'

'I think so, but Da always has the excuse that he can't leave the farm. It doesn't run itself, is what he always says. Are you coming in?'

Joe shook his head. 'I've to be up at five and if I come in I'll never get home. I'll see Bernie and Augusta on Friday, after we've been for the engagement ring. We can have a bit of a celebration then.'

Molly slid her arms around his neck. 'I'll see you on Friday and I'm so happy, Joe, I really am!' She meant it. She only wondered why she had hesitated for so long.

Bernie was waiting up for her. 'I can't go to bed until I know for certain that this time she really has agreed,' she'd told Augusta when the old lady had suggested they go up.

'It's a quarter to midnight now and I can hardly keep my eyes open. I'm too old for missing out on my sleep,' Augusta had grumbled and had taken herself off upstairs.

Bernie had tidied up and relaid the kitchen table for

breakfast, then she'd gone into the little sitting room at the front of the house and put more coal on the fire. It had been an unsettling evening, she'd thought as she settled herself more comfortably on the sofa, but she was excited and pleased for Molly and had said as much to Augusta.

'I am myself. They make a lovely couple. Now, what about you?'

'Me?' Bernie had echoed.

'Yes. I think you and our Bertie would make a lovely couple too. I intend to ask him how he feels about you next time he's home, but I'd very much like to know how *you* feel about *him*?'

'You never did mince your words, did you?' Bernie had replied, rather taken aback.

'Don't be evasive!'

'I'm not! I just haven't really given it much thought.'

'Well, think about it now.'

Bernie had leaned her elbows on the table. 'Well, I do like him a lot and we get on very well together and he takes me to some great places.'

'And so he should. He's away at sea for months on end with nowhere to spend his money except the crew bar and he isn't a one "to have drink taken", as you would say.'

Bernie had nodded. 'One pint and he says he's flat on his back so it's just not worth it. But I wouldn't say I was madly in love with him.'

'You don't have to be besotted. Believe me, a good marriage is based on things like trust, mutual respect and genuine affection. Love, or whatever you want to call it, can come later.'

Bernie hadn't been so sure about that. She *had* really loved Jimmy McCauley, the young deck hand she'd first met on the ferry coming over from Dublin to Liverpool. 'I'll really give it some thought, Aunt, I promise.'

To her surprise the old lady had reached across the table and taken her hand. 'I'd like to see you settled, Bernie. I won't be here for ever and he's a good lad, though I say it myself. He'd take care of you.'

'I know,' she'd answered.

Augusta had got up and taken a small wooden box from one of the cupboards. 'I want you to have this, Bernie. I don't have much in the way of good jewellery but this belonged to my mother.' She'd held out a gold brooch set with seed pearls and small rubies. It was of an ornate Victorian design and Bernie could see it had some value.

'I can't take it, Aunt! It looks valuable. It should go to Maud or Vera.'

'I wouldn't give either of them the time of day! I want you to have it and to wear it. It will be something to remember me by. I intend to write to Bertie and tell him that I've given you the "family heirloom" because I dearly want you to become "family".'

Bernie could see she was adamant and so she had taken the brooch and pinned it to her dress. 'I'll treasure it,' she'd promised, feeling very touched.

Now she sat and fingered the sharp edges of the gold.

Yes, it had been a very strange day all right and she wished Molly would hurry up and come home.

The room was warm and cosy and soon she was dozing. She was still asleep when Molly finally arrived.

'Well? Tell me everything!' she demanded, waking abruptly.

'I said yes and we're going for an engagement ring on Friday. We're getting married next May, here, at St Francis de Salles.'

Bernie hugged her. 'Oh, Molly, that's just great! Seeing as how I'm a widow I can't be a bridesmaid but can I be your matron of honour?'

'Sure, I wouldn't dream of having anyone else! Aren't you my oldest and dearest friend?'

Chapter Four

ITA KEEGAN HELD HER cold hands out to the turf fire and shivered. Autumn had come in suddenly with a heavy frost that morning and a bitterly cold wind this afternoon – a wind that was rapidly stripping the leaves from the trees in the yard.

'Maria, fill that kettle while I put down more turf; this fire's half dead and your da will be in for his tea in a few minutes,' she instructed her daughter.

'Ma, it's not my fault the fire's so poor looking, haven't I only just got in this minute?' Maria complained as she filled the heavy black kettle. 'And isn't it the job of those two eejits to see to the turf and the fire and the pair of them in the door a good half-hour before me?' She shot a look of annoyance at her two younger brothers, who were poring over a comic book that had come in a parcel from Denis, their oldest brother, who lived in Boston.

Ita glared at her sons. 'You two, put that thing down and fill up the turf box and the buckets, or there'll be no tea for either of you. I'm frozen to the bone slaving in that dairy all afternoon.' She worked hard and she wasn't getting any younger. As well as running a home, she helped Paddy to do the milking and she made butter and cheese, which she sold, along with the eggs she didn't need, in Tullamore on Thursdays. Only three of her six children were at home now. Molly was in Liverpool and Denis and Mick were in Boston. She glanced at Maria. The girl was finding it almost impossible to find anything other than odd jobs. Would she have to see Maria follow in Molly's footsteps?

She tied on a clean apron and began to set the table. There was cold ham, some late tomatoes, cheese and home-made chutney and buttered barmbrack. They had had rashers and cabbage and potatoes at dinnertime.

'Maria, pass me another plate, child. Mr O'Sullivan is helping your da out today.'

Maria did as she was bid and then seized the sweeping brush as her brothers staggered through the door with buckets full of turf. 'Ah, would you look at the mess they're after making of the floor, Mam! Wouldn't you think by now they'd have sense enough not to leave a trail of dust after them?'

'And wouldn't you think they'd have the sense to shut the door too and me trying to keep the kitchen warm,' Ita rejoined, slamming the offending door shut.

'You're always giving out to us,' Tom grumbled as he tipped a bucket of the fuel into the large wooden box beside the range.

'Con O'Brien gave me this to give to you.' Aiden placed a letter on the table.

'Mr O'Brien to you – have some respect! Here's your da now and the tea not whet,' Ita said with some irritation. The letter was from Molly; she could tell by the stamp. The post was very late today. No doubt Con had been chatting to everyone on his rounds.

When they were all seated and the meal was under way Ita finally opened Molly's letter. The teacup she'd been holding in her left hand clattered as it was replaced hastily on the saucer. 'Holy Mother of God! She's finally getting married!'

Paddy Keegan looked up in surprise. He was a big man with a weather-beaten face, grey eyes and thick auburn hair that was now turning grey. 'Molly?'

'Who else? She's finally agreed to marry Joe Jackson.'

Paddy nodded slowly. He'd never met the lad but he approved. Joe sounded decent enough and he was a Guard: if they were as well paid over there as they were here, Molly wouldn't want for much. Years ago she'd been sweet on a lad called Billy something but it had all fizzled out and he was glad. Billy had given some weak-sounding excuse not to come over with Molly when young Bernie O'Sullivan was getting wed. Obviously, in Paddy's opinion, the boy hadn't wanted to meet Molly's family.

'Our Bernie says he's a fine feller and he's been asking Molly for years,' Dessie O'Sullivan put in.

'So when is it to be then?' Paddy asked.

'Next May so she says and' – Ita paused, frowning – 'she's getting married over there. She says that Liverpool has been her home for over seven years and will continue to be her home when she's married, so she's decided to get married in St Francis de Salles and she wants to know will we all go over?'

Paddy looked doubtful. 'Sure, it's not that easy. She should know that.'

'That's exactly what she said you'd say! Don't you be using it as an excuse to miss your daughter's wedding. We can get someone in to see to the beasts while we're away and we won't be gone for weeks on end. Sure, a few days away will make a nice change.' Ita was firm. She would more than welcome a few days in Liverpool.

'Does she say I'm to be a bridesmaid, Mam?' Maria asked eagerly. It was the only chance she'd get to dress up in a fancy frock. She had no other sisters, both Denis and Mick had been married in Boston and it would be years and years before the two eejits sitting beside her would be old enough – if they could find girls daft enough to marry them.

Ita smiled at her. 'Of course she does.'

Paddy was still looking unconvinced.

'Wait until I tell Tess; she'll be only delighted – and, Paddy, won't *I* only be delighted to look after things here for you for a few days,' Dessie offered, thinking it would be money in his pocket. Tess would be pleased to hear the news *and* that he had got his offer in before Paddy had had the chance to ask anyone else.

'There now, that's settled. I'll write and tell Molly we'll all be over and we won't be disgracing her. We'll all have new outfits.'

Paddy looked alarmed. 'You'll have me bankrupted, woman!'

'You'll have a new suit, Paddy Keegan, if I have to drag you into Michael Farrell's myself! That one you have is a disgrace.'

''Tis good enough for Mass on Sundays,' Paddy protested, but he knew it was no use. He could see by the set of Ita's lips that she'd made up her mind, and once she'd done that there was no moving her. This wedding was going to cost him a small fortune, just when he'd had his eye on one of those new tractors that would save so much time and effort. They were hard to come by but he'd been reliably informed by a man he knew above in Dublin that he could get him one – there would be a couple coming over from Holyhead sometime before Christmas. Ah, well, maybe he'd be able to get one this time next year.

'Will you write to her after tea, Mam?' Maria enquired eagerly. There hadn't been so much excitement since Molly came home last and that had been ages ago. 'I'll clear up and see to the fire,' she offered.

'I will so. She'll be eager to hear if we're coming or not and I've a list of questions to ask her,' Ita replied.

When Molly and Joe returned to Arnot Street on Friday evening after spending the afternoon in town and then going for a celebratory drink in the bar of the Imperial Hotel, Bernie could hardly contain her excitement.

'Oh, let me see what you bought her, Joe, and congratulations!' she cried, kissing him on the cheek and reaching for Molly's hand all at the same time.

'For heaven's sake, let them get in the door!' Augusta chided but she was smiling. 'Congratulations, Joe. You've been patient long enough waiting on this one to make up her mind.'

Joe bent and kissed the wrinkled cheek. He was fond of Augusta Hayes. She had a kind heart in spite of her sharp tongue.

'Oh, it's just *gorgeous*!' Bernie enthused over the single diamond in the plain setting.

'Lovely. Not too ostentatious,' Augusta agreed.

'And we've decided to take a trip over to Ireland. I'd like to meet my future in-laws and I'm sure they'd like to meet me before next May,' Joe informed them.

'And we decided it would be nice for Joe to meet everyone who can't come over for the wedding. All my aunts and uncles and cousins.'

Bernie grimaced. 'You'd need months to get round everyone. When do you plan to go and for how long?'

'Just a long weekend. Joe has some leave due to him and he can't take it at Christmas so we've decided to go next month,' Molly informed them. It had all been Joe's idea. She'd warned him that there were literally hundreds of relations. Her da was one of nine children and her mam had ten brothers and sisters and they all had big families, which were scattered across three counties.

'Is it obligatory to have more than three or four children in Ireland? Is there something about it in the Constitution?' Joe had joked.

'No, I . . . I suppose it just . . . happens.' Molly had never really given it much thought. 'Some families here have lots of children. Look at Nellie O'Sullivan and her neighbours. Nellie had six kids and had them all at school too and then didn't she go on and have another five.'

'Aye, *look* at them!' Joe had replied grimly. He had firm views on this, as he did on many things. Too many children packed into cramped and unsanitary houses, inadequately fed and poorly dressed: it was no wonder so many of them died in infancy, and that in his opinion was more than a crime, it was a sin. Nor was it fair on the poor women: the constant pregnancies; the grinding battle of daily life; the endless worry about putting enough food on the table. No wonder so many of them died young too. He had no intention of putting Molly through all that or of having more than three children, no matter what anyone said.

'November! You must be mad!' Bernie cried now.

'Won't the ferry crossing be desperate and the place cold and damp and miserable?'

Molly shrugged. 'No one goes to Ireland for the weather, Bernie. You know that. It can be cold, wet and miserable in the middle of summer.'

'That's true enough,' Bernie agreed.

'Well, I think it's very commendable of you and I'm sure your parents will think so too. And I'm sure there will be a hundred and one details about the wedding you will want to discuss with your mother, Molly,' Augusta said, polishing her best sherry glasses and placing them on the table next to the bottle of Empire Pale Sherry that Bernie had bought.

Molly nodded her agreement. It would be nice to go back and see the family and show Joe off to them all. Strangely, she didn't think of it as *home* now.

Bernie duly handed round the sherry. 'Here's a toast to both of you. God bless you and may you be as happy as Jimmy and I were.'

'And may you both have good health and be together for many, many years to come – and be blessed with good, dutiful children,' Augusta added, swiftly dismissing her two daughters and the bitter disappointment they had caused her from her mind.

'Have you had any thoughts yet on where you'll live?' Bernie asked.

Molly sipped her sherry. 'I haven't.'

'I've started to make enquiries about houses to rent.

Quite often you hear about things from people,' Joe informed them.

'The houses in Weybridge Street are nice. Big but not too big; old but not too old. I'd like something with a bit of character but with modern conveniences too.'

'Would you not think of starting off in a flat?' Augusta asked.

Molly shook her head, remembering the appalling, vermin-infested room she and Bernie had shared at Nellie's and the far nicer but still slightly cramped rooms they rented in this house. She wanted a house all to herself. 'We'd only have to move in a few years and it would be expensive making new curtains and things.'

'I suppose you're right. Have you much more work, Molly?'

'I've just two small commissions. I'll have them both finished before we go to Ireland and then . . .' She shrugged.

'And then I'd start looking for a house in earnest if you're to have it ready to move into by May,' Bernie advised.

Joe looked thoughtful. 'If we find something we like I'd move into it straight away. I get a rent allowance.'

'Which I suppose at the moment you give to your mother? Won't she object to losing it?' Augusta probed.

Joe grinned. 'Still as blunt as ever, Aunt Augusta! I do and if she objects then she objects. I won't lose any sleep over it. We're not going to lose a good house because Mam's not happy about it.'

Bernie refilled Molly's glass and gave her friend a conspiratorial look. Joe Jackson was certainly not a 'Mammy's boy'. 'You'll have plenty of time to do all the soft furnishings for it, Molly. Will you be making your own wedding dress too?' Fondly Bernie remembered the beautiful dress Molly had made for her to get married in.

'I don't know. I might buy one. It all depends on how much time I have. I'd really like to get quite a few more commissions: the money would come in very useful.'

'I've told you that I have savings and I'll provide for you, Molly,' Joe said quietly.

'You made quite a hole in them today paying for this and, besides, I'd like to contribute something to our new home,' Molly replied, turning her left hand over so the diamond caught the light and blazed with red, green, violet and gold prisms.

'Keep your money and buy the most gorgeous wedding dress you can find,' Joe urged.

Bernie laughed. 'Don't go falling out already over money! I'll take her shopping, Joe, and she'll take the sight from the eyes of everyone the day she walks up the aisle, don't you worry.'

Joe smiled down at Molly. 'She takes the sight from my eyes every time I look at her.'

Chapter Five

AT LEAST THE CROSSING had been calm and the ferry hadn't been too crowded, Molly thought as the train made its way across the Irish midlands towards Tullamore. She was half dozing, her head resting against Joe's shoulder, while Joe watched the flat green fields and brown patches of bog flashing past. A watery sun was making a valiant effort to shed its pale gold rays across the land, despite the grey clouds that were being blown across its face by a strong northerly wind.

Joe was looking forward to this visit. He didn't mind being 'shown off like a prize bull at a fair' as Bernie had put it. He wanted to meet Molly's family, wanted to learn more about her, to try to envisage her life as she'd been growing up. He felt that a close family was important. He only had one sister, Annie, and she was married, but they had always got on well together and he liked her husband. Both Mam and Da had their funny ways but there were very few big rows or arguments between them. He settled his head back against the seat and closed his eyes. It would be a busy few days but he was sure they would be enjoyable. As long as he was with Molly there was very little that could upset or annoy him.

Paddy was waiting for them at the station with the trap. He was well wrapped up against the cold but cast frequent anxious glances up at the sky. He hadn't worked outdoors all his life not to know the signs. They'd have rain before long so he'd have to get them home quickly.

'It's a welcome sight you both are; now get up into the trap. There's rain on the way,' he greeted them, kissing Molly on the cheek and shaking the hand Joe extended to him.

'I'm very pleased to meet you at last, sir.' Joe's tone was both sincere and respectful.

Molly's da had to look up; Joe was much taller than him. 'Ah, we'll have none of the "sir". "Paddy" will do just fine, or maybe even "Da".'

'I think I'll settle for "Paddy", if that's all right?'

'It is so. Now let's be on our way. Ita will eat me if I bring you home soaked to the skin.'

Molly gazed around as they left the station yard; nothing seemed to have changed much. The trees that lined the road had lost their leaves, except for the occasional evergreen, and the fields along the Charleville Road were devoid of cattle. Here and there a few sheep were grazing. In the distance the grey crenellated turrets of Charleville Castle could be glimpsed, surrounded by skeletal trees. From the houses and cottages further along plumes of blue-grey turf smoke rose into a sky now the colour of gunmetal.

'I'd almost forgotten what turf smoke smelled like,' she said.

Joe smiled at her and Paddy shrugged. 'I just hope your ma has plenty of turf on the fire; the wind is bitter.'

Molly pointed out the ancient ruin of Ballycowan Castle on the canal bank at the twenty-ninth lock and Paddy was thankful that they hadn't much further to go. Finally, as they reached the two-storeyed farmhouse where Molly had been born and reared, the first heavy drops of cold rain began to fall, sending half a dozen chickens scurrying for the shelter of the barn.

'Come on in with you quickly!' Ita urged, appearing at the door. Molly noticed with a dart of concern how much her mother had aged since her last visit. She definitely looked thinner.

Molly hugged Ita tightly. 'Mam, it's so good to see you!'

'Saints above! Haven't you become very grown up?' Ita took in the smart grey coat with the velvet lapels and the matching velvet beret perched over the shining auburn hair, the silk stockings and the high-heeled black patent-leather court shoes. She also noticed the lipstick and the pencilled eyebrows. She'd be having a word about the make-up later; Molly would be the talk of the parish if she turned up at Mass with her face painted.

'I *am* grown up!' Molly laughed. 'And this is Joe.'

Ita's sharp eyes noticed the sparkle in Molly's eyes; nor did she miss the note of pride in her daughter's voice and she smiled. Molly obviously loved him.

'Come into the kitchen where I can see you properly, Joe,' she urged.

Joe had to duck his head to avoid banging it on the beamed ceiling.

Ita liked what she saw. He was tall and well built, his dark brown hair was cut short and he had open, honest features. He was a fine-looking lad – but not really a lad any more, he was nearing thirty. Still, that was no bad thing. Any wild oats would be well sown.

'You're very welcome, Joe, and it's a relief to her da and me that she's getting married.'

Joe laughed. 'It's a relief to me that she finally accepted me!'

After dinner the rain stopped and the sky cleared and Ita agreed to go with Molly to see Tess, Bernie's mam. Bernie had made up a parcel of things she considered her mam would find useful and Molly had promised to deliver it. Joe had put on a pair of wellington boots and old coat of Paddy's and was accompanying his future father-in-law on a tour of inspection of the fields and outbuildings.

Molly put her arm through Ita's as they walked along

the narrow road towards the hump-backed stone bridge over the canal, beyond which lay the low, thatched cabin that had been Bernie's home.

'You are happy, Molly? You are sure?' Ita asked.

Molly smiled. 'I am very sure and I'm very happy, Mam.'

Ita nodded and then glanced at the narrow gold band on her own finger. 'Your da never had the money to be spending on a fancy ring for me.'

'Did you mind?'

Ita smiled. 'Not at all. Wasn't I getting the finest man in the parish and we had a lovely wedding. Nothing fancy, mind, but it was the happiest day of my life.'

'Do you mind that I'm not getting married here?' Molly asked, absently plucking a dead stalk of cow parsley from the hedgerow beside her.

'Not at all. I'm looking forward to the break away from here and it's your decision: Liverpool is your home now.' Ita sighed. 'I've never had any kind of a holiday. I've never been out of Ireland. Imagine that and me with my family scattered all over the world.'

'Maybe one day the lads will send you the money to go to Boston.'

'And maybe one day pigs might fly! Ah, I'm not giving out about them. They have their own families to provide for and they do send a bit of money from time to time. Now, I hope you have all the answers ready for Tess has a hundred questions to ask about Bernie. She worries about her so.'

Molly laughed. 'Bernie is fine, really.'

'You'd better sound more convincing than that,' Ita warned.

Tess was standing at the door, a heavy black shawl clutched around her. She waved as she caught sight of Molly and her mother and then went inside to put on the kettle.

'Molly! Haven't ye turned into a fine-looking woman! I would hardly have recognised ye!' Tess cried as they came into the small, dark kitchen that served as a living room as well. It was poorly furnished with few comforts and no modern conveniences at all. Tess still cooked on an open fire.

'It's grand to see you again!' Molly gave the older woman a quick hug. 'And I brought you this, from Bernie.'

Tess took the parcel and placed it on the table. She'd open it later. 'Ah, she's a thoughtful girl, not like that bold strap Claire who'd not give ye the time of day.'

Ita raised her eyes to the ceiling. Tess was having a hard time with Claire who was Maria's great friend. Tess *had* thought of sending Claire over to Bernie but she doubted Bernie would welcome her sister. Claire tended to be lazy. 'I brought a bit of blackberry pie for us to have with our tea. I baked four this morning with the berries Tom and Aiden picked for me last week. I could have got another two had the pair of them not started fighting and trick-acting and spilled a half a basket full.'

'Aren't boys a heart-scald! Sure, ye'll find that out,

Molly, when ye have a few of your own. What have ye done with Joe?' Tess was a little disappointed that Molly had not brought her fiancé to meet her. She'd heard such glowing reports of him from Bernie.

'He's gone off with Paddy on a tour of inspection,' Ita informed her, cutting the piece of pie into three.

'I think Da wanted to have a chat to him and I know Joe wanted to have a private word with Da.'

Tess nodded. 'Sure, isn't it only to be expected that they'd want to get to know each other? Now, will ye tell me truthfully, Molly, just how *is* that daughter of mine?'

Joe looked out across a wide field to where a group of bullocks grazed beneath the shelter of the thick blackthorn hedge. He was city-born and -bred and knew very little about agriculture but he instinctively knew that Paddy Keegan was proud of his land and his stock.

'I don't know much about it but they look like fine animals. Plenty of flesh on their bones,' he ventured.

'If I could only get a decent price for that flesh I'd be a good deal happier. They're this year's calves and I sometimes wonder if it's worth bothering at all. I'll have to be bringing them inside soon and that means they'll be making a big hole in the silage.' Seeing the concern on Joe's face the older man grinned. 'Ah, take no notice of me, lad. Farmers are always complaining. I'll be after thinking that your job is no picnic either.'

Joe shrugged. 'It's not bad. It can get a bit rough at

times, especially on a Saturday night when the pubs let out. My beat isn't in one of the quietest parts of the city – just the opposite, in fact.' Joe thought of Scotland Road on a Friday and Saturday night; you often spent the time dodging flying fists and boots and occasionally bricks and bottles.

'You should see Tullamore on fair days. There're a fair few drunks, I can tell you.'

Joe grinned. 'I think I could cope.'

'No doubt you could.'

Joe became serious. 'I will look after Molly. She'll never want for anything. It's not a bad job and there are prospects. It's steady, the pay isn't a fortune but we get paid a rent allowance, a boot allowance and overtime. It's a job for life and with a pension at the end of it. I don't mind a drink now and then but I don't smoke or gamble and I'll never raise a hand to her.'

Paddy nodded. He could tell the lad was sincere. Molly would be all right; she'd be happy with him. 'And what about this business of hers? Ita tells me she was doing well, earning quite a bit herself.'

'We've talked about it and she says she really doesn't mind giving it up. If it was up to me I'd be quite happy for her to go on with it and whatever she earned would be her own. I wouldn't expect her to use it for housekeeping.'

Paddy shook his head; he didn't agree with him. In his opinion it looked as if a man couldn't afford to keep his wife if she insisted on working. It was a matter of pride. It was different of course if a man had no work, if they were living in poverty, but Joe had a good, responsible job. The police were looked up to, respected, feared even, pillars of society, well able to keep a wife and family and in comfort. He agreed with the Police Authority and its rules and regulations.

'Well, maybe it's for the best that she gives it up. She'll have enough to do looking after you and then the children.'

Joe smiled. 'And I hope that it won't be too long before we're able to announce that you're to be grandparents.'

'I hope so too and maybe we'll get to see them for we'll never see the three we have in America.'

'I promise we'll visit as often as we can. I grew up in a city but I'd like my children to have some time in the countryside.'

Paddy pulled the collar of his coat up as a cold squall buffeted them. 'It might well be a safer place for them, the way the world is going, with that Hitler feller persecuting the Jews and building up his army and navy and that Mussolini invading Abyssinia.'

Joe nodded. There were dark warnings in all the newspapers from the politicians and the League of Nations about what was going on in Europe and sometimes he, like Paddy, wondered where it would all end.

Paddy shook off his pessimistic mood. 'It's turning bitter; we'd better be getting back. You've a bit of peace and quiet tonight and then it's off on a round of visiting. You are to be inspected by all and sundry.'

'So I understand.'

'God help you!' Paddy muttered under his breath.

Joe grinned. He had excellent hearing.

'And I've yourself to blame for me having to have a new suit.'

Joe laughed. 'Ah, you know what the women are like. I've to be done up to the nines in my dress uniform, no less.'

'Ita is looking forward to the outing and I have to admit that I've never been further than Dublin.'

'We're looking forward to you coming over and I promise I'll take you on a tour of Liverpool's high spots,' Joe offered.

Paddy chuckled. 'Sure, I wouldn't mind a look at some of the "low spots" either, but don't tell Ita I said that!'

After supper that night Molly was concerned to see her mother looking very tired. She had also noticed that Ita had a racking cough.

'Mam, sit down and have a rest, you look worn out.'

'I'm just getting older, Molly. I'm not able for some of the things I never used to give a second thought to.'

'You're a lot thinner, Mam, and you've got a bad cough. Have you been to see Dr Fahey at all?'

'I have not and, sure, there's no need. It's just a bit of a tickle at the back of my throat.'

Molly wasn't giving up. 'It's more than that and why have you lost so much weight?'

'Molly, don't fret so! I don't eat as much as I used to, that's all.'

'You've lost your appetite too? Mam, I'm going to make an appointment and come with you to see the doctor. I'll have no peace of mind to go on planning this wedding until I know there's nothing wrong with you. I mean it!'

'Is she always this bossy, Joe?' Ita asked.

Joe grinned. 'She can be as stubborn as a mule.'

Molly was determined. 'Stubborn or not, you're going to see Dr Fahey.'

'Paddy, will you tell this one here it will be a waste of money?' Ita appealed to her husband.

Paddy was lighting a cigarette. 'Ah, now, don't go getting me involved. Anyway, it would be no harm, Ita. You've had that cough for months now.'

Molly was alarmed. 'Then for heaven's sake why didn't you make her go to the doctor, Da?'

'You know your mam, Molly!'

'Oh, it's all a fuss about nothing. Sure, it really only bothers me at night.' But Ita knew Molly wouldn't be pacified until they'd taken the trap into Tullamore and paid a visit to the surgery.

Molly discussed her worries about Ita's health with Joe next morning while her da hitched up the trap and Ita was putting on her hat and coat.

'You do understand, Joe? If there's anything seriously wrong with her we'll have to postpone the wedding. I just couldn't concentrate on anything. I wish Da had written to me.'

'Don't worry too much, Molly. She does look tired but she works very hard and she's not getting any younger. I'm sure it's nothing serious. Maybe just a rest and a good tonic will help.'

Molly bit her lip. 'Oh, I hope so. Living so far away doesn't help at times like this. If I'd been here I would have noticed that she was losing weight; I would certainly have been aware of the cough. You don't think . . . ?' She couldn't even voice the fear that was nagging at her.

Joe put his arm around her. 'Molly, I honestly don't think she has consumption. I mean that. That's what's worrying you, isn't it?'

She nodded. 'There's no cure for it, Joe. You know that. And, if . . . if it is that, I'll have to stay and nurse her.'

He kissed her forehead. 'Of course you will but I think you're reading too much into a cough. Take her to see the doctor; let him put your mind at rest, love. I've promised to give your da a hand, though I doubt I'll be much use.'

She nodded and felt a little better. Her mother didn't look quite so pale this morning and she hadn't had a single bout of coughing.

Two hours later it was a very relieved Molly who left the doctor's surgery with her mother. Dr Fahey had known them for years and he had given Ita a very thorough examination. She needed to rest more, he told them both. Yes, it was a stubborn cough but there was nothing sinister about it. He had prescribed a cough mixture and a tonic and had advocated a rest each afternoon and maybe some extra help around the house.

'I'll not be paying out good money to have some bold strap of a girl do the housework when I've a daughter of my own,' Ita declared as they left.

'Mam, I'm sure Maria won't mind doing a bit more but I'm also sure that you could find someone who would be really glad of a few extra shillings. You don't have to have a young girl. A married woman would be more suitable; someone to do the really heavy work. The washing; the scrubbing; dragging the furniture out to clean behind it. Ask the parish priest, he's bound to know of a decent woman who'll be more than willing to come in a few times a week. You have to rest, Mam. You had me worried sick!'

Ita nodded slowly. Maybe Molly was right. She'd speak to Father Seamus after Mass and she'd sort out with Paddy how much they could afford to pay a cleaner. Only now would she admit to herself that she really hadn't felt well for quite a few months. Rest and a tonic would work wonders and she'd be back to her old self for Molly's wedding.

Chapter Six

BERNIE HAD WASHED HER hair and attempted to style it the way they had shown in that new magazine she had bought called *Woman*. It was the very latest of magazines, so Mr Chapman in the newsagent's had informed her, and so she'd paid her tuppence and bought a copy. She gazed intently into the mirror. It didn't look quite right. She'd struggled with the Amami setting lotion and the metal Lady Jane grips which were supposed to give you lovely deep waves and even though she'd clipped her hair into place it didn't quite resemble the picture.

She sighed and reached for the hairbrush. Why was she going to so much trouble? She'd even bought a new jumper. She'd seen them in work: new winter stock and just *gorgeous*, Jean Hopkins, her friend from ladies' fashions, had enthused. She'd chosen the royal blue with the white Fair Isle pattern around the neck and cuffs. She'd sewn a little white piqué Peter Pan collar to the neck but it hadn't had the desired effect. Now she wished she'd chosen the bright scarlet. Red suited her; the blue was too dark.

'Oh, for heaven's sake!' she muttered to herself. If Molly had been here she would have chided her that she was making a big effort for Bertie Hayes's visit home, but Molly was off visiting her family in Ireland with Joe. She sat down on the bed and began to brush her hair. Well, she *was* glad he was coming home. He was good company; she liked him; it made a nice change to be taken out instead of going to the cinema alone or with Molly or one of the girls from work. Bertie certainly spared no expense when they went out but, as she'd said to Molly, when else was he to spend his money? And he always brought some nice gifts for his mother and that put Aunt Augusta in a good mood.

Bernie glanced at the big metal alarm clock on the chest of drawers. She'd better get a move on; he'd be arriving any minute. The blue jumper would have to do and now that her hair had been given a good brushing it didn't look bad at all, falling in soft waves that framed her face.

'I was wondering if you intended to stay in that bedroom all night? What have you been doing?' Augusta asked when she came downstairs.

'Oh, just getting changed and doing a bit of sorting out,' Bernie answered evasively. She noticed that the old lady had put on her best black wool crêpe dress and was wearing the single row of cultured pearls Bertie had brought her on his last visit. Her silver-grey hair had been neatly brushed into its usual bun at the nape of her neck.

'Your hair looks nice – softer – but I'm not too sure about the jumper, even if you did give half a week's wages for it. Still, it does match that blue and green plaid skirt, I suppose. You girls are so fussy about everything matching.'

Bernie was sorry she'd mentioned how much the jumper had cost. She grimaced. 'One of these days you'll keep your opinions to yourself, Aunt, but I have to admit that I'm a bit disappointed in it myself.'

Augusta smiled a little grimly. 'There was a time not so long ago when you'd have thought that but would never have dared say it.'

Bernie bent and kissed her on the cheek. 'Ah, but I know you a lot better now.'

'What time did he say he'd be here? I can find neither his letter nor my reading glasses.'

'Around seven. His train is supposed to get into Lime Street at half past six.'

'Make up the fire, there's a good girl. No doubt he'll be frozen stiff.'

Bernie gave the fire a good poke and then emptied half the contents of the brass coal scuttle into the grate. 'There, that should burn up well in a few minutes.'

Augusta looked around the little room with some satisfaction. It was nicely furnished now and looked cosy and welcoming. Molly and Bernie had done wonders with it. Molly had made the soft furnishings and Bernie had kept the best pieces of furniture she'd had from her home with Jimmy. The rest she had eventually sold, after they'd been in storage at Heller's for nearly a year after he'd died. It now looked what it was, a *home*, instead of just rented rooms.

Bernie went into the kitchen to check that the tea tray was laid. She hated this waiting. She'd always been impatient, even as a child. Everything was in order so she went back and sat with Augusta until the loud hammering on the front door made them both jump.

'Oh, wouldn't he put the heart across you!'

'He always was what you'd call boisterous!' Augusta agreed, thinking her son could have announced his arrival a little less noisily.

'Sure, do you have to nearly take the doorknocker off its hinge!' Bernie said, opening the door, but she was laughing.

Bertie Hayes stood on the doorstep grinning broadly. 'Hello, Bernie! I didn't know if you'd be in or not and Ma is getting a bit deaf.'

He wasn't nearly as tall as Joe Jackson but because he was so broad-shouldered you didn't really notice that, Bernie thought. He was quite a bit older than her, being almost thirty-two, and had hazel eyes that twinkled, a shock of unruly reddish-brown hair and – like Joe – an open, honest face.

'Now, would I go out when you're expected home? Sure, she'd murder me. Come on in with you, it's so cold out there it would perish the crows.'

Bertie stacked his seabag against the hallstand while she closed the door and pulled the heavy chenille curtain across.

'Hello, Ma. You're looking well.' He bent and kissed Augusta on the cheek.

'You're freezing, lad. Take off your coat and pull a chair up to the fire,' his mother instructed firmly.

'It's not that bad. To listen to the pair of you you'd think we lived in the Arctic.'

'It sometimes feels like it,' Bernie said.

'You should be out on deck in a force eight gale and with the icicles hanging off every bit of rigging.'

Bernie shivered. 'No thanks!'

Bertie took off his heavy Navy reefer coat and sat down, fumbling in his jacket pocket. 'I thought you'd like this, Ma. It's made from some kind of shell.' He handed a small box to Augusta. It contained a brooch shaped like a fan and embossed with a type of mother-of-pearl. The setting was gold filigree.

'That's pretty. It will look lovely on your good winter coat,' Bernie enthused.

Bertie delved into the other pocket. 'And perhaps you'll like these, Bernie?'

She opened a similar box to find a pair of earrings, again shaped like small fans and made of the same iridescent shell. 'They're beautiful! I've never seen anything like them before.' She clipped them to her ears and stood admiring them in the mirror above the fireplace.

'So, you'll be staying for over a week this time,' Augusta remarked. Usually his visits were fairly brief.

'I am. I've signed off with P&O.'

'What for?' his mother demanded. They were a long-established company whose ships sailed to the Far East and Australia.

He shrugged. 'I'd like shorter trips. I'm hoping to try Cunard; they've a brand-new ship due to go into service soon. The biggest ship in the whole world, so I hear, and they do short Atlantic crossings for most of the year. I've seen most of the world now.'

His mother raised her eyebrows but said nothing, hoping his desire for shorter trips was something to do with seeing more of Bernie.

When Augusta finally went to bed Bertie patted the empty seat on the sofa beside him. 'Come and sit here.'

Bernie moved to the sofa and smiled at him. 'I can remember a time in this house when we were allowed no "gentlemen callers". Now, she goes off to bed and leaves me alone with a man.'

'Ah, but not just a man. I'm her favourite son, don't forget.'

'And it's great that you get home to see her more often these days. She's getting old, don't forget.'

'But just as indomitable. And I come to see you as well.'

'I know you do and I'm just as pleased to see you as she is.'

'And with Molly jaunting around Ireland showing off her fine catch to the relations I have you all to myself.'

'He *is* a fine catch.'

'I'm not saying he isn't. He's a good bloke – for a copper! I expect all I'll hear are wedding plans now.'

Bernie laughed. 'Not at all. She hasn't really made any yet, apart from deciding to get married here.'

'There's some would say I wasn't a bad catch myself.'

Bernie glanced at him from beneath her lashes. 'Your mam for one.'

'She's biased. But I've never been without a ship, I've a few bob saved and no bad habits.'

Bernie laughed. 'Except one,' she challenged.

'What?' he demanded, disconcerted.

'You can't stay in one place for longer than a month *and* there's something else that will always come first with you.'

'What?' He was looking at her quizzically, his head on one side.

'The sea. You've salt water in your veins. Now, enough of this desperate conversation. Where are you taking me tomorrow night?'

He sighed. He could never pin her down. He was sure she was fond of him; his mother assured him she was and advocated giving her time, but time was one thing he didn't have. He wasn't around for months on end and he was afraid that one day she might meet someone else. He had even contemplated giving up the sea, though he knew he would find it desperately hard to live and work on land.

'I thought we might go to the Grafton Ballroom.'

Bernie smiled. 'Well, seeing as we're going somewhere posh, I want to look my best, so I'd better get my beauty sleep.' She kissed him briefly on the lips and rose.

'Goodnight, Bernie, luv. See you in the morning,' he said with a note of disappointment in his voice.

'You're to have a lie-in tomorrow, as it's your first day home. Your mam's instructions, remember. I'll see you when I get in from work. There's blankets and a pillow in the kitchen.'

He bent to take off his boots. He always slept on the sofa when he was home, as there were only two bedrooms, but when he heard Bernie's footsteps on the stairs he wished he were going up with her.

Despite the cold weather she wore her best pale blue crêpe de Chine dress the following evening.

'You'll catch pneumonia dressed like that,' had been Augusta's comment when she'd come downstairs.

'Aren't I going to wear a cardigan and my heavy coat over it? And it's bound to be very warm in the ballroom,' Bernie'd answered with some spirit.

Bertie was all done up in his good serge suit with a clean shirt and shining boots. Sensibly, in his mother's opinion, he had his reefer jacket over his arm.

'Enjoy yourselves,' Augusta said as they prepared to leave.

Bernie laughed. 'Oh, I'm sure we will.'

They went for a drink first. Gregson's Well was situated on the corner of Cobden Street and was a small, cosy pub. Bertie bought the drinks while Bernie settled herself at a table near the blazing fire in the small parlour. She looked around admiringly: it was a comfortable, cheery room. The firelight was reflected in the shining brass ornaments that adorned the window ledges. Everything looked well cared for.

'It's really nice here,' she commented, sipping her sweet sherry.

'Would I bring you anywhere that wasn't?'

'You're really very good to me.'

'You're worth it, Bernie, and I . . . well, I wanted to talk to you before we went to the ballroom.'

'What's so important?' Bernie shot a glance at the only other occupant of the room: an elderly gentleman engrossed in a copy of the *Racing Post*.

'He won't bother us. He's too busy studying form,' Bertie said, fiddling with the beer mat and feeling nervous.

'Well?' Bernie pressed; she was wondering just what it was that was on his mind.

'I . . . I'm changing shipping company to be nearer to you.' He lowered his voice while glancing at the man with the newspaper. 'I love you, Bernie, and . . . and . . . will you marry me?'

Bernie twisted her rings around on her finger. 'I'm very fond of you, Bertie, I really am, but I don't know if I love you. We haven't been walking out for very long—'

'I know that and you know that if I were home more often I'd see more of you. That's why I want short trips,' he interrupted.

Bernie sighed, thinking of Augusta's words about trust and mutual respect. 'Can I think about it? It's all a bit sudden. I'm not turning you down flat, I just want time to sort out how I really feel about you.'

Bertie took her hand, feeling relieved and hopeful. 'Take all the time you need, Bernie. I want you to be sure. I'll wait.'

She smiled shyly as she squeezed his hand. 'I won't make you wait too long, I promise. Now, shall we finish these drinks and go and "trip the light fantastic" as they say?'

Chapter Seven

CHRISTMAS THAT YEAR WAS a very busy time as Molly had obtained four new commissions and was house-hunting in earnest. Bertie had managed to do two trips to New York on the *Aquitania* and still be home for the holiday and he had told his mother in confidence that Bernie had agreed to consider his proposal of marriage.

'Give her time. Don't rush her into anything,' had been Augusta's advice.

January of 1936 was a bleak month with ice and heavy snow which made conditions underfoot treacherous. Ashes were spread on the pavements to prevent people slipping, although many pavements were made even more dangerous by groups of young boys making slides of them with the aid of shelves from their outraged mothers' ovens. The hooves of the shire horses used to pull the carts were tied up in sacking to prevent them slipping but there had been many accidents and the poor, patient animals had had to be put down.

On the twentieth of the month King George V died, plunging the whole country into mourning.

Augusta draped black crêpe across the window of the parlour and a picture of the deceased monarch was displayed in a prominent position on the sideboard.

'Don't you think it's going a bit too far? It's not as though a relative has died,' Bernie confided to Molly as they sat in the mournful little room looking at a magazine for brides-to-be that Molly had bought.

'I suppose it's different for her – for everyone like her. We're too young to remember what it's like to live in a country ruled by a monarch. Mam and Da will remember, Ireland was still part of the British Empire when they were young,' Molly replied.

'I don't suppose they'll do much mourning. They remember the long, hard fight for freedom and it's not really over yet. Aren't there all kinds of trade restrictions imposed on the Free State?'

Molly nodded. 'I remember Da complaining about them but I don't suppose we should say too much. Everyone would be up in arms.'

Bernie sighed. 'You're right, but it does put a damper on things. Who'll be the next one?'

'The eldest son of course. What's his name?'

'Edward, I think. Will they have a big "do" for him?'

'When he gets crowned, you mean?'

Bernie nodded.

'I suppose so. I just hope it doesn't clash with my wedding. Joe might not be able to get the time off.'

Bernie looked horrified. 'Sure, they'll *have* to give him time off to get married! You've everyone coming over and the church booked and Reece's Restaurant booked for the reception.'

'I know. Oh, I suppose we'll just have to keep our fingers crossed.'

'I'm going to say a novena just to make certain,' Bernie said firmly.

The plans for the wedding progressed and Molly was relieved that no date appeared to be set for the coronation of King Edward VIII. Ita had written to say that she was now feeling much better. The cough had gone and she had more energy. She was going to buy her outfit in Liverpool as it was years since she'd had anything at all stylish and Tullamore wasn't great on style. Maria's bridesmaid dress was also to be purchased in Liverpool but Paddy insisted he was having his suit from Michael Farrell's as they were doing a new line in suits now, so he'd been informed. You didn't need to go to all the bother of getting measured up, you could buy one 'ready made' or 'off the peg'.

'Sure, we've had "off the peg" for years over here,' Bernie remarked when Molly read out the letter, thinking of the coats and two-piece costumes they'd both bought over the years.

'I think Mam should have a nice two-piece in a pastel shade with a hat to match,' Molly said. She'd been giving a lot of thought to her mother's outfit lately. 'Mam's only ever had a decent dark coat for winter and a lighter-coloured one for summer. She always says they're "serviceable" but I want her to have something *different*. Something a bit . . . *frivolous*. After the wedding she can wear it to Mass for the summer months.'

Bernie grimaced. 'I don't think "frivolous" would go down well in Rahan.'

'Oh, rubbish! Let them talk! I want Mam to look *special*! She deserves it.'

Bernie laughed. 'You don't have to eat me! Where will you take her for it?'

Molly was thoughtful. 'Lewis's or Owen Owen.'

'It will cost you a pretty penny.'

'I can spare it. Joe is insisting on totally furnishing the house, if we get it. All I've got to pay for are the curtains and cushions and as I get the material and trimmings at trade they won't make too big a hole in my savings.'

'Have you heard any more about the house?' Bernie enquired.

'We should hear this week if we've got it.' Molly touched the little gold cross around her neck. She'd been praying hard that they'd get the house in Oxbridge Street, just a few streets away from Weybridge Street, which she'd admired so much. The houses were identical and her mind was full of plans for the colours she'd have in each room.

Joe had said he'd decorate, aided by his father who was willing to leave his precious pigeons to help out. Effie had offered to help Molly scrub the place out, if it needed it.

'We are still going for your wedding dress at the weekend?' Bernie said anxiously. Time was getting on; it was now late March and there was still so much for them to do.

'Of course. I've made the appointment for one o'clock so you can come with me in your lunch hour.'

'I've never had the courage to go into Hendersons. They have a uniformed commissionaire on the door. It looks so *grand*.'

Molly smiled at her. 'Isn't our money just as good as that of all the toffs?' But despite her words she too was a little apprehensive; the store was one of Liverpool's most exclusive and one she would never have frequented had both Joe and Augusta not urged her to do so.

Bernie nodded. She was sorry Bertie wouldn't be home for the wedding but he had been so fortunate in getting a job on the brand-new *Queen Mary* whose maiden voyage was set for May 27. He was so excited about it. It was all he'd talked about on his last leave. He'd only been with Cunard for a short while and he'd been really lucky to have been picked as a crew member. Then she brightened a little: he'd said that he might bring her something really special after his first trip on the new ship – a bit of jewellery, maybe a ring. She'd laughed but then she'd said a ring might be nice which was tantamount to saying she would agree to become engaged. Molly's wedding would be over by the time he got home so she wouldn't be stealing any of Molly's thunder by announcing her engagement.

It was a wild March day with a strong wind blowing and the occasional sharp heavy shower as Molly stood in the doorway of Frisby Dyke's on Lord Street, sheltering while she waited for Bernie to appear. She didn't want to look bedraggled when they had walked down to Church Street to confront the commissionaire outside Hendersons.

'Have you been here long? I got away as quickly as I could but you know what Saturdays are like! I'd hoped the wind and rain would have kept people at home but we've been as busy as ever.' Bernie jammed her scarlet beret firmly on her head.

Molly smiled at her. 'You look nice.'

'Well, we've both got to look halfway decent. Shall we risk it? I think the rain is easing off and I've got my umbrella.'

They both stepped out of the shelter of the doorway and, heads bent against the powerful blast that was blowing up from the river, walked towards the junction of Lord Street and Whitechapel.

To their relief when they reached Hendersons the commissionaire opened the plate-glass door for them with a polite, 'Good afternoon, ladies, let me take those umbrellas.'

They stepped into the foyer with its deep-pile sage-green carpet embossed with the letter 'H' in cream.

'Oh, it is *grand*!' Bernie whispered in awe.

'Hush! Try to look as though we always shop here. Don't gape!' Molly whispered back, straightening her velvet beret.

The ground floor was large and imposing and almost entirely given over to cosmetics and high-class haberdashery.

'Which floor do we need? Should we ask?' Bernie again whispered, eyeing the incredibly smart sales assistants.

Molly nodded and headed for the nearest counter with its array of fancy jars and bottles. 'Excuse me. We have an appointment in the bridal department. Could you tell me which floor we need?'

'Third floor. I'd take the lift if I were you or you can walk if you prefer; the stairs are just over there.' The girl pointed in the direction of the wide, carpeted staircase.

'Thank you. We'll take the lift; it might be quicker,' Molly replied.

They both made an effort not to stare as if mesmerised as they walked to the lift. It was all a little daunting.

'I'm beginning to think I might have felt more comfortable going to Lewis's,' Molly confided as she pushed the button for the third floor and the lift doors silently closed.

When they emerged they couldn't help their jaws dropping. Neither of them had ever seen such clothes as those displayed.

'Oh, Moll, this really is high fashion. Just look at that *gorgeous* outfit!' Bernie hissed.

They both stood and admired the coat and dress in apricot crêpe. The collar of the coat was deep and trimmed with fur, which had been dyed the exact same shade as the coat. A large picture hat of Bangkok straw accompanied the outfit, trimmed with silk ribbon and artificial roses.

'Wouldn't Mam look stunning in that,' Molly finally said.

'Wouldn't *I* look "stunning" in that! That colour is gorgeous! How much does it cost?'

'There's no price ticket on it. I suppose if we have to ask the price we can't afford it.'

Bernie sighed. Molly was probably right. It would be way beyond her lowly means. She intended to go to Blackler's for her outfit. 'Come on. I think the bridal bit is over there, at the back.'

It was an area partitioned off with stylish frosted-glass panels. Inside there was a small reception area with a delicate-looking couch covered in oyster brocade. The young woman behind the ornate, highly polished desk looked rather snooty, Bernie thought.

'May I help you, miss?' The tone was rather clipped.

Molly approached the desk, straightening her shoulders. 'Yes, I have an appointment. Miss Mary Keegan.'

The woman smiled. 'Ah, yes. If you would like to take a seat I'll inform Miss Armstrong that you are here.'

'I hope this Miss Armstrong is a bit more pleasant than your one behind the desk,' Bernie whispered when the receptionist was out of sight.

'So do I but I'm not going to be put off,' Molly said firmly.

To their relief Miss Armstrong was very pleasant and put them both at their ease immediately. Molly judged her to be in her mid-thirties and admired her upswept blond hair and smart black and white dress.

'Now, have you a particular style in mind? Is there anything you definitely don't want to see?' Miss Armstrong asked.

'I don't want anything fussy. Definitely no frills,' Molly said firmly.

The assistant nodded. 'I agree with you entirely. You have a lovely figure, you're tall, and your colouring is very striking. I think we should make the most of those assets. I have three dresses I think would look stunning on you.'

They were shown into a wide cubicle with mirrors on three of its walls and hooks on the wall for their coats. Eventually Miss Armstrong reappeared with three of the most beautiful dresses they'd ever seen.

'Now, if you'd like to undress I think we'll try this one first.'

Molly did as she was bid and was thankful she'd worn her best white bra and matching camiknickers. Both Bernie and the assistant helped ease the confection of silk organza and duchesse satin over Molly's head.

'Oh, Molly! It's just *gorgeous*!' Bernie breathed as Miss Armstrong fastened it up and adjusted the bodice and skirt.

Molly felt transformed as she gazed at herself in the mirror. The dress was a sheath of duchesse satin overlaid with delicate silk organza. The bodice was tight with a high neck and a mandarin collar and long sleeves. The collar was adorned with two rows of seed pearls and two further rows embellished the cuffs of the sleeves. Unusually, the neckline came to a 'v' at the back and was fastened with tiny pearl buttons. The skirt, which was almost straight at the front, billowed out at the back into a cloud of silk organza which then fell into a short train. Molly thought it looked just like a cloud of gossamer. It was elegant, unusual and utterly gorgeous.

Miss Armstrong produced a small pearl tiara and a full-length veil of silk tulle and placed it on Molly's head.

Tears pricked Bernie's eyes as she looked at her friend. Molly looked amazing, utterly amazing.

'Just perfect!' Miss Armstrong announced and Molly nodded slowly.

'I can't find the right words, Moll! You look so . . . Oh, gorgeous and beautiful and amazing just aren't enough!'

'She's all of those things and utterly elegant too,' Miss Armstrong said and she meant it. The dress was exactly the right one for the girl. This was a part of her job she really enjoyed, when she saw the look of astonishment and pure pleasure that came over the faces of the brides-to-be.

'This is definitely *it*! It's the one I want.' Molly was totally sure. She hadn't really had a picture in her mind of what she wanted but this dress was perfect.

'Try the other two on, just to be sure,' Miss Armstrong advised, starting to undo the row of pearl buttons.

Molly tried the other two and while she agreed with Bernie that they were both beautiful dresses, her mind was made up.

The dress was carefully packed into a large box with layer upon layer of tissue paper. The tiara and veil were packed just as carefully.

Molly hadn't even asked the price but now she broached the subject tentatively.

Miss Armstrong smiled. 'It's not as expensive as it looks. It's eight guineas which is excellent value and the accessories come to another four.'

Bernie thought you could buy a good bedroom suite and a dining table and chairs for that amount but she said nothing. She knew Molly had been a diligent saver for years and she never wasted money. This was a really special occasion and she didn't begrudge her friend one little bit.

'Now, do try it on at least three weeks before the wedding day, then if it needs altering at all, if you lose weight or gain weight, we can make the necessary adjustments.' Miss Armstrong took the notes and coins Molly handed over.

Molly mentally calculated how much of her savings she had left. She had shoes to buy and underwear. There was Maria's outfit and she intended to contribute to her mam's too. Bernie was to be her matron of honour but was insisting on buying her own outfit and they'd decided that something more practical than a long dress that would never be worn again would be better. There were the flowers and the cake too, but she had budgeted carefully and the wedding dress hadn't been as expensive as she'd imagined.

'We saw a lovely coat and dress as we came in. Would it be possible for my friend to try it on?' she enquired, ignoring Bernie's look of horror.

'Of course. If you'll describe it to me I'll bring it in here.'

'It's apricot crêpe and the coat has a fur collar in the same shade. Oh, and could you bring the matching hat, please?'

When the assistant had left them Bernie found her voice. 'Holy Mother of God! Are you mad? I can't afford it. I've about four pounds and ten shillings put by. I'm going to Blackler's. They have some nice things and aren't too dear. God knows how much that suit costs!' she hissed.

'I'll make up the difference. I've done my sums and I can afford it. You'll take the sight from the eyes of everyone!' Molly urged.

'It's not me who is supposed to be taking the sight from the eyes of everyone! It's you. It's *your* day; I've had mine, remember? It's not even as if Bertie will be home to see me.'

'But didn't you tell me that when he comes home he's bringing a ring? You'll be going somewhere really posh to celebrate and it will do for when he takes you down to Southampton to see his new ship.'

Bernie bit her lip. She was going down to Southampton early in June. Bertie was going to get permission to take her over the *Queen Mary* for a day. It was quite usual for family members of the crew to be allowed this privilege and to have lunch or dinner on the ship. The new liner was supposed to be the height of luxury and the apricot outfit would be perfect.

Before there could be any further discussion on the matter Miss Armstrong arrived with the crêpe ensemble over one arm and the hat balanced on her right hand. 'It's very, very smart. The latest colour for spring and summer and the latest style too.'

Bernie tried it on, noticing for the first time the delicate embroidery on the yoke of the dress and the way the skirt was gathered into soft pleats at the hip on the left side. The coat was so light and she touched the fur collar almost reverently.

'The colour suits you very well. Not everyone can wear that colour but you definitely can. Now, let me get the hat at the right angle.'

Bernie submitted to having the hat tried on at various angles and then Miss Armstrong stepped back, satisfied.

'You look just like a picture of Princess Marina I saw in a magazine and you know how elegant she is!' Molly enthused. Bernie looked so different, so 'chic' – a word she had read in the same magazine.

'Except that she's much taller than I am. It is beautiful though, isn't it?' Bernie sighed.

'A nice pair of cream court shoes and a cream handbag would be perfect – or if you preferred black patent leather?' the woman finished, seeing the slightly anxious look that crossed Bernie's face. Obviously they were both working-class girls and cream shoes would be a bit impractical.

'Either would look good,' Molly agreed.

Bernie took a deep breath and asked the price.

'It is a bit on the expensive side. It's six guineas and the hat is one pound eighteen shillings.'

Before Bernie could make any comment Molly said they would take them both. She'd brought twenty pounds out with her, what Augusta would view as a small fortune and which was indeed a lot of money in anyone's book.

The apricot ensemble was duly packed in a box, as was the hat. Molly handed over the money and was thanked profusely and reminded to try on her dress; then they both left the shop in a slight daze.

'Oh, Moll! Did we really spend that amount of money?' Bernie said as they emerged into Church Street.

Molly laughed. 'We did so and won't we both look so gorgeous that we'll be the talk of everyone for months!'

Chapter Eight

AUGUSTA THOUGHT BOTH DRESSES were the loveliest she'd ever seen. She realised they were expensive but neither of the girls enlightened her as to just *how* expensive they had been.

The time just seemed to fly. As the weather got warmer the trees that lined some of the city's streets unfurled fresh green leaves and in the parks the spring flowers made colourful displays.

Bertie had made his last trip on the *Aquitania* and was looking forward to joining the new flagship of the Cunard Line towards the middle of May. He'd come home bearing gifts for both his mother and Bernie and had given Molly a beautifully wrapped box containing his wedding gift to her and Joe.

'It will be a shame to open it. Who wrapped it up like

this?' Molly had asked as she carefully laid it down on the top of the chest of drawers.

'The girl in the shop. They go in for all kinds of fancy things over there,' he'd replied.

'We never wrap things up like that. Look at this ribbon, Moll. I've never seen ribbon like it before.' Bernie had fingered the big pale pink and silver bow carefully. It didn't feel like the ribbon she was used to selling. That was soft and satiny; this was much stiffer and it had a silver shimmer to it.

'I just hope you and Joe will find it useful. They said it was the latest gadget and that every home should have one,' Bertie had informed them.

'Now you'll have the pair of them eaten up with curiosity until the wedding day,' Augusta had remarked, slapping Molly's hand gently as Molly had poked and prodded the parcel.

Bertie had laughed. 'Well, it's not long to wait now.'

Bernie was rushing home from work to get changed as Bertie had made plans to take her to the Stork Hotel for a meal and then on to the late show at the Empire. It was to be a very special occasion, he'd told her, and Augusta had informed her that he had bought a gold dress ring in New York, as a sort of 'stop-gap' to the engagement ring. She knew he was expecting an answer and she had made up her mind. She couldn't stay a widow all her life; it was time to look to the future.

'Look, there's a tram coming! If we run we'll catch it,' Jean, her friend, said as they stepped into the street.

'As long as it's not packed,' Bernie replied as they both broke into a trot, which was all they could do on the crowded street.

'I thought he wasn't coming to meet you?' Jean said, catching sight of Bertie on the opposite side of the road.

Bernie slowed down. 'He isn't. Are you sure it's him?'

'It is. Look. You must have got it all wrong, Bernie.'

'Oh, damn!' Bernie said irritably, her gaze fixed on Bertie.

Jean tugged at her arm. 'Who is *that*?'

Bernie's eyes narrowed and she gave a shocked little gasp as a girl of her own age came up to Bertie and hugged him.

Jean pulled herself together. 'Come on, Bernie, let's get the tram!'

Bernie didn't reply. She felt cold. He had someone else! All the time he had been courting her, taking her to dances, to the cinema, he'd been taking *that one* out too! She'd trusted him implicitly. She'd even decided to marry him! Had he brought *her* a ring too? Or was he meeting her, Bernie, to tell her it was all over, that he was going to marry someone else?

'Come on, Bernie!' Jean half dragged her towards the tram and bundled her inside. 'It was probably nothing. A misunderstanding.'

'It didn't look like a misunderstanding from where I was standing! The two-timing . . . I could murder him, so I could!' she exploded.

Despite all Jean's reassuring words she continued to seethe all the way home.

'What in the name of Holy God is wrong with you?' Molly asked as Bernie flounced into the kitchen.

'That two-timing, sneaking . . . rat!'

'Who?' Molly demanded.

'Bertie Hayes! Didn't I just see him with another girl? With my own two eyes I saw her rush up to him and hug him! As brazen as you like in the middle of Lord Street! Well, he can take his ring and—!'

Molly pushed her down on to a chair. 'Are you sure it was him? It gets so crowded on Lord Street at that time of day.'

Bernie was shaking with anger and humiliation. 'Of course it was him: I trusted him, Moll! He said he loved me and all the time he was seeing *her*! I was going to marry him . . .' Bernie laughed bitterly but her eyes were full of tears.

Molly couldn't believe it. 'There's got to be an explanation, Bernie!'

'What? Oh, he's running true to form all right. Typical bloody sailor: a girl in every port, even this port. How many more are there that I don't know about? He wanted shorter runs to see more of me, he said, and to see *that one* too!'

'Bernie, calm down! I don't for a single minute believe he has a string of girls. He's just not like that.'

The tears were trickling down Bernie's cheeks and Molly put her arm around her. 'How do we know what he's like? He might be a totally different person when he's not here. Oh, Moll, I feel so hurt and so desperately humiliated. I hate him!'

Molly squared her shoulders as she heard Bertie's key in the lock. 'Here he is. Now let's see what he has to say for himself.'

Bertie was whistling as he came into the kitchen but the sound died as he saw Bernie's face. 'What's the matter, Bernie? You're upset. What's happened?'

'I think you've got some explaining to do,' Molly said coldly.

'I saw you, Bertie Hayes! I saw you with that . . . that floozie!' Bernie cried, getting to her feet, her fingers clenched into fists.

'What floozie?' Bertie sounded mystified.

'That girl who ran and threw her arms around you in the middle of Lord Street not half an hour ago!'

Comprehension dawned on Bertie and he shook his head. 'You mean Lily Williams? She's married to my mate, Jackie Williams. He couldn't get home this time. He'd bought her a necklace and I said I'd give it to her. I've known Lily for years and she's as straight as a die. She works further up Lord Street and so I said I'd meet her when she finished.'

'But why did she throw her arms around you?' Molly demanded.

'It was a quick, friendly hug, that's all. Like I said, I've known her for years. Look, if it's going to cause this much trouble I'll get Jackie to write to you or I'll bring Lily down here to see you. Bernie, you didn't honestly think I had someone else?'

Bernie was beginning to calm down. 'I didn't know what to think. You never mentioned that you had to meet her.'

'I didn't think it was all that important, Bernie. Come on, luv, dry your eyes. I'm really sorry if I've upset you but I just didn't think! I'm so sorry, Bernie, I really am. I'd never willingly hurt you. Couldn't you have trusted me?'

Molly sighed with relief. She believed him. 'Let's forget all about it.'

Bernie was beginning to feel slightly foolish for jumping to conclusions, but it had looked so . . . *believable* at the time.

Bertie took her in his arms. 'It's all a storm in a teacup. I love you; I'd never do anything like that. Now, go and get changed or we'll be late.'

Bernie nodded but a little voice in her head was asking: Was he telling the truth?

Augusta had been to visit a cousin who was ill in hospital and when she returned she could see something was wrong. Molly looked worried.

'What's wrong now? Has there been bad news from home?'

'No. Nothing like that,' Molly replied and then told the old lady the whole chain of events.

'He's telling the truth, Molly. He's known Lily for years. She used to live at the bottom of this street; her name was Lily Irwin then. They played together as children. If I thought he was seeing someone else behind Bernie's back I would have quite a lot to say on the matter, you can be certain of that. Nor would I have encouraged her. The last thing I want is for that girl to be heart-broken again.'

Molly nodded slowly. 'I'm so relieved. I believed him but I don't know if Bernie did entirely.'

'Then when they come in I can put her mind at rest. I just hope he hasn't produced the ring and she's turned him down!'

In fact Bernie had been very quiet all evening and Bertie had decided it wasn't the right time to produce the gold dress ring. He could have kicked himself for not mentioning the fact that he'd promised to meet Lily.

'I suppose all this nonsense has spoiled the evening?' Augusta stated when they returned home.

Bernie shrugged.

'He has known Lily Williams since they were both five years of age and she lived at the end of this street. She's a very nice girl and I went to her wedding. She has eyes for no one other than Jackie. Bertie here was a fool not to have told you he was meeting her, on behalf of Jackie, but let's hear no more about it. Did he give you the ring?' Augusta asked pointedly.

A wave of pure relief washed over Bernie, silencing the doubt that had nagged at her all evening, and making her realise that she loved Bernie more than ever. 'No. I . . . I haven't exactly been the best of company, have I?' She smiled up at Bertie. 'I'm sorry.'

'And I'm sorry too.'

'Well, for heaven's sake give her the ring and we can celebrate something!' his mother instructed.

'Honestly, Mam, you're the living end!' Bertie cried but he delved into his pocket and brought out a small leather box.

Bernie held out her hand and Bertie slipped the ring on her finger.

'Congratulations! Now I'll have a daughter-in-law I can get on with. Molly, get out the best glasses while I fetch the sherry. Two weddings in the family – isn't that something to celebrate?'

Bertie put his arm around Bernie and she reached up and kissed him on the cheek. 'Let's get Molly's big day over with first.'

Before Molly could quite believe it the week of the wedding arrived and she found herself down at the Pier Head to meet her family coming off the Dublin ferry.

'Mam! Da! Over here!' she cried, waving frantically as she spotted them in the crowd emerging from the ferry.

'Oh, isn't this a shocking crush? Haven't I nearly had the bag pulled out of my hand twice already!' Ita exclaimed, hugging Molly with one arm while clutching her big and rather battered carpet-bag with the other.

'Let's get away from the crowd. Maria, hang on to your ma and you lads hang on to me,' Paddy instructed.

Molly shepherded them quickly towards the waiting line of trams and buses. 'I'll get you home. I bet you're in need of a cup of tea, Mam.'

'I am so. There was only beer, spirits and mineral water on that.' Ita jerked her head in the direction of the ferry boat.

Molly laughed. 'Oh, well, that was Da and the lads catered for.'

'My arms are aching with carrying this case. I had to put some of their stuff in too,' Maria complained, casting her brothers a look of disdain. 'When will we be going for the outfits, Molly?'

'Will you give us time to draw breath, child? Haven't we only just set foot on dry land?' her mother admonished.

Molly could see how excited her sister was. 'Tomorrow, Maria. You'll have had a good night's sleep so we can spend the whole day sorting you and Mam out. Joe has a rest day so he's offered to take Da and the lads to see the sights of Liverpool.'

'Thanks be to God for that. I was wondering what we'd do with these two. You are sure that Augusta's neighbours don't mind putting us up? We are strangers, after all.'

'Not at all. They're very nice; you'll feel right at home with Mrs Stockbridge and Mrs Harper,' Molly assured them.

There had been great discussions as to where Molly's family would stay. Effie Jackson had suggested that Maisie Dobbs, her next-door neighbour, might be approached but Molly had prevaricated. Both Maisie and her future mother-in-law were terrible gossips and would give you a headache in half an hour. Augusta had agreed to ask the two neighbours she'd been friendly with for years and Molly had been relieved. They were both women of her mam's age but their families had married and left and so they could easily accommodate hers. She'd offered to pay them but her da had insisted that he do so. He was also insisting on giving her money towards her own, Maria's and her mother's outfits, plus the flowers and the cake and the reception.

'If you'd been living at home and getting married at Killina wouldn't I have had to foot the entire bill?' he'd said when she'd protested.

They had been introduced to Augusta and Bernie informed Ita that her cousin Nellie O'Sullivan was only itching to meet her and would be paying a visit tomorrow night.

'That's grand, Bernie. I'd like to meet her and thank her for putting you up when you first came over here,' Ita had replied. Then Molly had taken them and introduced them to Mrs Harper and Mrs Stockbridge and helped them settle in.

The following morning they were all up early and after breakfast Ita and Maria came into Augusta's house.

'Where're Da and the lads? Joe will be here any minute,' Molly asked.

'Just coming. Your da was giving them a good talking to about minding their manners. Aren't they fascinated with the electricity? Flicking the light switch on and off by the minutes. I told the pair of them if they didn't stop it would be a belt they'd be getting. You'd be after thinking I'd put no manners on them at all but isn't your da as bad? Spent hours chatting to Mr Harper about how much time and energy having the electricity would save on the farm. It would save me a great deal of time and energy too, I told him. No range to keep going. No lamps to fill and clean and trim. I could have a lovely cooker like everyone here seems to have, pretty lamps you just switch on, a kettle that boils up at the flick of a switch, and Maria is mesmerised by the set of curling tongs Herself next door has and has a puss on her that she can't have a set.'

'Oh, you'll get the electricity in time, Mam,' Molly soothed, thinking how used she'd got to everything. 'Here's Joe now.'

Joe greeted Ita and Maria warmly and kissed Molly on the cheek. Then: 'How are you today, Aunt Augusta? I brought you these. I thought you'd like them.' He handed her a small bunch of violets and anemones. He never forgot the old lady had been so good to Molly and liked to treat her.

'I'm not too bad; I can't complain. They are lovely. Thank you, Joe. I'll find a vase for them.'

'They'll cheer her up. She's been feeling a bit down lately, so Molly says. I suppose it's no fun being in constant pain as she is with her arthritis,' Joe confided to Ita.

Ita smiled. He was such a thoughtful lad. 'Ah, here's Himself and the lads. Now, Joe, don't you stand for any trick-acting out of them.'

'I won't, but I'm sure they'll be fine. I've a great day planned for us all. A tour of the city then a ride on the ferry to New Brighton. The lads will love New Brighton. It's a seaside place with a real fort, a lighthouse, a tower and a fun fair. That should keep them amused.'

Ita cast her eyes to heaven. 'I'll be able to do nothing with them when I get them home, Joe. Rahan is going to seem very dull after all this.'

'Ah, they'll be just grand. They'll settle back down,' Paddy said amiably. He too was looking forward to the day and he'd already given Ita a nice wad of money to spend, so that should keep her and Maria happy too.

'Right, we'll be off then. I promise to have them all back safe and sound by teatime,' Joe promised.

'We'll have a cup of tea and then we'll be off too,' Molly said as the men left, preceded by two very excited young boys.

Ita sipped her tea thoughtfully. 'I've been wanting a word with you, Molly, just the two of us.'

'What's the matter, Mam? It's not that cough again, is it?'

'It is not. Aren't I fit and well, thanks be to God. No, it's you. Well, you and Joe and you being his wife.'

'Mam, what are you trying to say?'

'You know your duties as a wife, Molly? You can't go refusing him his rights, even if you don't always feel . . .' Ita gave an embarrassed little cough and took a sip of tea.

'Mam, you don't need to worry about things like that,' Molly said quietly. Her mother was trying in a clumsy way to tell her the facts of life. She felt ashamed and embarrassed herself. Ita did not for one minute suspect that she already knew quite a bit about sex and its inevitable outcome and she couldn't enlighten her. Maybe one day she'd feel she could tell her mother the whole sorry tale of her affair with Billy Marshall, but not now. 'Come on, put all that out of your mind and drink your tea. I'll hurry Maria up and then we'll be on our way.'

Ita felt excited herself at the prospect of some real shopping in the big stores both Molly and Mrs Harper had described. It had been years since she had been up to Dublin even and she had noticed when they'd been travelling on the tram that everyone looked so smart and very stylish. She felt very drab and old-fashioned and Maria had said that everything she owned was just so babyish that she was dying of embarrassment. Well, they'd both enjoy the day.

Molly took them to Lewis's in Ranelagh Street, which to Ita's eyes seemed huge. It was on five floors with a basement as well and even had a small zoo!

'How do you find your way around?' she asked.

'You get used to it. Now, we want the second floor. Ladies' fashions,' Molly replied as she guided them towards the lift.

'You're sure this contraption is safe?' Ita whispered.

Molly laughed. 'Oh, Mam! Of course it is.'

'Well, I'd feel safer using the two good legs God gave me to climb the stairs,' her mother said, still doubtful.

'Don't be so . . . unadventurous,' Maria exclaimed. Just wait until she got back and told Claire O'Sullivan, her best friend, about everything. She'd never seen anything like the display of make-up and perfume that she'd glimpsed on the ground floor of the store.

'Now, Mam, what colour do you think you would like? Effie has told me that she's considering a navy and white costume, which I think is very dull but she says is practical.'

'It is,' Ita agreed but then frowned. 'I don't know what colour I'd like, Molly, and that's the truth of it.'

'What about lilac? It would suit you and I've never seen you in anything like it.'

'I don't know.' Ita looked very doubtful as they arrived at the second floor.

'Mam, be a bit more adventurous,' Molly urged.

'She's right. Go on, Mam. Give it a try.' Maria was on Molly's side.

Ita finally chose a lilac two-piece with a white crêpe de Chine blouse embroidered with the little mauve flowers. 'The skirt is lovely on you, Mam. I never realised you had such good legs,' Molly said.

'That's because it's not at all decent for a married woman of my age to be showing off her legs to all and sundry!' Ita retorted, but the bias-cut skirt draped beautifully and the short fitted jacket showed off a remarkably trim figure for a middle-aged woman, she thought.

Maria raised her eyes to the ceiling. 'Would you just listen to her!' she hissed to her sister.

Molly smiled. Maria was indeed growing up. 'We'll find a lovely pair of high-heeled court shoes and a matching handbag, and a very smart hat; and then no one will recognise you.' She grinned conspiratorially at Maria.

'Holy Mother of God! Me in high heels! Sure, I'd never be able for them!' Ita exclaimed.

'You will, Mam,' Molly said firmly.

The costume and complementing blouse were duly purchased and they went in search of matching accessories. An hour later Ita was in possession of an outfit that she declared was 'suitable for the gentry', no less. A large lilac and white picture hat had been purchased, along with white high-heeled court shoes and a small white clutch bag which she said looked lovely but was of absolutely no use whatsoever in carrying everything she crammed into her usual bag.

'You're not meant to go stuffing all that rubbish into it,

Mam!' Maria said, with some exasperation.

'It's a "special occasion bag", Mam. I agree it's definitely not practical,' Molly added.

'When will I ever have a "special occasion" to use it again?' Ita wondered.

'Oh, Mam!' both girls chorused in unison.

It was decided that a cup of tea was called for before they began the search for Maria's outfit.

'They've a nice café on the fifth floor,' Molly said, leading them once more to the lift.

'Imagine? Five floors up,' Ita marvelled.

Maria cast her eyes to the ceiling. 'Mam, didn't Denis write and tell you they have buildings in Boston that are *twenty* storeys high!'

'Ah, well, you'd expect that in America,' Ita said.

They chose pale peach taffeta with an overskirt of white organza for Maria's dress. It was very fashionable, the girl thought. Her first really smart dress. The neckline, however, caused some friction between Molly, Maria and Ita.

'Isn't it very low? Sure, your da will have a fit!'

'Mam, it's lovely!' Molly protested. It was what was called a 'sweetheart neckline' and was very popular. There was nothing remotely immodest about it, she thought, and she could see by her sister's face that she agreed. Maria was acutely embarrassed. 'She can wear the gold cross and chain you bought her when she got her Confirmation. It will look lovely,' Molly insisted.

'Molly's right, Mam.' Maria loved the dress. She'd never had anything like it before and Molly had promised her high heels and the smartest of head-dresses they could find. If there was going to be all this argument over a simple thing like a neckline, the battle for the high heels would be hard fought!

'Well, I suppose you're right, Molly,' Ita finally agreed.

'I am. She's not a child any more. I was younger than her when I first came here,' Molly reminded her.

'Ah, but you always had more sense than this one ever had,' Ita replied with spirit and Molly sighed. She hadn't had that much sense back then; otherwise she would never have become infatuated with Billy Marshall and almost ruined her life.

'Right. Let's tell this poor woman that we'll take it and then we'll go and look for shoes and a head-dress.'

There had been a real argument over the shoes, just as Maria had expected. But, thankfully, Molly had won and the first pair of elegant high-heeled shoes Maria'd ever had were now safely paid for and packed in the box by her side. Even if her da had ten blue fits she wasn't taking them back! The head-dress was gorgeous too. It was a little Juliet cap that sat perfectly on her head. It was decorated with tiny peach and white flowers and the sales assistant had said they couldn't get a more perfect match to the dress.

They were all exhausted but happy when they arrived home at half past four.

Augusta had been dozing in the chair but made to rise as they came into the kitchen. 'Did you have a good day? Did you get everything you wanted?'

'Stay where you are, Aunt, I'll put the kettle on. And yes, we got everything.' Molly smiled. 'They'll both look gorgeous.'

'Are Paddy and the lads back?' Ita enquired.

'They are indeed. Molly, Joe said he'd be down later on but he had a few jobs to do so he went home. Oh, those two boys could hardly contain themselves but I'd say they were worn out.' Augusta smiled too. 'They've gone to have a wash and brush-up. They've been on all the amusements and they went paddling in the sea as well so they were a bit wet and windswept, but they'll be in for tea.'

'I can imagine! Let me give you a hand, Molly,' Ita offered, although she felt quite worn out herself.

'Sit there and have a rest, Mam. It's not often you get the chance,' Molly replied.

'Can I go and hang up my dress? I don't want it to be all creased,' Maria asked anxiously. She wanted to try on the shoes again too. She would have to get used to wearing them.

'Ah, go on. Take it next door and hang it up and tell your da he's to come in for his tea,' Ita instructed.

'Well, tomorrow I've to go and see the girl who is doing the flowers and I've the table plans to take to Reece's. Would you like to come with me, Mam?'

'Of course. And I'd like to go and see the church too,' Ita replied.

'Another busy day. You'll be worn out by Saturday, Molly,' Augusta said.

Molly nodded. There were only three days left before she became Mrs Jackson. She was excited and nervous all at the same time. It was best to keep as busy as possible!

Chapter Nine

ON THE THURSDAY NIGHT Molly and Ita and Bernie went into Liverpool for a bit of supper and a drink.

'Well, isn't Da going out with Joe and his da and his mates tomorrow night?' Molly said when Ita protested.

'Ah, but you'd only expect the men to go and have a drink. I don't know that it's at all respectable for women to do the same.'

Bernie cast Molly an amused look but said nothing.

'Mam, we're not going out to get drunk! We're three "respectable" women going for a bit of supper and a glass of wine or something. I asked Aunt Augusta if she'd like to come too but she said she was too old for such things; she prefers a glass of sherry by the fire in the parlour. But she thanked me for asking and said we should all enjoy ourselves. Now, I'll hear no more about it,' Molly finished firmly.

Ita thought that she'd prefer to sit and have a glass of sherry in the small but nicely furnished parlour with the old lady but she could see Molly was determined.

'What about Joe's mam? Did you not think to ask her too?' Ita asked.

Molly grimaced. 'God, Mam, she'd give us all a headache in half an hour. She just never shuts up! Besides, I think Joe said his sister was coming down to do Effie's hair tonight.'

'Well, if we don't get a move on it will be too late to go anywhere,' Bernie had urged.

Despite her misgivings Ita had enjoyed herself. They'd had a very nice meal at the Bijou Café in Slater Street, which was just off Bold Street, one of the city's most fashionable roads. It was a small establishment that served good plain food at reasonable prices and was frequented mainly by people such as themselves. Afterwards they'd gone to the Lounge Bar of the Imperial Hotel, which was quite a grand hotel on Lime Street, and which Ita had remarked was a vast improvement on the Bridge House Hotel, Tullamore's small and only hotel that catered for commercial travellers and the like.

After a frantic Friday, Ita, Molly, Bernie and Maria were quite glad to sit and have a glass of sherry with Augusta after Paddy had gone off with Joe on the 'bachelor party' and Tom and Aiden had been seated at Mrs Stockbridge's kitchen table with some comic books, glasses of Vimto and a packet of Smith's crisps, with dire and dreadful warnings from Ita as to what would befall them if they didn't behave themselves.

'I can't remember things being as hectic the day before your wedding,' Molly remarked to Bernie.

'You've a very short memory. Wasn't Mam in a terrible state worrying about *everything* and Da falling in the door dead drunk and the kids like a bag of cats! I was nearly after leaving them all to it and coming up the road to you! But everything was fine next day. Da had a bit of a head on him but he soon recovered.' Bernie laughed then shook her head, thinking of the day she had married Jimmy McCauley. It had been a beautiful wedding and she'd been so happy. She would always look back on it with bitter-sweet memories.

'Well, everything is in hand and there isn't anything we can do about the weather, except pray to God it's a fine day. So let's enjoy these few hours,' Ita said, sipping her sherry and thinking she could get quite used to all this. In addition to the fact that her elder daughter was getting married tomorrow and she herself had the smartest outfit she'd ever owned, it was proving to be a real holiday. It was a total change from getting up and raking out the range, cooking breakfast, helping to milk, washing up, washing and ironing, collecting the eggs and spending hours in the dairy churning butter. And here everyone seemed to have such labour-saving devices. Yes, she was enjoying herself.

As they undressed for bed, Molly fingered the delicate white silk organza of her dress, which was hanging up behind the bedroom door, covered with tissue paper. 'Were you nervous, Bernie, the night before?'

Bernie was brushing her dark hair vigorously but she paused. 'A bit, but I just couldn't wait to see Jimmy's face when he saw me in all my finery and I kept thinking: He'll be good to me, I'll never know the hardships Mam has known.' She sighed heavily. 'How little I knew.'

'But you *were* sure he was the right one?'

'I was *certain*. Even though we had so little time together I was very happy, Moll, and you will be too and I pray to God and His Holy Mother that nothing awful ever happens to Joe. He'll be good to you too, Moll. You've got everything to look forward to.'

'I know, it's just that sometimes I stop and think: It's for *life*, and who knows what life brings?'

'Life will bring happiness, security and lots of lovely children,' Bernie answered firmly.

Molly laughed. 'Not too many and not too soon, I hope!'

'Oh, you never know. Now let's try and get some sleep. You've got to look your best tomorrow.'

To Ita's great relief when she drew back the bedroom curtains next morning the sky was a clear blue and bright sunlight flooded the quiet street.

'Thanks be to God! Now, I think I'll just have a cup of tea before I wake Himself,' she muttered, glancing at the sleeping form of her husband, who had arrived back after midnight smelling strongly of whiskey. Still, hangover or not, he would have to be up in a few minutes.

Despite her nervous excitement Molly had slept well and she was up before both Bernie and Augusta.

'What time have you been up since? I was going to bring you your breakfast in bed as a treat,' Bernie yawned, coming into the kitchen at half past seven.

'A quarter to seven. I've the kettle boiled. It's a gorgeous morning, thank God! Aunt said she doesn't want to be disturbed before half past eight but I expect Mam will be in soon. I wonder what time Da got in? I hope he's not too much the worse for wear this morning. I know I can trust Joe, he doesn't drink much, but Da does like a drop of whiskey.'

'He'll be fine. Joe will have made sure he got home. Now, you're to have first turn in the bathroom and take your time: it's your day. Don't you be worrying about Aunt and me.'

'Oh, it really won't take me long. I had a bath last night.'

Bernie sipped her tea and smiled. 'Take all the time you want.'

Half an hour later Ita arrived. 'Good, you're both up and about. I can't get your da out of that bed! Bernie, come on in with me. The sight of yourself might bring him to his senses!'

Bernie laughed. 'It might and it might not! Mam had to chuck a bowl of cold water over my da to bring him to his senses!'

'Holy Mother of God! I hope it doesn't come to that!' Ita said fearfully, shepherding Bernie towards the door.

She returned ten minutes later, grinning.

'Well, is everything all right?' Molly asked, helping herself to another cup of tea.

'It is so. He's up and about. Looking a bit sheepish but nothing to worry about. I left your mam pouring him tea and muttering something about men not having the sense they were born with.'

Molly laughed. 'I gather he enjoyed himself.'

'Indeed he did. Now, will I take Aunt a cup of tea?'

Fifteen minutes later Ita arrived with Maria. Ita looked agitated and Maria looked mutinous.

'What's the matter?' Bernie demanded.

'It's this one here! Isn't she demanding to have her hair curled with those electric tongs while Mrs Stockbridge is trying to get them all organised next door, and her da is complaining of the worst head he's ever had in his life?'

'Is that all? Bring the tongs in here and I'll do her hair. Go and get yourself ready. Sure, we've all to be ready in just over an hour. We've to be at the church for ten. Give himself a hair of the dog and he'll be fine.'

'Saints above, Bernie, I don't want him reeking of drink at this hour of the morning!'

'Well, a cup of tea and two aspirins then. Now, Maria, go and get those tongs and we'll make a start,' Bernie instructed.

It was a miracle they were indeed all ready on time, Ita

thought as, resplendent in the new outfit and quietly basking in the praise bestowed on her by both Mrs Harper and her husband, she shepherded her two sons and Paddy into Augusta's house to wait for the cars that were to take them to the church. Both boys were excited. They'd never ridden in a car before; it sort of made up for having to be scrubbed clean and dressed in their new Norfolk jackets, stiff-collared shirts and scratchy new trousers. Paddy was feeling a bit better and looked smart in his new suit although he wasn't quite sure about the bowler hat.

Bernie had wrought wonders with Maria's hair and Ita was quite startled at the transformation. Maria looked so grown up and Ita had to admit she was a very attractive girl. Bernie herself looked very, very smart in the apricot crêpe coat and dress with matching hat.

'That's a beautiful outfit, Bernie! I never saw the like of it before.'

'It was also a very expensive outfit but I think it was worth it,' Bernie replied with satisfaction. She had never felt so utterly *elegant* in her life and she wished Bertie were here to see her.

'Wait until you see Molly, she'll take the sight from your eyes, Mam!' Maria exclaimed.

'Will I go up and see her?' Ita asked.

'You will so,' Bernie replied emphatically.

Accompanied by Maria, Ita and Bernie went upstairs and Bernie opened the bedroom door to reveal a tall, slim vision of elegance swathed in shimmering duchesse satin and silk organza. Molly's thick auburn hair had been fixed in deep waves and the pearl tiara nestled neatly into them. The yards of silk tulle veiling seemed to float around her. Tears sprang to Ita's eyes and her white-gloved hand went to her mouth as a cry of wonder and love rose in her throat.

'Is that all you can manage, Mam?' Molly laughed.

'Oh, Molly! Wait until your da sees you and Joe and . . . everyone! I can't believe it's *you*! My little Molly, so . . . beautiful, so . . . elegant! You look like a lady, you really do!' Ita hugged her carefully.

'I won't break, Mam!' There were tears in Molly's own eyes as she hugged her mother tightly.

Bernie intervened. 'Right, I think I heard a car arrive. Maria, Mrs Keegan, we'd better get downstairs. We're to go first with Aunt Augusta, then the car will come back for Molly and her da,' she informed them, ushering them all out.

Paddy was rendered speechless when, after the others had gone, Molly came slowly down the stairs.

'Da, will you pull yourself together and go and get my bouquet from the scullery sink,' she said quietly, hooking her train more securely over her arm.

'Begod, but I think you'd outshine the gentry in Dublin!' Paddy exclaimed.

'I'll be happy if just Joe thinks I'm beautiful, Da.'

'He will, Molly. Begod, he will!' Paddy kissed her on the cheek before going to fetch the bouquet of peach and white roses, white carnations and trailing green smilax.

As they approached the church Paddy took her hand and squeezed it. 'Is this the happiest day of your life, Molly? Are you absolutely certain he's the one for you?'

'I am, Da, truly I am and yes, I'm happy. Nervous, but happy.'

Paddy smiled. 'Then enjoy the day.'

Maria and Bernie carefully arranged her train and her veil and she took her father's arm and held it tightly as they entered the portals of the church and the first bars of the wedding march from *Lohengrin* thundered out.

Every head in the pews in front of her turned and she smiled to herself at the looks of amazement she caught, and then she saw Joe, tall and straight and resplendent in the dark blue and silver dress uniform of the Liverpool City Police. Her heart skipped a beat and as he turned towards her she felt a thrill of excitement and a surge of love such as she'd never felt before wash over her. She smiled and he smiled back, an expression of love mixed with admiration and astonishment on his delighted face.

Joe passed his helmet to his best man. His hand was shaking. He'd never seen her look like this before. So beautiful; so utterly *radiant*. Her face was shining with love and in a few brief minutes she would be his for ever.

Tom Foley, his best man, nudged him and he stepped out of the pew to meet her, gently taking her hand as she passed her bouquet to Bernie.

It was a fairly long service; the Nuptial Mass was always

over an hour, Bernie mused, gazing at Molly and Joe as they knelt at the altar-rails. She prayed that they would be happy and that they would have a long, trouble-free life together.

Ita and Paddy were praying for the same thing, as was Augusta. Maria knew she should be praying but her gaze and concentration wandered to the figure of one of Joe's cousins in the pews on the opposite side of the church. She'd caught his admiring gaze and she'd smiled. He looked very handsome and she determined to get to know him at the reception, despite the fact that she knew her mam's eagle eye would be on her. She bent her head dutifully. One day she wanted all this and she wanted to look just like Molly. Maybe Mam would let her come over here to work; she could stay with Molly. Bernie nudged her as she rose to take Communion and Maria got to her feet, composing her thoughts and her expression.

When the service was over, Joe took his wife's hand and gently placed it on his arm. 'I love you so much, Molly!' he whispered.

The triumphal chords of the bridal march from *A Midsummer Night's Dream* drowned Molly's reply but she smiled up at him, her eyes shining.

After the photographs had been taken and the confetti thrown and the couple congratulated by everyone, the bridal party made their way by various forms of transport to Reece's Restaurant in the city centre.

'Oh, this is very nice,' Ita remarked with great approval

as she was handed a glass of sherry by a waitress in her black and white uniform.

'I hope we get a decent meal. I'm starving,' Paddy informed her, taking a glass of whiskey from the tray the waitress proffered.

'I'd go easy on the hard stuff! Haven't you a speech to make? And would you keep your eye on those two or they'll be up to all kinds of mischief and disgracing us. I just know they'll put the heart across me before the day's out.'

'Ita, will ye stop fussing! Leave them alone; they'll be grand. It's your one over there who'll be putting the heart across you.' Paddy jerked his head in the direction of Maria, who was openly flirting with one of Joe's cousins.

'I'll soon put a stop to that before she loses the run of herself altogether! It's that dress and those shoes. Haven't they gone to her head?' Ita headed in the direction of her younger daughter, a look of grim determination on her face. She wasn't after having Joe's family thinking Maria was a bold strap of a tinker. No, indeed!

Bernie, who was only half listening to Effie's effusive compliments about Molly's, Ita's and her own outfits, grinned with some amusement as she watched Ita disengage her daughter from a flirtatious conversation with young George Jackson. She didn't blame the girl. He was a good-looking lad and why shouldn't she have a bit of fun? There weren't many opportunities for Maria in Rahan.

'Bernie, would you come and help them organise people? We're nearly ready to sit down,' Molly intervened, gently steering her friend away from her gregarious mother-in-law.

'I wasn't really listening to her; I was more interested in Maria's antics.'

'Mother of God, what antics?'

Bernie grinned. 'Calm down, Mrs Jackson, your mam has everything under control. Enjoy the day that's in it. Go and sit yourself down next to your husband and eat your dinner and have a nice glass of sparkling wine.'

Molly squeezed her hand. 'I'll do as I'm told! Did anyone ever tell you that you've become very bossy in your old age, Mrs McCauley?'

Bernie laughed. 'Don't I need to be with Aunt Augusta? I have to hold my own.'

Molly glanced across to where the old lady, resplendent in black lace and a black hat with a large feather attached to the side of it by a silver brooch, was sitting talking to Joe's sister's husband. 'Well, she is going to be your mother-in-law one day . . .'

Bernie raised her eyes to the ornate plaster ceiling and gently shoved her friend towards her seat at the top table.

Chapter Ten

BERNIE LISTENED CAREFULLY as she crossed the landing and quietly eased the door to Augusta's room open. The old lady hadn't been at all well this last week and she was worried about her. Augusta flatly refused to have the doctor, saying it was just a chill and all he'd say was stay in bed, keep warm and he'd call again at the end of the week – and charge five shillings.

The old lady appeared to be sleeping, if a little restlessly, so Bernie went back to her own room. She was wide awake now, she thought, climbing into bed and pulling the covers up to her chin. She had so much on her mind that it was no wonder sleep eluded her. She was a little worried about Molly too. Molly was pregnant; in fact she was due in a couple of weeks. Bernie smiled to herself. It was hard to believe that it was almost a year since Molly and Joe had been married and Molly had been rather stunned when she'd found she was pregnant.

'Well, it does happen,' Bernie had laughed when Molly had imparted the news.

Molly had shaken her head in disbelief. 'But I just didn't think . . . I never expected it to happen so soon.'

'Are you happy about it?' Bernie had asked.

'Of course I am. Everyone is delighted, Joe especially, and he's so . . . sensitive about it.'

'Sure, I wouldn't expect him to be anything else,' Bernie'd answered and over the months she'd watched her friend bloom with happiness and health.

Then there were all the arrangements for her own wedding. It was to be a very quiet affair, to be true, but it still needed planning. The main problem was that Bertie would only be home for a very short period so the timing was crucial. She twisted the engagement ring around on her finger. At first it felt very odd to be without both the wedding and engagement rings Jimmy had given her, but she'd become used to it. She now wore them on the third finger of her right hand. The square-cut ruby set in gold that Bertie had brought her on his return from the maiden voyage of the *Queen Mary* now graced the third finger of her left hand.

She sat up in bed and hugged her knees. What a day that had been when she had gone with him to see over the huge luxury liner. It was impossible to sleep now, so she got up and pulled on her dressing gown and went quietly downstairs to the kitchen. She'd make herself a cup of

Ovaltine. The weather hadn't been cold but the fire was still in as Augusta always felt chilly these days. She stirred the embers into life as she waited for the milk to boil.

Sitting at the table, her hands around the mug, she noticed that the sky was getting light. It would soon be dawn and she would have to go to work but until then she would enjoy the peace and savour the memory of that day in Southampton. It had been one of the real highlights of her life. She had seen many ships before, some of them very big, for Liverpool was still a very busy port, but nothing had prepared her for the sight of the massive black hull that seemed to reach almost to the sky itself, the gleaming white decks, the three red and black funnels. Bertie had escorted her, proudly showing her first his rather cramped quarters, which he assured her were far more spacious than those he'd ever encountered before. Then they'd taken what he called an 'elevator' and she called a lift up to the first-class dining room. The ship was quiet, except for the cleaners. There were no passengers on board. She had wandered, open-mouthed at the sheer opulence of the magnificent rooms. She had never seen anything like it before in her life.

'It's hard to believe that this is a *ship*!' she'd exclaimed.

'It most certainly is and built for one of the most treacherous oceans in the world. No ship is unsinkable but she's as safe as they make them,' he'd replied with pride.

She was so glad she'd worn the apricot outfit. She'd noted the admiring looks she'd received from the members of the crew they'd encountered and he'd said she looked as elegant as any first-class passenger he'd seen. She'd been treated to her lunch in the second-class dining room, which she'd thought was almost as grandiose as that of first class. Then they'd toured the open decks and she'd marvelled at the swimming pool, the sun deck and the promenade deck with its teak steamer chairs, now neatly stacked. Finally at the end of the day she'd gone into Southampton with Bertie to do some shopping, after first leaving her case in the lovely room in the quiet little hotel Bertie had booked her into. It had been a perfect day.

'I would have liked to have seen over her myself but at my age I couldn't stand all that travelling,' Augusta had said after Bernie had finished describing her tour.

The thought of the old lady brought Bernie out of her reverie. She really was worried about her. If Augusta was no better when Bernie got home from work this evening, she'd insist on the doctor. She wanted her up and about and well enough for the wedding at the beginning of June. That reminded her of the list of things she had to do that she'd attached to the back of the kitchen door. There would only be a handful of guests. Molly and Joe – Molly had declared that she would attend even if they had to wheel her there; Jean, her friend from work, who was standing for her; Augusta, Bertie and his best man Jackie Williams, Flo and Charlie McCauley, her parents-in-law; and Nellie and Matty O'Sullivan, the only representatives of her family as her mam and da were not coming over. Bertie's two brothers couldn't make it and Augusta refused point blank to allow Bernie to invite his two sisters. She sighed heavily. There was no use arguing with her. Still, it would be a grand day. After the Mass they were all going for a meal and a drink at the Bradford Hotel in Tithebarn Street.

She'd made sure that Augusta had everything she'd need for the day before she went off to work and Mrs Harper said she would look in on her a few times. She intended to call in to see Molly before she came home and so she was grateful for their neighbour's kind offer.

It had been a busy day and she was tired as she walked up Oxbridge Street to the house Molly and Joe rented but she smiled as she opened the front gate. It was by far the smartest-looking house in the street. Joe had planted the little front garden with spring bulbs and although the daffodils were now past their best, the tulips still looked good. Fred Jackson had forsaken his pigeons long enough to help Joe to paint the outside of the house in cream and forest green, and the cream-coloured curtains, trimmed with forest green and held back with scalloped tie-backs, which could be glimpsed in Molly's gleaming bay window, matched the paintwork beautifully.

Bernie climbed the three steps to the front door, which was flanked on either side by matching box trees in pots, and lifted Molly's shiny brass doorknocker.

After a little while the door opened and Molly smiled at her. 'Come on in. I'm sorry I was so long but being the size of an elephant slows me down.'

Bernie smiled back. Molly was dressed in a cream- and russet-printed maternity smock and a russet-coloured skirt but it was impossible not to notice the fact that she was heavily pregnant. She looked well, but tired.

'I can't stay too long, Moll, Aunt isn't well at all. In fact if she's no better when I get home, she's having the doctor whether she likes it or not!'

Molly looked concerned; she was very fond of the old lady. 'Her chest is no better then?'

Bernie shook her head as she followed Molly into the bright, comfortable kitchen. Molly made to put on the kettle.

'Sit down, I'll do that.'

'Aren't you the guest? You look worn out too. I'll do it. I'm not ill, just pregnant.'

Bernie sat down. 'Is Joe at work?'

Molly nodded. 'His shift finishes at eleven.'

'Are you not worried being on your own all day?'

Molly shook her head. 'Not at all. I've a phone number I can ring if anything happens.'

Bernie still marvelled that her friends were the proud possessors of a telephone. Very few people actually had their own; they used the red-painted public telephone boxes.

Molly eased herself into a chair opposite and pushed a cushion behind her back, grimacing. 'So, how are all the plans coming along?'

'I've still got to sort out the flowers and decide on the menu for the meal. And Nellie is driving me mad about what she is to wear.'

Molly smiled. 'I didn't think she had an extensive wardrobe.'

'She hasn't. She still finds it hard to make ends meet but apparently half the street have offered their best things for her to choose from.' Bernie thought how generous people were in a neighbourhood where no one had much. 'She says she can't decide between a navy two-piece, a light green coat and a brown and cream dress.'

'Tell her the brown and cream dress would be nice. It will be June so it shouldn't be chilly, and I've a brown and cream hat and cream gloves and a brown bag she can borrow. God knows what I'll wear myself. Sometimes I wonder if I'll ever fit into any of my decent clothes again!'

'You will, Moll, and that's very good of you. She says she doesn't want to let me down.'

'You're still insisting on wearing the apricot ensemble you had for my wedding? You won't consider buying something new?'

Bernie shook her vehemently. 'No indeed! Didn't that outfit cost an absolute fortune? I've only worn it twice and I'm not going to pay just as much again for something I'll hardly ever wear. No, it's so elegant it's just perfect.'

Molly sighed. She could see her friend was adamant. 'Well, at least all the excitement of the Coronation is over and done with. I was worn out with making red, white and blue paper flowers and streamers but I have to admit that when they'd finished decorating the street it did look lovely.'

Bernie nodded as she poured the tea. There had been a terrible scandal when the relationship between King Edward VIII and Mrs Wallis Simpson had come out. Well, the woman had been divorced not once but twice, and that was scandalous in itself! she thought. She could see why the woman was totally unsuitable to be the Queen of England but secretly she thought it so *beautiful*, so utterly romantic, that he'd given up his crown to marry her. It wasn't a view shared by many; most people were shocked and saddened. Still, the new King seemed to be a decent-enough man and his wife looked far more attractive than that skinny American hussy. The two little girls were lovely. They looked just as little princesses should look: all golden curls and frilly dresses and with little gold crowns too. The newspapers had been full of pictures of them on the balcony of the palace with their parents, waving to the crowds. Sighing, she remembered her Irish roots. A President just didn't seem to have the same glamour at all.

Molly's voice broke into her reverie. 'What's wrong with you? You look desperately worried.'

'I was just thinking about it all and wondering if I wasn't becoming a bit less . . . Irish. Should I be singing the "Soldier's Song" or "The Fields of Athenry" to remind myself that even though I've chosen to live here I'm not English?'

'Don't you have some funny notions, Bernie McCauley? I helped decorate this street; we joined in the party and we toasted the new King and Queen and we sang all the songs but I didn't feel less Irish. Now, will you stop giving out about it all and drink your tea!'

Bernie laughed. 'You could always put things into perspective. I'd better get off home and see how Aunt is and then I'm putting my feet up. No dashing around tonight for me.'

When she arrived home it was to find an anxious Mrs Harper waiting for her.

'What's wrong? Has she taken a turn for the worse?' Bernie asked.

'She's having terrible trouble breathing.'

'Oh, God! Would you mind very much going up to Mrs Stockbridge and asking her if Tom would go for Dr Davies? It sounds as though she needs to be in hospital.'

The woman nodded and left and Bernie ran quickly up the stairs.

Augusta was propped up on pillows but Bernie instantly saw that she was indeed very ill.

'Don't try to talk, Aunt. I've sent for Dr Davies. You really are poorly.'

Augusta made a feeble attempt to protest but she was too exhausted: it was such an effort to get her breath.

Bernie adjusted the pillows and tidied Augusta's silver-grey hair. Her honorary aunt was seventy-nine: a good age, so many said; and until recently she had been as indomitable as ever. Now, however, she looked frail and withered. Bernie was afraid to confront the fact that Augusta was dying. She was so fond of her; she looked on her as a grandmother for she'd never known her own grannies, and in a few weeks she was due to become her mother-in-law. She'd often confided in her, asked her advice, argued with her and laughed with her. Tears pricked her eyes. Oh, how she'd miss her. She sat holding Augusta's thin, gnarled hand until the doctor arrived.

He was a quietly spoken but firm man and Bernie trusted him. 'It was good of you to come so soon.'

'I was told it was very urgent. Now, let me have a good look at you, Mrs Hayes.' He gently raised her up and sounded her chest.

When he'd finished and Augusta was once more settled on the pillows he took Bernie to one side.

'It's pneumonia, I'm afraid. I could send her to hospital but I know how she feels about hospitals.'

Bernie nodded. 'I know. She says no one ever comes out of those places alive, which is nonsense. Is there anything you can give her that will help?'

'I'm afraid not. Just keep her warm and comfortable. She's an old lady; she's exhausted. She can't fight it.'

'So, she . . . she's dying?' Bernie's throat constricted with pain.

'I'm afraid so. Has she asked for any of her family?' His tone was kind; he could see how upset Bernie was.

'No. Bertie is away at sea, Harold is in London and

George is in Dover. I'll send them a telegram but I know she won't want either of her daughters here.'

'You should inform them. It could be that she changes her mind,' he advised.

Bernie nodded reluctantly. She knew both Maud and Vera had telephones and that Molly had Vera's number. She'd have to go down to the public phone box on the corner and phone Molly. She'd get one of the neighbours to sit with Augusta while she went.

Chapter Eleven

MOLLY AND JOE ARRIVED at a quarter to midnight. Bernie was sitting at Augusta's side, wiping her hot forehead with a damp flannel. She intended to sit up all night with the old lady.

'Molly, you didn't have to come! It's so late,' Bernie whispered.

Molly eased herself down in the chair Joe pulled across for her. 'Of course I did. Aren't I just as fond of her?' She leaned across and gently stroked the parchment-like cheek. 'Aunt, it's me, Molly. How are you feeling?' she asked quietly.

Augusta opened her eyes and tried to speak but her words were a mere whisper. 'Molly, child, I . . . I wanted to see you for the last . . . time.'

'I know, but hush now and rest. Bernie and I will stay with you and Joe is here too.' Molly tried to keep her voice steady.

'Are those two coming?' Bernie hissed.

Molly nodded. 'They said it would take a while to get here. Does she know? You know how she feels about them.'

Bernie shook her head. 'Sure, how could I tell her? I don't want to upset her but Dr Davies said they had to be informed and I suppose he's right. They are her own flesh and blood; I'm not even a daughter-in-law yet. Oh, I wish Bertie were here! It's going to be awful having to tell him and when she . . . she's gone and there's the funeral and everything he'll be the only one who won't be here.'

'It can't be helped, Bernie. They haven't arrived in New York yet and it's a four-day voyage home to Southampton and another day's journey to Liverpool. There is no way he can make it,' Molly soothed.

'Have you sent for the priest?' Joe asked quietly.

'I have so and Dr Davies too. They should both be here any minute. I thought it was them when you arrived.'

She had barely finished speaking when footsteps were heard on the stairs and Mrs Harper ushered in both priest and doctor. The doctor took Augusta's pulse and shook his head slowly. Father Stephens took the stole from his pocket, kissed it and placed it around his neck. Bernie knelt beside the bed while Molly bent her head reverently as the Last Sacrament was administered.

Both girls were near to tears and Joe was feeling very anxious about Molly. She should be at home in bed, he thought, but he understood how she felt and hadn't argued with her when she'd begged him to bring her here. Well, it wouldn't be long now. Poor Augusta. She'd had a hard life with little comfort in it until recently. She'd struggled to bring up her family alone and she'd remained alone after they'd grown until Molly and Bernie had moved in as lodgers.

He raised his head as he heard the sound of a car coming down the dark, silent street. It looked as though the relations were about to arrive.

'Don't worry. I'll go down and see them,' he said firmly as both girls looked up worriedly at the sound of the car door being slammed.

He greeted Vera Hesketh and her sister Maud and their husbands in the narrow lobby.

'I'm afraid she hasn't long,' he informed them.

'Has she said anything? Have our brothers been contacted?' Vera asked rather imperiously, or so Joe thought.

'No. She's barely conscious. Bernie has sent telegrams to Harold and George and as soon as the *Queen Mary* docks in New York Bertie will be informed. The shipping agents have been contacted.'

Vera nodded and walked past him and straight up the stairs, followed by Maud.

'I think we'll stay down here, in the parlour. It must be a bit crowded up there,' Richard Hesketh said.

Joe nodded. It would be, with Molly, Bernie, the doctor and the priest and now Vera and Maud in there. 'I think that's best. Both the doctor and the priest are here. If you don't mind, I'll stay upstairs, but on the landing. Molly, my wife, is due to have a baby very soon.'

Bernie looked up as the two women who would soon become her sisters-in-law entered the room. She took in the smart, expensive clothes and shoes but also caught Vera's quick and slightly disdainful glance at the old-fashioned furniture and plain bed linen and she felt her temper rise. But she said nothing.

Molly got to her feet. 'She . . . she's very sick. She's had the Last Rites and I don't know if she even knows we're here now.'

Vera Hesketh sat down in the chair Molly had vacated and leaned over the old lady. 'Mother, it's Vera. Can you hear me? Maud is here too. We would have come sooner if we had been informed that you were dying.'

Father Stephens breathed heavily through his nose and cast his eyes to heaven. Not the most tactful of greetings, he fumed to himself.

'I would have thought that an enquiry as to how she felt would have been better,' Bernie said quietly.

Augusta seemed to rally a little. She opened her eyes and tried to raise herself against the pillows, clutching the sheet between purple-veined fingers. 'Who . . . who . . . sent for you two?' she gasped weakly.

'Molly did and quite rightly too, but not before time,' Vera replied.

'Mrs Hesketh, I think a little less aggressive a tone would be in keeping with her condition. You are agitating her,' Dr Davies said reprovingly. The woman's manner was beginning to grate on his nerves.

Vera totally ignored him. 'How *are* you feeling, Mother?'

Bernie could have slapped her. 'Aunt Augusta is *dying*!' she hissed.

'Bernie . . . send . . . send the pair of them . . . away!' Augusta managed to get out, her dark eyes bright and clear.

'Now, Mother, you don't mean that. We have come all the way from Southport and at some inconvenience too. There are no trains at this time of night. Richard had to drive us.'

'Please, please have some consideration for her. Don't upset her even more,' Bernie begged, casting an appealing glance at the doctor.

Dr Davies approached the bed and placed his hand on Augusta's forehead. She had sunk down into the pillows and her eyes were closed. He took her wrist between his strong fingers and then he shook his head. 'I'm afraid she's gone,' he informed them.

Bernie leaned her head against Molly's shoulder and tears slowly trickled down her cheeks. Poor Aunt Augusta. Well, she was out of her pain now.

Molly brushed the tears from her own cheeks. 'Come on, Bernie, let's go downstairs. We can't do anything for her now,' she urged.

'She was so . . . so good to us, Moll! Oh, I wish Bertie had been here, he was her favourite and he'll be so upset!' Bernie sobbed.

Between them Molly and Joe got her downstairs and into the kitchen.

Richard Hesketh put his head around the door. 'I . . . er . . . gather that Mother-in-law has passed away?'

'She has, I'm afraid,' Joe informed him, thinking how aloof this man who was to be Bernie's brother-in-law was.

'Dreadful shame. Very sorry.' He disappeared.

Dr Davies came in next. 'I'm very sorry. She was one of my favourite patients. Spoke her mind, indomitable but kind-hearted. I've signed the death certificate.' He handed it to Joe who took it and placed it on the mantelshelf.

'Father Stephens will be down soon. He's saying a few prayers.'

'Thank you, doctor, for everything,' Molly said a little unsteadily.

'And in my professional opinion, you, Mrs Jackson, should be at home and in bed.'

Molly managed a watery smile. 'I know but . . . I had to be here.'

'Well, goodnight or should I say good morning?'

'Not that there's anything "good" about it, but thank you.' Bernie sniffed, dabbing her eyes.

The doctor had only just left when Vera appeared, followed by Maud and both their husbands.

'Did she give any instructions about the funeral?' Vera asked and then, not waiting for an answer, she carried on. 'I imagine not. I don't suppose she had any insurance or paid into a Burial Club of any kind so we will have to make all the arrangements and pay the bill. We've been discussing it and we think it's best if we contact Thompson's.'

'She wanted the Co-op. She told me so,' Bernie said.

'Oh, not the *Co-op*! They're so . . . ordinary!' Vera only just stopped herself from saying how *lower class* it was to have them.

'I think we should respect Aunt's wishes,' Molly said firmly.

Vera was losing her temper. All this was just so annoying. Her mother had been a difficult old woman, outspoken in the extreme, which could be very embarrassing. She had made it very clear that she wished to have absolutely nothing to do with them, which was very unfair. She could have had a comfortable life in one of the lovely homes in Southport that catered for old people. But no, she had insisted on staying here in this pokey little house, taking in lodgers. She looked frostily at Molly, formerly one of those lodgers. 'I don't recall that she was any relation at all to you – to either of you.'

'She asked us to call her "Aunt" years ago! She *chose* to think of us as family,' Molly answered, just as coldly.

Bernie got to her feet. 'We're not having Thompson's or anyone else! Bertie and I will pay for her funeral and she'll have the Co-op.'

Vera was outraged. Then she caught sight of the brooch that was pinned to Bernie's dress, and her eyes narrowed. 'I see you've already helped yourself to the only decent bit of jewellery Mother had. That was my grandmother's brooch and now, as the eldest daughter, it belongs to me.'

Bernie stared at her, shocked. 'Aunt Augusta gave it to me! I didn't ask for it; I asked her for nothing.'

Maud's laugh was cutting. 'A likely tale! The house is only rented; she had to take in lodgers so there's no money to speak of and it is the only thing of value she owned, apart from her wedding ring, so you decided to help yourself!'

Bernie's shock was giving way to anger. 'I took nothing! I would never steal from anyone, least of all someone I was fond of and I was very fond of her! In a few more weeks she would have been my mother-in-law and what's more Bertie knows she gave this brooch to me. She wrote and told him; it's down in writing. So you can take yourself back to Southport and if I never see you again it will be too soon!'

'How dare you speak to me like that you . . . you common little Irish emigrant! Just who do you think you are? Coming over here and inveigling yourself into this family. If you think I believe for one minute that cock and bull story about Mother writing to Bertie—'

'I hope you realise that it's a serious matter to accuse someone of stealing?' Joe's voice was calm but there was a note of menace in it. He was furious at the slur cast on Bernie and, having recently been promoted to sergeant, he was sure of his ground. 'Are you prepared to stand up in court and repeat your accusations? Don't forget Bertie will be home, Mrs Hesketh. He will be able to produce written proof that the brooch was a gift from Augusta to Bernie. I'd be careful if I were you; you're skating on very thin ice indeed.'

Vera glared at him. They were all tarred with the one brush! 'You haven't heard the last of this! When Bertie gets home I intend to have a serious talk to him. Richard, go and unlock the car, we're going home. Maud, get your coat and your bag.'

Bernie was shaking with anger and humiliation. 'Go on, get out of this house. She never wanted you here in the first place!'

When the front door had slammed shut behind them all, Joe put a hand on Molly's shoulder. 'Are you all right, luv?'

She nodded but she didn't feel right at all. 'Put the kettle on, Joe. We could all do with a cup of tea. Bernie, calm down; don't upset yourself. They're a pair of hard-hearted snobs, so they are. Take no notice of them.'

Bernie was still shaking but she sat down at the table, her hand going to the big brown teapot. Augusta would never pour tea from that pot ever again.

'She went too far,' Joe said grimly.

'She did so. What did the pair of them ever do for Aunt? They wanted to shut her away in some home! What way is that to carry on? She wasn't ill or doddery or losing her mind.'

Joe poured the tea. 'We'll have to contact the funeral director's. They'll do everything.'

'Sure, it doesn't seem right for her not to be waked. It's not decent,' Bernie muttered, thinking of the prolonged ceremonies that accompanied death in her own country.

'It's not the custom here, Bernie. It's not what she would have wanted either.'

'Didn't she drape the parlour in black crêpe when the old King died?'

'That was different. She'll have a decent send-off just the same and even though I know you won't agree with me, those two have every right to be there – though I doubt they'll come,' Joe added, seeing Bernie bristle at his words.

Molly shifted uncomfortably on the chair and bit her lip.

Joe looked at her hard. 'Molly, there's something wrong, isn't there?'

'It's just . . . well . . . I think this baby has decided to put in an appearance.' As she finished speaking a pain tore through her and she groaned and gripped the table hard.

'Oh, Holy Mother of God! Joe, get an ambulance or the doctor or *someone*!' Bernie cried, entirely forgetting about the recent events.

Joe was concerned. 'Bernie, you stay with her while I go and phone for an ambulance.'

'No! I want to go home! I'm supposed to be having this baby at home. Everything is arranged: the midwife, Dr Taylor and all the things for the baby are there. I've got plenty of time yet to get home.' Her last words ended in another groan followed by a scream.

'Molly, I don't think there's going to be time to get you home and you can't have the baby here, not with herself lying upstairs,' Bernie urged. 'Just try and stay calm. Joe, go and phone for an ambulance and tell them to hurry!'

Joe didn't wait for Molly to protest; he was out of the door before she could say a word.

Molly clutched Bernie's hand tightly. 'Oh, Bernie, I'm terrified! Labour can go on for hours and hours, sometimes days!'

'Molly, I can remember Mam having our Iggy and she wasn't hours and hours and I don't think you will be either. It's the shock of Aunt and then those two frights of daughters that's brought it all on.'

Molly tried to smile. 'Baby must be in a hurry to see his da and his Aunty Bernie.'

'Well, you just tell Baby to wait a bit longer; there's no rush. Oh, Jesus, Mary and Joseph, hold on to me, Moll!' she finished as Molly screamed again. Bernie grimaced as Molly nearly crushed the bones in her hand to bits and then she smiled as she remembered a saying of her mam's. 'As one candle goes out, another is lit.' What Tess meant was that as one person died, another was born. Bernie said a silent prayer for Augusta, now in heaven she was certain, and for Molly's baby's safe delivery. Then she said another: for Joe to get a move on and come back. She didn't want to have to deliver Molly's child herself.

Chapter Twelve

TO BERNIE'S RELIEF JOE had appeared a few moments later and a few minutes after that they'd heard the clanging of the ambulance bell. Still protesting, Molly had been taken to hospital, accompanied by Joe and Bernie.

They had sat for what seemed like hours in the waiting room. Joe had pleaded with the sister to be allowed in to see her for just a few seconds but his requests had been met with stony-faced refusal that bordered on outrage that he should even contemplate doing such a thing.

'She was in so much pain,' he said pitifully to Bernie.

'I know, and she'd feel better if *someone* was with her.'

'I was right to bring her here, wasn't I, Bernie?'

Bernie nodded, but she thought that Molly might blame them at a later date. When you felt the way Molly must be feeling now, she reasoned, you wanted safe, familiar things and faces around you. She decided to change the subject to something a little lighter.

'Have you decided on names? I know there was a bit of an argument.'

'There was. If it's a boy I wanted Peter or Andrew but Molly wanted an Irish name: Keiran or Damien, she thought. At least we were agreed on a girl's name: Lucy Elizabeth.'

'I like Lucy but I'm not sure about Elizabeth,' Bernie mused.

'After the princess and St Elizabeth of course.'

Bernie nodded. 'I think you should stick to your guns and have Peter. It's a saint's name so the Church can't object and back home everyone is called Keiran or Damien.'

'Peter Andrew Jackson. I think it's got a nice ring to it, don't you?'

'I do so. I'll back you up,' she promised.

'Mr Jackson, you may come in now!' Sister announced. 'But only for a few minutes; she's very tired.'

'What about me? I've been her best friend since we were five years old. She's like a sister to me,' Bernie pleaded.

Sister relented. 'Well, seeing as her mother can't be here, you may come in.' She turned to Joe. 'Your wife is fine, just a few stitches, and you have two fine sons.'

Both Joe and Bernie gaped at her then Bernie threw her arms around Joe and began laughing. 'Twins! Holy Mother of God! She's had twins!'

Joe started to laugh too but Sister was not amused.

'If that's how you're going to behave I'll have no alternative but to send you away!'

They both instantly became serious.

'Sorry, it's just that . . . well, you've got to agree it's a huge surprise!' Bernie apologised.

'It's certainly that. And we've only got one cot and one of everything!'

'Oh, don't be worrying over things like that,' Bernie scolded Joe gently.

Molly was lying back against the pillows and Bernie thought she'd never seen her friend look so utterly exhausted – or so happy.

Joe seemed to be at a complete loss for words as Molly indicated the two cots, one either side of the bed.

'Go, on, have a look at them'. Molly smiled. 'You can pick them up; they're *yours*!'

Joe bent and kissed her. 'Oh, Moll! Are you all right?'

'I'm fine. Tired and a bit sore and a bit shocked too, if the truth be known. No wonder I was the size of an elephant. Sister said twins often come a bit early.'

Joe gazed down at the tiny form of his son, swaddled in a towel.

'Pick him up and I'll pick the other one up, if I may?' Bernie urged, looking at Molly for approval.

Molly nodded. 'Poor little things. I had no clothes for them so they wrapped them up in towels.'

Bernie looked down into the screwed-up little face. 'I can't see any resemblance to either of you.'

'Oh, Bernie! Hasn't he got auburn hair like me?' Molly said.

'I mean apart from that.'

'He's— They've got your Irish colouring, Molly,' Joe said, gently holding the tiny infant.

Bernie laughed. 'I just hope they haven't got her Irish temper too! Now what are you going to call them? Don't inflict awful Celtic names on them, Moll. Just remember they're half-English and they're going to live here.'

'We could call one Peter and the other Andrew?' Joe suggested hopefully.

Molly nodded; she was too tired to argue. She just wanted to go to sleep.

'There, that's settled!' Bernie said with a note of triumph in her voice.

Sister came bustling in. 'That's long enough. Now, put those babies back in their cots; it doesn't do to be cuddling them too much. Little as they are they get used to it and then cry to be picked up and she isn't going to have time to be doing that all day, believe me. And she's very tired. It's hard enough bringing one child into the world, let alone two. Off you go; you can come in at visiting times,' she instructed.

Molly was almost asleep so they laid the babies back in their cots and left.

'I'll have to go and see Mam and Da and tell them the news. I can hardly take it in but I've never felt so proud and happy and grateful in my life!' Joe said, shaking his head in amazement.

'Do you want me to send a telegram to Molly's mam and da? It would save you a job. And we're going to have to go and buy things, like another cot, more blankets, more nappies, more vests and nightdresses. Oh, the washing!' Bernie finished with a wail of dismay.

'Would you mind?' Joe asked, the disruption to their quiet, ordered life beginning to dawn on him for the first time.

'Not at all. Won't I only be delighted?' Bernie suddenly fell quiet, remembering Augusta. 'Oh, Joe, isn't it a shame that Aunt Augusta didn't live just a few more days? She would have loved to have seen them.'

Joe nodded, a little sadness dampening his spirits.

'Well, at least I've something *good* to tell Bertie now. I'll send a telegram to the shipping agents too,' Bernie said, thinking it might help lift her fiancé's spirits a little. He was fond of Molly.

Bernie was waiting at Lime Street Station when Bertie arrived home just over a week later. The station concourse was packed as four trains had arrived almost simultaneously. She had difficulty finding him and was becoming anxious. Then at last she saw him, his seabag thrown over one shoulder.

'Oh, I'm so glad to see you, really I am!' she cried with relief, almost throwing herself into his arms.

'I'm glad to see you, too, Bernie, luv! How are you? How are things?'

'I'm all right . . . now.' She smiled up at him as he put his arm protectively around her. They began to push through the mêlée. 'I'm so, so sorry about your mam. But she didn't suffer and that's a blessing, so it is.'

'I've never felt so . . . confused about things. When I got both telegrams I opened the one about Molly's twins first. I was so surprised and dead pleased for them and then . . . I found out about Mam. My heart dropped to my boots, Bernie. The worst thing was not being able to do *anything*. I felt so *helpless*. It was almost as bad as the grief. She had a long life but a hard one, until you two came along. Did everything go all right about the funeral?'

Bernie nodded. 'There was a row with your sisters, the night she died. Vera accused me of helping myself to that brooch your mam gave me, the one that belonged to your grandmother.'

'The one Mam wrote and told me she was going to give you?'

Bernie nodded. 'She backed down in the end; Joe asked her was she prepared to stand up in court and accuse me of stealing? Of course she wasn't but she said she wants to have a serious talk with you. No doubt she'll try and talk you out of marrying a "common Irish emigrant".'

'Is that what the stuck-up bitch called you?' Bertie was angry; he could see Bernie was hurt.

She nodded.

'Well, I'm not going to wait until she descends on us. I'm going out to Southport to give her a piece of my mind and I'm going to take Mam's letter with me! Don't worry, luv, I'll not have her over the doorstep ever again. Did they come to the funeral? Did she say anything else to upset you?'

'No. Both she and Maud were stony-faced and didn't speak to anyone and they didn't come back to the house like everyone else, thank God! Harold and George came and went home next day.'

'At least they were there,' Bertie said, his tone full of regret.

'How could you have known that she was going to . . . die?' Bernie soothed.

'If only she could have hung on for another week!'

'Life is full of "if onlys". You can't blame yourself and she wouldn't want you to. It's your work and that's that! That's what she'd say, so come on now, we're going up to see Molly and the boys. I promised her and it will cheer you up: they're gorgeous! They've got little screwed-up faces and red hair like Molly but Effie swears they've got Joe's nose and eyes and because they've got long backs, she says they're going to be tall like Joe.'

'Well, Molly's not small either,' Bertie pointed out.

Bernie managed a smile. 'Unlike me?'

He bent and kissed the top of her head. 'I like my women small!'

'Oh, you've got more than one, have you? Where do you keep the rest of them?'

'Ah, Bernie, you know you're the only one for me!'

'I know. Come on, Molly will be waiting.'

Bertie duly admired the babies but didn't quite have Bernie's enthusiasm. Molly looked tired, he thought.

'So, you're still finding it all a bit daunting?' Bernie said, cradling little Andrew while Molly changed Peter's nappy.

'You could say that. Mam has written to say that if I'm agreeable she'll send Maria over to help me – if Joe doesn't mind, of course.'

'What are you going to do?'

'Write and tell her I'd be glad of the help, of course. I'm worn out; I get hardly any sleep.'

Bernie was thoughtful. 'And will she be a help?'

'She will. She's not a bad girl.'

Bernie sighed. 'You know what will happen? When our Claire hears, she'll want to come over too and I'll be pestered to death. She's a lazy little madam and bold with it too!'

Molly bit her lip. If Bernie didn't want Claire to come and live with her it would make things a bit difficult. Yet she could understand Bernie's fears and she was getting married soon too.

'She might be a bit of company for you, Bernie, while I'm away. Don't forget you'll be all alone in that house,'

Bertie suggested. He was sure Bernie could more than handle her sister.

'He's right. You always had Aunt there before,' Molly added. Bernie was keeping on the house in Arnot Street. 'And if she gets really stroppy you can always count on Nellie to help sort her out.'

Bernie sighed. 'I'll see. Now give that lad to me and you take this one: he's a bit wet,' she informed Molly as she handed the baby over.

'Joe is still trying to get the day off for your wedding but if he can't I'll have to bring Effie. I can't manage these two on my own. Will that be all right?' Molly asked.

'Yes, but I hope he can come, I really do. You know what Effie's like; she never shuts up.'

'She won't have much time to gossip,' Molly said grimly.

To Bernie's relief Joe had managed to swap his rest day with a colleague and a week later he accompanied Molly and his sons to the church of St Francis de Salles.

A sleeping infant in her arms, Molly stood in one of the front pews beside Joe in the church. Bernie looked lovely, she thought. The apricot colour really suited her and she looked radiantly happy – as happy as the day she'd married Jimmy McCauley. Molly prayed with all her heart that Bernie would never again suffer the heartbreak of losing her husband. Bernie deserved to be happy and Bertie Hayes idolised her. Molly looked around at the few guests and knew that they were all praying for the same thing. Life had changed so much for her and her friend since they'd left Ireland and she wondered what the future would bring. She hoped Bernie would soon become a mother for despite all the weariness and worry it was a wonderful thing to be. She wouldn't change her life and she was certain that at this minute, with Bertie's gold ring on her finger, the new Mrs Hayes would agree with her.

'Congratulations! I know you're going to be very, very happy!' She hugged her friend as tightly as she could.

'Thanks, Molly. I think you might be right,' Bernie replied with shining eyes.

Joe shook Bertie's hand. 'Break her heart and you'll have me to answer to!' He laughed but in his heart he meant it. He knew just how much Bernie meant to Molly.

'I'll not be doing that! And I can trust you to keep an eye on her while I'm away?' Bertie replied.

Joe nodded. 'If she needs anything she knows she's only got to ask.'

'Right, we'd better all get ourselves up to the Bradford Hotel for a bit of celebration,' Bertie said, ushering his new bride towards the church gate.

Bernie smiled at him. It would be a far quieter celebration than she'd had the last time when half the parish of Rahan had been invited and the dancing had gone on until four in the morning, but she was older now and, she considered, wiser. A nice meal and a few drinks with the people closest to her would suit her very well.

Chapter Thirteen

ITA WAS HOT AND tired as she drove home from Tullamore. The weather was very hot for early June and she was certain there would be a storm by evening; already there was that heaviness in the air. The leaves on the trees that flanked the Mucklagh road were dusty and still, and the cow parsley, which grew thickly in the ditches, hardly stirred as she passed. She wiped the perspiration from her forehead with a handkerchief. There wasn't much further to go now; she was dying for a cup of tea, but she felt quite contented. She had sold all her eggs, butter and cheese and she'd purchased some groceries from Deegan's and other necessities that they didn't produce themselves from various other shops in the town. She'd also met quite a few people she hadn't seen in a while and had spent some time catching up on all the news. Then she'd met Tess O'Sullivan and offered her a lift home.

'Isn't it very warm for the time of the year? Sure, there's thunder in the air, I'm thinking.'

'You're right, Tess. I'm glad we're nearly home now. Will you come in for a cup of tea?' Ita had already noted Tess's only half-filled shopping bag and knew Dessie had had very little work of late. Tess would welcome a bit of soda bread and a slice of sponge cake with her tea.

'Ah, that's good of you, Ita. Aren't I dying for a cup? Have you heard how Molly is coping? You and me know full well what it's like.' Tess had had twelve children.

'She's not doing too badly but she says they're a bit fretful and cross at times and she's tired. I wish I was nearer but at least Maria is going over next week. That will be a big help to Molly. She's a good girl and a good worker if you keep after her.'

Tess rolled her eyes expressively. 'Aren't I demented with Claire begging and pleading with me to let her go to Bernie? You know what she and Maria are like.'

Ita nodded. They were inseparable and the only fly in the ointment of Maria's delight in being sent to Liverpool was that Claire wasn't going with her. 'Will you be after letting her go?'

'I'd pack her things this very minute but I haven't heard from Bernie as to whether she wants her or not! Every day Claire has me destroyed altogether, asking has Con O'Brien brought a letter and when none comes isn't she as cross as a bag of cats? If I haven't heard by the end of this week, sure, I'll have to write to Bernie again and I really didn't want to do that.'

'What does Dessie say about it?'

'Ah, you know Dessie. He's not much of a one for making decisions; he's only interested in where he's going to get the money for a few pints of porter in the Thatch on Saturday night, and he hasn't had much work lately.'

Ita nodded. 'Well, they'll be cutting the turf at the weekend. Paddy will be looking for help. That should keep Dessie happy for a while.'

'And meself too,' Tess replied thankfully, thinking of the money that would bring in.

Ita suddenly dragged on the reins and brought the pony and trap to a sudden and unexpected halt.

Tess almost slid off the seat. 'Mother of God! What's wrong?'

'Isn't that Ger Rooney with that new tractor he has? Coming towards us. Sure, we'll never both be able to stay on the road. Won't I have to back up to the nearest laneway?' Ita began expertly to back up the trap.

'He shouldn't be allowed on the road with that thing! These lanes weren't made for big heavy machinery like that. Be careful we don't end up in the ditch, Ita,' Tess warned, glancing warily over the side of the trap. At this time of the year the roadside ditches were camouflaged by vegetation.

'Well, if we do he can damned well pull us out!' Ita replied with some spirit. She mentally thanked God that

Paddy wasn't yet able to afford a tractor. Tess was right; these lanes weren't at all suitable for them.

When they finally arrived home there were huge, heavy grey clouds gathering in the sky.

'I'll get Paddy to see to this animal. Come on in with you, Tess, before it starts to rain,' Ita said, waving to her husband, whom she'd caught sight of coming out of the barn. 'Paddy, will you unhitch the trap? Tess and me are desperate for a cup of tea. Weren't we run off the road by Ger Rooney and his tractor and didn't I have to back the trap almost to the gates of Rahan Lodge!' she called.

Mentioning the tractor was not very tactful on Ita's part. It was a sore point with Paddy as it was the tractor he hadn't been able to afford because of Molly's wedding. 'That lad should be more careful on the roads with that thing. Sure, he's no consideration at all.'

'Maria, put on the kettle,' Ita instructed as she entered the kitchen.

'Isn't it on already, Mam? I have the cups laid out too,' Maria answered. She was on her very best behaviour these days. She didn't want to give her mother the least excuse to stop her going to Liverpool. She was highly delighted to be going. She might even get to see George Jackson again.

'Aren't you a good, thoughtful girl. Sure, it wouldn't cross Claire or Eileen O'Sullivan's mind to do such a thing. Wouldn't they have to be told to do it?' Tess said rather crossly.

Maria refrained from defending her friend but placed a fresh cake of soda bread and a light Victoria sponge sandwiched with blackberry jam on the table.

Both women sat down thankfully.

'Won't she be a huge help to Molly? Isn't she well able to do all kinds of things?' Tess said, pushing back a few wisps of grey hair from her damp forehead.

'She can cook and clean and wash and iron, leaving Molly time to see to the babies,' Ita said.

Maria poured the hot water into the teapot and said nothing. She didn't mind doing all those things just as long as she got some time to herself. Time to go out and have fun. Molly had written to say that they could afford to give her a little pocket money until such time as the twins were older and Maria could look for a job.

'And then when the babies are older she can find some kind of decent employment, like Molly did when she first went there.'

'Ah, now, Ita, I wouldn't go comparing them. Doesn't Molly have a gift for the soft furnishings?'

'She does and I suppose it is a pity she had to give it up but she couldn't have coped with two babies and a business.'

Maria poured the tea while Ita sliced up the soda bread and spread it thickly with rich, creamy butter.

'I have got some new things to take with me and Da says he'll give me some money so I can buy what I need without having to ask Molly for things like a winter coat or a pair of shoes,' Maria announced.

'Well, if Claire goes to Bernie she won't be after getting a few pounds from *her* da,' Tess said, sipping her tea.

'Sure, she won't need it. She'll be able to get a job and have a wage,' Maria answered with a note of envy in her voice.

A week later Ita and Paddy were standing on the platform of the station in Tullamore waving goodbye to another daughter. It didn't seem all that long ago since she'd stood here and waved to Molly and Bernie, Ita thought a little sadly. Now they were both married, Bernie for the second time, and Molly was a mother herself. At least Molly wouldn't have to wave her children goodbye as they took the emigrant ship and maybe never see them again. There was work in England; there always had been, although there was a depression at the moment. Paddy had read in the newspaper that thousands of unemployed men from Jarrow had marched to London to demand that the government do something to help them. Yet despite that, it was a rich country compared to Ireland. Ireland was poor. And Molly herself had a good life. Joe had a good, secure job. They had a nice house in a good area and, most of all, they had their health and strength. She really didn't worry too much about Molly. Maria, however, was a different matter. She would worry and fret about her until she was safely married, the way she'd worried about Molly.

Ita sighed and turned away as the train steamed out of the station. 'We'd best get home, Paddy. There's so much to do and now I'm short of Maria's help. There's only Tom and Aiden left to us and no doubt they'll go too when the time comes. We reared a family and for what, Paddy? So we could spend our old age alone and half forgotten?'

'Ah, not half forgotten, Ita. Won't Molly and Maria be just across the Irish Sea? And, you never know, the two lads might not have to go. I'm not getting any younger and the homeplace will go to them in the end.' Paddy was more optimistic.

That cheered Ita a little and she smiled as he helped her up into the trap.

Maria had found the journey exciting. There had been a little time to have a look at the shops in Dublin before going for the ferry and then she'd met a lad from Sligo on the boat who was going with his older brother to Chicago, via Liverpool. He had kept her entertained during the journey and had even bought her a mineral water from the bar. Before long she found herself at the Pier Head where Joe was waiting for her.

'You made it safe and sound then?' he greeted her as she waved farewell to her travelling companion. She'd grown up, he thought. She was an attractive girl. Slim and tall like Molly but with light brown hair and blue eyes.

'I did so. How's Molly?'

'Tired. I do what I can to help but she'll be glad to see you.'

Maria smiled as she gazed around. It was great to be

here again. There was so much going on, even at this time in the morning, whereas at home there was nothing, absolutely nothing happening at all of any interest. She was looking forward to seeing Molly's home and her two nephews.

'Let me take your case and we'll go for the tram. It won't take us long to get home,' Joe informed her, taking the small case from her.

It was a very quiet street, Maria thought. Curtains were still drawn, giving the neat houses a closed-off look. The early-morning sunlight glistened on the dew on the tiny front lawns and the bright array of summer flowers. At the far end a man was delivering bottles of milk from the back of a horse-drawn cart, placing them on doorsteps. Of course the milk had been delivered when Molly had lived in Arnot Street but Maria still found this very odd; she was used to going out to the dairy with a big jug any time milk was needed.

'Here we are,' Joe announced, opening the gate.

'Oh, this looks grand, Joe.'

He grinned. 'Painted it myself with the help of Da. I'd never lifted a paintbrush before we moved here.'

Molly was up and dressed and eagerly waiting. 'Did you have a good journey? You did well to come when the weather is so fine; it can be desperate in winter.'

'It was grand and I didn't find it long or boring. I got these in Dublin for the twins.' Maria fished two blue knitted hats out of her case. 'Sure, it's a bit warm at the moment but they'll come in handy later on.'

Molly kissed her. 'They will, thank you. It was very thoughtful of you. Come on upstairs and meet your nephews and I'll show you your room.'

In the big, sunny front bedroom with the wide bay window two cots were set side by side. Maria peered into them.

'How do you tell which is Andrew and which is Peter?' she whispered. She could only see two identical sleeping babies.

'Andrew has green ribbon threaded through his matinée coat and Peter has blue,' Molly answered.

Maria nodded. It seemed a sensible idea.

'Let's not disturb them; they'll be awake soon enough. Come and see your room.'

Maria was delighted with the room. True, it wasn't terribly big, but it was painted pale pink and white and the curtains and bedspread were of pink and white gingham. There was a chest of drawers with a nice mirror on top, a single wardrobe, a white wicker chair with a pink cushion trimmed with white lace, and on the floor was a new rug. She liked the pictures on the walls and on the wide window ledge was a vase of fresh flowers. Despite everything she had to do Molly had made the room as welcoming as she could.

'Oh, it's just lovely, Molly, really it is!'

'I'm so glad you like it. Now, leave your case and your jacket up here and we'll go and have a bit of breakfast before those two wake up and start demanding theirs!'

Joe only had a bit of toast and a cup of tea as he was dashing off to work but Molly and Maria had rashers and eggs.

'I only usually have tea and toast but you must be starving,' Molly said as Maria dutifully laid the table. 'How is Mam? I thought she was looking thin when I saw her last. Mind you, that was at my wedding.'

'She's grand altogether and I don't think she looks thin at all. Sure, she eats like a horse, same as the rest of us,' Maria answered, tucking into her breakfast. 'I've a couple of pounds of smoked rashers in the case, wrapped in greaseproof paper so they won't spoil my things. She says you can't get decent rashers over here but these are fine.'

'It's good of her to send them. I'll thank her when I next write.'

'Claire is just waiting to hear from Bernie to see if she can come over. Won't it be great if she can?'

Molly looked thoughtful. 'I don't know if Bernie wants her to come. She hasn't made up her mind yet.'

Maria was dismayed. 'Why doesn't she want her to come?'

Molly shrugged. 'She says she's lazy and that she's a bold strap.'

'She is not!' Maria was indignant. 'And she's not lazy. She wants to find a job and earn money for herself.'

'I'm glad to hear that; she can send some of it home to her mam. Mam tells me they've been hard up down at

Cappaloughlan although now Da's cutting the turf I suppose he'll have Dessie helping him.'

'Is Bernie coming here at all soon?' Maria asked, mopping up the egg yolk with a crust. She was hoping to put a word in for her friend.

'She's coming up tonight, after work. Joe won't be home until late and Bertie is away,' Molly informed her.

Maria nodded. 'Right. I'll wash up and if there is any washing that needs doing I'll make a start on it.'

'Thanks. There's always a pile of things: nappies mainly. I soak them in two buckets of cold water. One for wet ones and one for soiled ones.'

Maria nodded. She really didn't relish washing dirty nappies but she wasn't going to complain. She was back in Liverpool and for good and tonight she was going to plead with Bernie to let Claire come too. Oh, wouldn't they have a great time together?

PART II

Chapter Fourteen

1940

'MARIA, WILL YOU SEE what's the matter with Andrew? He's making a shocking row down there,' Molly called downstairs, hearing her son's loud wails.

'It's all right, Molly! He's just fallen and bumped his head. Nothing serious; he'll be fine. Peter pulled the cart away from him. They've been fighting again!' Maria called back up. She had settled well into life here, she thought, even though there was a war on. She took so many things for granted now; things they still didn't have at home. She got on well with everyone and she had begun to walk out with Joe's cousin Georgie. Of course Molly watched her like a hawk and she'd been given the 'serious talk' about not disgracing herself or her family – not that she had any intention of doing so. Bernie had at last relented and Claire had come over from Ireland too. She herself had pleaded her friend's cause, reminding Bernie how much of a help around the house she was to Molly and insisting she was certain Claire would be just as helpful. And Claire desperately wanted to work and have money of her own and escape the dreariness of life at home, just as Bernie herself had. So Claire had arrived and now, Maria thought, life was almost perfect.

Molly was balanced on a stepladder in the front bedroom, putting up the thick blackout curtains that she had taken the opportunity to wash, the weather being fine. She wished Joe were home; he was much better at sorting out the twins when they started fighting. At almost three years of age they were a handful at any time but they were getting steadily more difficult and she found their tantrums increasingly stressful.

She got down from the ladder and pulled the curtains over. Well, at least they kept out every chink of light. She wouldn't have Freddie Mercer the ARP warden hammering on her door complaining. She picked up the new ration books from the top of the dressing table. How on earth did they expect you to live on such meagre amounts of food? she wondered irritably. Wearily she pushed the books into her handbag and went downstairs.

Maria was bathing a bump on Andrew's forehead and Peter was pushing a small wooden cart around the kitchen at great speed and with a look of triumph on his animated little face. Despite their Irish colouring they both looked more like Joe than Molly.

'Peter, will you stop that! Take the cart outside. You know it's not supposed to be in here and it's not nice to fight with Andrew.' Molly turned her attention to her tearful son. 'You're sure he's all right? He's not sleepy or anything like that?' she fussed, gently stroking the thick auburn curls.

'He's grand! You do fret so. There now, Aunty Maria has made it all better. Get down now and go out and play with Peter and no more fighting!' Maria lifted the child down and gave him a gentle push in the direction of the door. She turned to Molly. 'Are the curtains up then?'

'They are so.'

'Isn't it desperate? Do you really think we'll get bombed? I mean we've been at war now for months and there's not a thing been dropped.' At first Maria had been very apprehensive but now it just seemed to add a bit of excitement to life. Everything was happening in Europe and that seemed so far away. Apart from having to carry a gas mask everywhere and the installation of an Anderson shelter in the back garden and the blackout regulations and now rationing, life hadn't really changed much.

'I hope not! Aren't we sick of that air-raid shelter already? It's horrible. It's damp and cold and cramped.'

'At least we have one of our own; we don't have to go to the public shelters,' Maria said, filling the kettle.

'Go easy on the tea, it has to last. Everything is rationed now so don't go heaping spoons of sugar into your cup either!'

'Aren't you very irritable today, Molly? What's the matter?'

Molly shrugged. She *was* irritable and it wasn't like her, but she had so many things on her mind, so much to worry about. Joe was desperate to join the Army but they wouldn't have him. He was in a 'Reserved Occupation'. He argued that there were plenty of older men in the police force to maintain law and order and wasn't it the duty of all young men to go and fight? They were adamant but he kept on trying. Yet she didn't want him to go and fight. It didn't bear thinking about and they'd argued over it. Then there was the fact that Maria was going to have to go and work in a munitions factory and she relied on her sister's help so much. Maria said she really didn't mind, she'd heard the money was great, better than what she earned now, for she only worked part time in the little drapery shop on the top road. Molly had been seriously thinking of writing to her mam about sending her sister home. She was afraid they would be bombed and why should Maria have to suffer that and work in a factory making ammunition? It wasn't her country; it wasn't her war. The Irish Free State was neutral. She'd discuss it with Bernie when her friend called this afternoon.

She sat sipping her tea and listening to the babbling voices of her sons as they played together, peacefully for a change. 'What is Claire going to do? Is she going to work in munitions, too?' she asked.

Maria nodded. 'We're to go out to a place called Kirkby. They make anti-tank shells there. She's heard that it can be quite dangerous work. You have to fill them with TNT, an explosive, and sometimes there are accidents.'

Molly shuddered.

'But she says we'll be earning a fortune!'

'Sure, it won't be much use to you if you have your hand blown off – or worse.'

Maria shrugged. The wages were twice and sometimes three times more than they were earning now. Claire was always complaining about what she called 'the pittance' of a wage she earned in Peegram's Grocer's. She had been living with Bernie for three years now. There had been some rows, for Claire was a strong-willed girl, confident and self-assured, but most of the time the sisters got on well. After all, they were very alike, both physically and temperamentally. Maria knew Bernie wouldn't admit it but she was glad of her sister's company while Bertie was away. Claire had worked at a variety of jobs. She didn't seem to stick at any of them for very long but Bernie had laid down very strict rules. If Claire didn't work and contribute to her keep, then it was back to Rahan. As she swore she would *never* go back, Claire made sure she had another job to go to before she left the one she was in.

Molly rose reluctantly and began to clear away the tea things. It was time for the boys' afternoon nap. At least they could look forward to an hour of peace and quiet.

'You haven't forgotten that I'm going out this evening?' Maria reminded her.

Molly smiled. 'I have not. Who is it? George Jackson or Teddy Soames?'

Maria grinned. 'George. Teddy was a bit too "flash", if you know what I mean?'

Molly nodded. She had thought the same herself when the lad had called for her sister. She much preferred Joe's cousin, who had joined the RAF.

It was two o'clock when Bernie arrived, a little out of breath. 'Did you find yourself puffing and panting when you were having the boys?' She laughed as Molly took her short, pale-pink loose jacket. She was almost five months pregnant and being small she joked that she really did look like a little barrel now.

'All the time. How are you, apart from the shortness of breath?' Molly asked as she settled her friend in an easy chair in the front room.

'I'm grand. I'm getting kicked to death but I don't mind that. He's very lively.' She adjusted the cushion Molly had placed behind her.

'It might be a girl and you might be thankful for it.'

'Are those two still as bad?'

'They wear me out. They are such bundles of energy and they seem to be going through a phase of fighting over every single toy. If one has something you can be sure the other one will want it. Joe can deal with them far better than I can at the moment.'

Bernie laughed and then, seeing the look of consternation that had come into Molly's eyes at the mention of her husband, she stopped abruptly. 'Is he still determined to join up?'

'He is and they are just as determined not to have him and I'm glad, Bernie. Won't it be dangerous enough here if they start dropping bombs on us?'

Bernie looked very serious. 'It will. It's getting worse, Moll. Haven't they've gone and invaded Norway and Denmark now? It's all over the newspapers.'

'Oh, Holy Mother of God! Will we be next?'

'I can see why Joe wants to go and fight, to keep us from being next.'

Molly stared at her friend hard and then she nodded slowly. Bernie was right but there already were soldiers in France: the British Expeditionary Force. Surely they could keep Hitler's army at bay? 'Have you heard from Bertie?' she asked.

'No. All I know is that the convoy is expected any day now.'

'It can't be easy for you, not hearing, not knowing.'

Bernie sighed. 'It isn't and it doesn't help that it said in the paper today that Hitler has ordered his U-boat captains to attack all ships, not just allied ones. Everyone is fair game.' Bernie hadn't argued when Bertie had transferred from the *Queen Mary* to a freighter on the convoys sailing from Nova Scotia to Liverpool: he'd been so determined; but she prayed constantly for his safety.

'Maria says Claire is going out to Kirkby to make anti-tank shells.'

Bernie rolled her eyes expressively. 'There have been more rows over that, Molly, I can tell you. I want her to go home; I don't want her to get blown to bits and have Mam screaming at me that I should have stopped her, but she's twenty and she says she'll do as she likes. It's the money that's the big attraction and she says there will be hundreds of Irish men and women coming over to get work in all the factories. There's plenty of work here now and she's right. But for the fact that I'm pregnant and you've got two toddlers they'd be having us working in a factory too. Did you know that?'

'I'd heard rumours. I was thinking of sending Maria home too and for the same reason but I'll probably get the same argument.'

'She is a bit more manageable than our Claire and maybe if your da wrote to her it would carry some weight. You know what my da is like: useless at being authoritative.' Bernie grimaced.

'I still don't know though; she's quite keen on George Jackson. She's off out with him tonight.'

'It's a good job I'm here then, to give you a hand to get the boys to bed. What time is Joe in?'

'About eight and you'll not be wearing yourself out with my two little devils.'

Bernie laughed. 'Won't it be great practice for when I have a little devil of my own?'

Joe arrived home to find Molly and Bernie tidying up the kitchen. He looked tired, Bernie thought, but she said nothing.

'The little monsters are in bed then? How have they been?' he asked, taking off his tunic and hanging it behind the door.

'Not too bad at all. At least, not since I've been here. Didn't they sit still all the while I was reading them a Winnie-the-Pooh story and then they went to bed as good as gold,' Bernie informed him.

Molly put his meal on the table. 'Isn't that a poor excuse for a dinner to put down to a man after a day's work? How we're expected to live on a few ounces of meat a *week* I don't know.'

'We'll just have to get used to it, Moll. You never know, it might do us all some good,' Joe replied cheerfully, tucking into the shepherd's pie that was all potato and very little meat.

When Bernie had gone, after extracting a promise from Molly that when Bertie got home they would all go out for a drink, Molly sat down in the easy chair in the bay window.

'They've invaded Norway and Denmark. It's getting worse, Joe.'

'I know, luv, and they still won't let me join up. It will be Belgium and France next.'

'And then us. Oh, Joe, I know it's selfish of me, I'm such a coward, but I'm afraid. I don't know how Bernie manages to keep so cheerful. I'd go out of my mind with worry if you were away and I didn't know when, or if, you were coming home. And we've had a couple of false alarms here with the siren going and us dragging the boys out of their beds and dashing down to the shelter!'

Joe reached over and took her hand and squeezed it. 'Everyone is afraid, Molly. We don't know what's going to happen next but if . . . if we're invaded I know every man and boy will fight to the last. Please God, it won't come to that. We have an Air Force and a Navy and that strip of water between us and the rest of Europe may well just save the day. Try not to worry, luv. I know it's hard but we have to keep going. Bernie is doing her best and you've got to admire her. It *is* hard for her, especially after losing Jimmy McCauley, and the convoys are taking terrible losses. We hear more than most people and the news isn't good. Bertie's convoy is due in in two days but, God help them, there's only a handful of ships left and two of the escorts are missing too. I couldn't tell her that. I just couldn't.'

Molly forgot her own fears at this news. 'Joe! Oh, Holy Mother, I hope he's safe. She couldn't stand it again – and in her condition! I'll pray as hard as I can to St Jude.'

Joe got up and kissed the top of her head. 'I'll get us the last drop of brandy. I think we both need it. What time will Maria be in?'

'Half past ten – and she's worrying me too.'

Joe handed her the glass. 'Why?'

'I've been thinking that I should send her home. She's had notification that she has to go and work in munitions and it's dangerous. I'd never forgive myself if anything happened to her and if . . . if we get bombed here and . . .' She took a sip of brandy. She didn't even want to *say* it.

'Have you mentioned it to her?' Joe could see her point. Maria was a citizen of the Irish Free State; it wasn't her war.

Molly shook her head. 'Bernie has been fighting with Claire over the same thing and Claire says she's twenty and she'll do as she likes.'

'She's Bernie's responsibility until she's twenty-one. Bernie is to all intents and purposes her guardian, just as you are Maria's. It's called *in loco parentis*. But, like Claire, Maria might not want to go. She's got used to living here – and then there's George, but I hear he's off next week to start training as a pilot. Mam says Aunty Vi doesn't know if she's delighted or dismayed. She's proud of him but worried too.'

'Oh, I don't know what to do!' Molly finished the last of her brandy.

Joe grinned. 'Freddie Mercer has the sharpest eyes of anyone I know. He can spot a chink of light a hundred yards away and he's down on you like a ton of bricks. It's amazing how a bit of power goes to some people's heads. Before all this started he wouldn't say boo to a goose.'

Molly managed a smile. 'And he certainly wouldn't say boo to his wife!'

Joe switched on the wireless, hoping to catch the news, and Molly sat twisting the empty glass between her fingers and thinking of Bernie. They'd both come to this country with such hopes and dreams. Some of those dreams had come true but they'd never envisaged that they'd be caught up in a war; that their own lives and those of the people they loved dearly – their husbands, their children, their sisters – would be in such terrible danger. That they would have to endure the daily worry, the privations, the terror of having the home you loved reduced to rubble around you as had happened in Spain and then Poland and now Norway and Denmark.

She'd write to Mam tonight, she decided. At least she could do something about Maria.

Maria nestled closer to Georgie. He had his arm around her and he looked down at her and smiled. They had decided to take a ferry ride to New Brighton and back. The little seaside town looked a little shabby and forlorn but they didn't plan to spend any time there. The upper deck of the ferry was deserted and a soft breeze lifted Maria's hair.

'You look so pretty tonight.'

'Why especially tonight?' Maria asked, although she was flattered.

'I think it's the way the wind is ruffling your hair. It's curly.'

'You do say the nicest things.'

'They're true! You know I don't go in for idle flattery, unlike some lads do.'

'You mean Teddy Soames? He was just too flash.'

'There won't be anyone else, Maria, will there?'

'No, not now. It's you I want to be with, Georgie.'

He kissed her forehead. 'I'm glad. I love you, Maria. From the first time I saw you at Joe's wedding I couldn't stop thinking of you. I was even planning to go to Ireland for a holiday, just so I could see you again.'

'You never told me that before! I love you too, Georgie, but I won't be able to see you as often now because I've got to go and work in munitions and the hours are terrible, so I heard.'

He pushed a strand of hair away from her cheek and kissed her. 'And I've got something to tell you, Maria. I've been posted to Biggin Hill. I'm leaving the day after tomorrow.'

'Oh, Georgie! Will you be able to get home on leave?'

'Not very often.'

'How I hate this war!'

'Will you write to me?'

She clung to him tightly. 'Every day, I promise! Will you write to me? Will you get home as often as you can?'

'Do you even have to ask that? You won't go taking up with anyone else, will you? You're my girl now.'

'Of course I won't! I *am* your girl!'

'Maybe one day, when all this is over, we can talk about our future.'

'I'd like that, Georgie,' she replied shyly and they spent the rest of the crossing without saying another word, too wrapped up in each other to notice the sky darkening and the stars appearing one by one.

Chapter Fifteen

ITA STARED AT THE newspaper Paddy had laid on the table and she hastily crossed herself. 'Oh, dear God! Where will it all end? Sure, there's nowhere safe from them at all! Thanks be to God this country is neutral.'

Paddy shook his head. 'Even that may not save us. Hasn't de Valera set up a National Defence Council and isn't he calling for more recruits to the Local Defence Force? Sure, soon half the country will be flocking to join up. The "phony war" as they call it over there looks as if it's over.'

Ita sat down and as she poured herself a cup of tea her hands were shaking. 'Do you think the Nazis will bomb the English cities like they did Warsaw?'

Paddy knew she was thinking of Molly and Maria. 'I don't know, Ita, and that's the truth of it, but the way they're going they will. No country has just let them walk in; they've all fought and fought hard but in the end it was no use. You can be sure that the British won't let them walk in either and they have their Empire behind them. They can count on men from all over the world. It will be a bitter fight, Ita.'

'Then they're to come home, both of them! Molly can bring those babies here, away from the bombs. I know that Tess is going to write to Bernie and tell her exactly the same thing.'

Paddy shook his head. 'Even if they agreed to come, all of them – and I don't think for a minute that either Molly or Bernie would agree – it's too late.'

'Too late!' Ita cried.

'Hasn't the British government banned travel to and from Ireland without special permits?'

'Then they can get one of those "special permits". I'll write to Molly this very minute.'

'Ita, she has responsibilities to Joe. She just can't up and leave, even if she could get a permit. I know you're worried – so am I – but just stop and think a minute.' He placed a hand on her shoulder. 'She's a married woman, Ita. Her place is with her husband. Liverpool is her home now.'

Slowly she nodded. 'But Maria can come home. She can get permission. She's a single girl.'

Paddy didn't want to discourage her but he doubted that his youngest daughter would agree to come home. He was very thankful that his two eldest sons were in America and that his two youngest were not old enough to join any kind of army or Defence Force. He remembered the sheer carnage of the last war. There had been many Irishmen who'd died in that one.

That evening a worried Tess came knocking at Ita's door. It was a pleasant evening and the half-door was open to let in the rays of the setting sun.

'Ita! Have you heard from Molly or Maria? Dessie was in town and all the talk is of the terrible things that are happening.'

'Come on in, Tess. No, I've not heard a thing but I've a letter ready for Con O'Brien to take in the morning.'

Tess sat down at the table. 'Oh, I'm destroyed altogether worrying about them all! My poor Bernie in the family way and Himself off on the high seas and with all them U-boats out there too, blowing the ships out of the water and the poor souls that's in them to kingdom come! The Lord have mercy on them!'

Ita could see that the situation called for something stronger than tea. She got up, opened the press and brought out two glasses and a half-bottle of port. 'Would she come home to you, Tess, do you think?' she asked as she poured them both a glass.

'She would not! Haven't I already asked her? How could she come running back here when he's out there facing death every day? That's what she said.'

'I was all for telling Molly to bring those two babies and herself and Maria home too, but Paddy talked me out of it. Both Molly and Bernie have husbands to consider now and they both look on Liverpool as their home. Maria is another matter. I've told Molly to ask Joe to find out about these special permits.'

'Ah, Dessie told me about them. He heard about them in town. Our Claire will need one too. Did you know, Ita, that they're all on rations over there? In Bernie's last letter didn't she say they were only allowed two ounces of butter and two ounces of margarine per person a *week*! Imagine?'

'Holy God! How would you manage on that? Sure, I get through about four pounds a week, what with the baking and the mash and the bread for the tea. I just wish there was a way of sending them a few pounds of rashers and a dozen eggs and some vegetables and a few cuts of meat.'

'Aren't we fortunate to live in the country, Ita?'

'We are indeed and away from any risk of bombs being dropped on us too.'

Paddy had heard their last few words as he came in. Every man he knew was seriously worried as to whether Ireland's neutrality would be respected. They were a very small country, unable to defend themselves. If the panzer divisions that were roaring across Europe, destroying everything in their path, were to cross the English Channel and succeed in bringing Britain to its knees, then what chance was there for Ireland? None at all, should Hitler turn his attentions to them. Then, whether they lived in a town or in the country, they would all feel the terrible yoke of fascism descend on them.

*

Bertie leaned over the rail of the *Andana Star* and watched the longshoremen loading the sacks of grain into the hold. The freighter was far from a new ship but at least she could keep up a decent speed, he thought. All around him ships were being loaded with every commodity from grain to oil, steel to canned food: everything the United Kingdom couldn't produce in sufficient quantity to feed its citizens and fight a war. The country depended so much on all these things and everything had to be transported across the Atlantic Ocean from Nova Scotia.

Bertie squinted in the weak sunlight. Here, in Canada, you could believe there wasn't a war on. Nothing was rationed; no invading armies threatened the peace; and no planes droned overhead. Even the dreaded U-boats kept their distance, preferring to wait in ambush around the Grand Banks. He shivered. No one liked to dwell on the days ahead and the risks they all faced. Well, at the end of his watch he was going ashore for a few beers with some of the lads – though no one was going to get drunk. There was an early start in the morning and, please God, they'd all make it home to Liverpool in just over a week's time. Canadian beer wasn't the same as the stuff you got at home, he thought, but at least it wasn't in short supply.

His thoughts turned to Bernie. He missed her and hoped she was well. He wished this damned war was over but he realised that it had only just begun. Still, it wouldn't be long now before he saw her again and he liked to think that he was doing this for her and the baby.

*

Bernie stood on the Landing Stage at the Pier Head peering into the gloom. It was barely light; dawn had only just broken. The sky was grey and a chilly damp mist swirled over the dark waters of the Mersey. There had only been a rumour that the convoy would arrive this morning but she had come here just the same. She pulled her jacket closer to her and shivered. She had said so many novenas and decades of the rosary that he would come home safely. He had to; he just *had* to.

Another two women joined her and after an hour they persuaded her to go and sit down on a pile of old packing cases they managed to find for her.

'We could be here all day, luv, and you can't stand for that long, not in your condition.'

'Thanks. I can't go home. I have to . . . know.'

'You don't have to explain to me, luv. I feel the same. I can't stay at home waiting for him to come in the door.'

Bernie tried to get comfortable but it was hard and the time passed slowly as the sky gradually brightened. How she hated this waiting. It was nearly three weeks since she'd waved him off and even though she knew he would post a letter to her from Canada, it wouldn't arrive until tomorrow at the earliest. It was a dangerous crossing both ways. Oh, she knew the country desperately needed the supplies the convoys brought in, but a shocking price was being paid in ships and men's lives. And even if he survived this trip, how many more would there be? For how long would their luck hold? She pushed the depressing thoughts to the back of her mind. It did no good at all to think like that.

'Is there still no sign of them?' she pleaded as the hands on the clock on top of the Liver Building reached eleven.

'Just the New Brighton ferry coming in. They could be safely in the estuary now, maybe passing Crosby, but we won't see them until they come further up the river.'

Bernie struggled to her feet. She was getting cramp and the baby was lying awkwardly. She walked to the edge of the platform and peered hard up river. She had excellent eyesight and she was sure she could just see three black specks on the horizon. 'Look! Look hard. I think it's them!'

The two other women joined her and they stared in tense silence until at last Bernie could make out the definite shape of three hulls.

'I can see them! It's the escorts. They can't be far behind!' Bernie's voice was hoarse with emotion. Her heart was beating in odd little jerks and she felt clammy. Please, dear God, let his ship be with them, she prayed.

The warships drew closer and then turned for Birkenhead on the opposite bank of the river. Behind them straggled the remnants of the convoy that had set out from Canada nearly ten days ago. There were only six ships left out of the fourteen that had sailed.

Bernie's hand went to her mouth as she searched the remaining ships for the *Andana Star* and then she gave a cry of relief. 'Oh, thank God! Thank God and His Holy

Mother! He's safe!' Tears of relief poured down her cheeks as the battered freighter drew closer.

One of the other women came and put her arm around her. 'Calm down, luv. Getting in a state won't be doing the baby any good. You'll be all right now. He'll be ashore soon enough, along with my feller and hers, thank the Lord.'

Bernie tried to compose herself as she was once more shepherded to the makeshift seat.

It was another hour before the crew came ashore, all of them looking gaunt and tired.

'Bertie! I'm so glad to see you!' She flung herself into his arms.

'Not half as glad as I am to see you! And not half as glad as I am to set foot on dry land. Safe, dry land,' he said, holding her as tightly as he could. It had been a terrible trip. He'd watched, helplessly, as ship after ship had been sunk. They'd managed to pick up some survivors but so many had perished. He'd watched a tanker, low in the water with the weight of fuel she was carrying, suddenly erupt into a massive ball of flames that shot skywards. To see a tanker explode was to see a vision of hell itself. The poor sods on board had never stood a chance. He shuddered at the memory. 'Let's get home, Bernie.'

She nodded and they walked towards the tram stop, still holding on to each other tightly, both thinking that this time they had been so lucky.

*

To the consternation of both Ita and Tess, Maria and Claire flatly refused to come home. Molly and Bernie wrote that they had reasoned, pleaded, argued and shouted, but to no avail.

When Tess had opened Bernie's letter she was so relieved to learn that Bertie Hayes had arrived home safely that she had burst into tears, but those tears of relief had turned to rage when she learned of Claire's obstinacy.

'Isn't she a brass-necked brat of a tinker! Isn't she the boldest strap that ever walked the earth!' she raged to Dessie.

'What's she done now?' he asked with some resignation.

'Doesn't she prefer to work in a factory making some kind of shells than come home here to us? That one has no thought for the sleepless nights she causes me; no thought for the grey hairs she's after putting on my head! No, doesn't she want to stay there and earn "more money than I ever earned in my life before"? And what good will all that money be to her if she has her hand blown off, or she's blinded, or she has a bomb dropped on her? It will pay for her wake and her burial – that's what!'

'So, she won't come home?' Dessie said flatly when his wife finally stopped for breath.

'She will not. Isn't that what I'm after telling you? Were you not listening to me at all, Dessie O'Sullivan?'

'I was so. Well, there's nothing we can do about it. If she won't listen to Bernie, then, sure, what can we do?'

Tess glared at him. '"Sure, what can we do?"' she

repeated with a whine in her voice. 'She's not twenty-one yet. We can *demand* she comes home. You can be certain that Paddy Keegan isn't sitting there saying, "Sure, what can we do?" There'll be a letter in very strong language going back to Maria Keegan. Didn't Ita tell me after Mass last Sunday that that was what he was going to do if she refused to come home? She said she was so worried that Paddy had said he would put her out of her misery.'

Dessie said nothing. Paddy would say that and no doubt he would write a very strongly worded letter to Maria. But at the end of the day the girl was over there and short of her father going himself and bringing her home, he doubted they would see Maria Keegan back in Rahan.

Chapter Sixteen

BERNIE WAS SICK AND tired of the whole situation and Molly was inclined to agree with her when they were discussing it sitting in the lounge of the Beehive pub as Joe and Bertie arrived back from the bar with the drinks: two very small sherries and two half-pints of mild.

'That's all he's allowing us and he says we're lucky to get it. There's lots of pubs with hardly anything to sell.' Bertie set the drinks on the table and they sat down.

'Oh, I don't mind. We don't get out very often so even a glass of lemonade would be nice,' Bernie said, sipping the overly sweet drink and trying not to pull a face.

'We were just saying we're both fed up with all the carry-on over Maria and Claire going home,' Molly said.

'Or not going home!' Bernie put in.

'Well, I think you should let them stay if they're both so set on it. Neither of them is a kid; they're young women and they know all the risks. It's not as if they haven't been told what could be ahead of them, of everyone. And it's getting you down, luv,' Bertie said. Bernie had enough on her plate with the baby and worrying about him without all this hullabaloo.

'It's getting us all down, Bertie, but how will we all feel if something happens to them?' Joe asked.

Bernie sighed heavily. 'Oh, let them take their chances with us.'

Joe looked grim. 'Things aren't looking good. I really don't want to worry you both even more but you'll hear it soon enough.'

Molly looked at him fearfully. 'What?'

'Both the Dutch and the Belgian forces are crumbling under the Nazi attack. Both countries are overrun and it can only be a matter of time before they have to surrender and then our lads will be cut off.'

'Jesus! What will happen to them?' Bertie asked.

Joe shook his head. 'God knows. They'll fight, as will the French, but who knows what the outcome will be? It will be in all the newspapers in the next few days.'

'Then maybe we should put Maria on the ferry as soon as we can,' Molly said, looking at Joe for support.

Bernie looked very doubtful. 'That will be easier said than done and as for Claire, well, I'll tell her what you've just told us and she can make up her own mind.'

On the way home Molly held on tightly to Joe's arm. She knew he was seething with frustration at being kept in the city when things were so desperate but the news was so bad that she needed him with her to give her courage and support.

The news got worse. It became known that the British forces were encircled on the French coast, trapped between the German Army and the sea at Dunkirk. Then began the evacuation. Every available ship, from fishing boats and pleasure craft to naval warships, set out for the French coast to bring home both French and British soldiers, many wounded. The Mersey ferries sailed out of the estuary and turned south heading for the Irish Sea, then St George's Channel and finally the French coast. Thousands lined both banks of the Mersey to watch them go. Many cheered but others were silent. The future had never looked so dark.

On June 18, with the remnants of the British Army safely home, the Prime Minister made a speech in Parliament. Joe read it out to Molly and Bernie as they sat in the kitchen.

'Let us therefore brace ourselves to our duties, and so bear ourselves that if the British Empire and its Commonwealth last for a thousand years, men will still say: "This was their finest hour".'

'So, we're alone?' Molly ventured. She'd never seen Joe look so grim.

'Yes, and against the most unmerciful enemy we've ever fought. It says here that the King is practising his shooting in the palace grounds and he says he'll die fighting there if necessary. The Queen won't leave him and take the princesses to Canada. They're very brave; an example to us all. They could all have gone to Canada, to anywhere that's safe; other royal families have done.'

'Will Bertie hear the news?' Bernie asked, for he'd sailed again and she knew he was on his way back home.

Joe nodded. 'They send messages to the escort ships.'

Bernie's hand went unconsciously to her 'bump', as she called her swollen stomach. She would be glad of Claire's company and help in the days ahead as she was sure Molly would be of Maria's. Both girls had stayed, even though all the dangers had been fully explained.

Maria had been horrified when Molly had informed her that it would be best if she went home.

'Molly, I can't! I just can't! It would be like running away and leaving Georgie. What would he think of me? I love him and I know that when the war is over, or maybe even before, he'll want us to get engaged. I'm not going home; I don't care what Mam says!'

Molly had had no idea that things were that serious between her sister and Joe's young cousin. 'You're far too young to be getting engaged!'

'Bernie was younger than me when she married Jimmy McCauley!' Maria shot back.

'That was different. Times were different. Everything is so uncertain now. You can't make plans for the future;

besides, I'm sure he will understand. He'll want to know that you're safe.'

'I'm not leaving, Molly! He doesn't get home very often and if I were back in Ireland I'd never see him! I won't go! Claire's not going and neither am I!'

Molly had sighed heavily as she realised Maria meant it.

As the glorious summer months progressed, the battle for the supremacy of the skies above Britain raged. Both Molly and Bernie followed the news avidly, as did Maria, for young George Jackson was stationed at Biggin Hill with his squadron and losses were heavy. Shipping in the English Channel had been bombed, the Channel Islands had been invaded and occupied and the convoys were still suffering heavy losses.

At the height of the Battle of Britain, Bernie's time was drawing very near and Claire had strict instructions to phone Molly immediately her labour started. Both the doctor and the midwife had been notified. On the night of August 17 they were both just finishing their supper when the rising wail of the air-raid siren sounded.

'Oh, damn! I'm tired and I was going to have an early night!' Claire said irritably. It was extremely hard work in the munitions factory and it was a long trek out to Kirkby and back. She quickly snatched up the blankets and the hurricane lamp.

Bernie got to her feet with some difficulty. 'You go on ahead; I can't move at all quickly now. I'll bring the cushions and the box of matches. I don't relish the thought of a night stuck in the shelter myself.'

Claire had already disappeared into the shelter as Bernie closed the back door behind her. The next minute she was hurled across the yard and fell gasping to her knees. There was a loud roaring in her ears that drowned out Claire's high-pitched screams. She heard the engines of the planes and the whistling noise as a stick of bombs fell; then the explosions shook the ground and she began to scream herself. Oh, Holy Mother of God! She had to get to the safety of the shelter! She pulled herself upright and found she was shaking uncontrollably.

Despite her terror Claire had dashed up the small garden. 'Bernie, are you all right? Get into the shelter, quick!' she shrieked above the roar of flames and falling masonry.

'I'm not hurt, just shaken. Give me your arm!'

Half running, half stumbling, they reached the safety of the shelter and collapsed on the wooden bench, clinging to each other in terror.

Bernie was the first to recover herself. 'That was close,' she said shakily.

'I think the next street has had a few direct hits and we've a hole in the roof but we're both all right, thanks be to God!' Claire replied through chattering teeth.

Bernie managed a weak smile. 'Didn't I tell you to go home when you had the chance?'

'Ah, Bernie, will you stop giving out to me about that!'

'How long do you think it will go on?' Bernie asked, thinking it may well be the turn of Arnot Street next.

'It's the first time we've ever had a real raid so how would I know?'

Bernie grimaced.

'What's wrong?' Claire demanded.

'I think I'm starting. Being blown almost flat on my face must have set me off.'

Claire looked horrified. 'You can't be! You can't have the baby in the middle of an air-raid! I don't know what to do and I can't go running for Mrs Nolan or Dr Joyce and I can't phone Molly!'

'We . . . we'll just have to hope it's over soon,' Bernie replied, thinking she didn't want to give birth here and with just Claire to help her.

Her pains got worse but two hours later they were both relieved to hear the all-clear sound.

'Oh, thank the Lord! Let's get out of here,' Bernie cried.

'I'll see you into the house and then I'll go and get help. I'll try to phone Molly but the lines might be down.' Claire was so relieved it was over.

Fires were blazing in the next street and the sound of fire engine bells clanging loudly could be heard as they emerged from the shelter. Bernie looked up at the roof of the house where a large hole had appeared.

'I suppose we're lucky just to have a few slates and the chimney blown off but I dread to think of the mess upstairs. Oh, God!' Another pain tore through her and she squeezed

Claire's arm so tightly that the girl winced. 'Go and get help, quickly!'

Claire saw her into the kitchen and then she turned and ran.

Bernie had never experienced such pain in her entire life and she was terrified that Claire seemed to be taking so long to come back. What was she *doing*? She didn't want to have the baby alone.

She was standing, leaning on the kitchen table and hardly noticing that everything was covered in a layer of dust, when Claire, accompanied by the midwife, finally arrived.

'Where have you been? You took so long!' she cried.

'Oh, it's shocking out there, Bernie! There are piles of rubble everywhere, the phone and electricity lines are down, and houses are still collapsing! I had to go the long way round and Dr Joyce is out as there are people with terrible injuries. Even more people are still buried.'

Mrs Nolan took control. 'Now, Mrs Hayes, try not to get upset. We'll cope just fine. Things are a bit . . . hectic but first of all let's get this place cleaned up as best we can.'

'The water's off. The main must be broken,' Claire informed them, turning on the tap.

Mrs Nolan looked grim. 'Well, we'll just have to manage. There is a war on.'

It was a saying both girls were to hear with ever-increasing frequency and would eventually come to hate.

Three hours later Bernie's son was born and even though she was totally exhausted she took the baby in her arms and felt that all the agony and all the hard work had been worth it.

'What are you going to call him?' Mrs Nolan asked, smiling, as she began to clear up, helped by a very relieved and still shaken Claire.

Bernie sank back on the bed they'd made for her from two chairs and all the cushions they could find. 'Albert Desmond Hayes. Albert after Bertie and Desmond after my da.'

'Hello, Albie Hayes, aren't you a fine-looking little lad!' Claire held out her finger and the baby grasped it tightly.

'Now, I'd advise you all to try and get some sleep. I'll call in to see you in the morning, and you, young lady, will have to leave early for work. Heaven knows what state the tram lines are in,' Mrs Nolan advised Claire.

Bernie and the baby were asleep and Claire was dozing in a chair when Molly arrived.

'Oh, thank God, you're both . . .' Her words trailed off as she caught sight of the little bundle in Bernie's arms.

'She had a little boy. They're both fine. It was all so sudden. We were on our way to the shelter and she was knocked over by the blast. It started her off.'

Molly looked around the kitchen. When she'd heard that bombs had fallen on this part of the city she'd been frantic. Joe was at work but she'd been determined to come and make sure Bernie was all right. It had been a terrible night for her too. She'd been startled when she'd opened the front door and found her mother-in-law on the doorstep.

'Effie! Come on in. Has something happened?' she'd asked, seeing the look on the older woman's face.

'I came up as soon as I could, Molly. It . . . it's bad news. Young Georgie's plane was shot down.' Effie had glanced at the kitchen door from behind which could be heard the sound of the twins' voices and Maria's laughter. 'The poor lass, she's so young!'

Molly had steered her into the front room. 'Is he . . . ?'

Effie had nodded wearily. 'Yes. He's dead. His poor mam is heart-broken.'

Molly had eased her down into a chair. 'I'm so very, very sorry. He was such a nice lad. She's going to be destroyed entirely. You know she wouldn't go home? She stayed because she . . . she loved him.'

Effie nodded and got up. 'I'll be getting back, Molly. I told them I wouldn't be long.'

'Sure, you've got to have a cup of tea at least! You've had a shock yourself.'

'No, I'll not bother, luv. I'm fine. I don't want them worrying about me.'

Molly had let her out, kissing her on the cheek, and then she'd gone into the kitchen.

'Did I hear the front door?' Maria asked, wiping Peter's sticky hands.

'It was Effie. She . . . she had some bad news.' There

had been no easy way to tell her sister. She'd taken Maria's hands and said: 'George is dead, Maria. His plane was shot down.'

The cry Maria uttered had gone through her like a knife and she'd gathered the sobbing girl into her arms. After a while she'd put her sons to bed and then tried again to comfort Maria as best she could until the siren had gone and despite everything they'd all had to go to the shelter. When the raid was over Joe had managed to phone her to tell her he was safe but that he would have to work late. He'd been deployed to where the bombs had fallen and she'd learned that there had been damage in Bernie's area. Wild horses wouldn't have kept her from coming here.

'Did you get hit? Everywhere is covered in dust,' she whispered. She didn't want to wake Bernie just yet.

'Not at all. There's a hole in the roof and the chimney has gone. There's a shocking mess upstairs but it's not bad compared to some.'

'Sure, you can't stay here. Go and start to pack your things and anything valuable, and pack clothes for Bernie and the baby too. You're all coming home with me until this place is fit to be lived in again. Maybe you can help to comfort Maria,' she finished sadly.

Claire looked at her quizzically.

'We got word last night that young George Jackson was shot down. He . . . he's dead.'

Claire forgot to whisper. 'Oh, poor Maria!'

Bernie stirred and opened her eyes, then a look of astonishment came over her face. 'Molly!'

Molly instantly took her hand. 'Didn't you pick a fine time to have your son?'

'How . . . how did you get here?'

'By tram for most of the way and the rest I walked. I came to make sure you were safe and what do I find?'

Bernie smiled. 'I think he'd had enough of being where he was and wanted to see what was going on.'

'He picked a great time to do that – in the middle of an air-raid! Now, I'm staying and when you've had a proper rest we'll get some kind of transport to take you home with me. I'll have no arguments about it; we'll manage. I'll get word to Joe somehow and Maria's at home with the boys. You just go back to sleep. Claire and I will pack.'

Bernie nodded thankfully and her eyes closed.

Molly smiled at her and for the first time in months she felt stronger, more confident. She was still afraid – you couldn't not be when you saw the terrible damage inflicted on the streets she'd come through – and she was heart-sore for Maria, but she would cope. They all would.

Chapter Seventeen

JOE HAD SOMEHOW MANAGED to arrange for an ambulance to take Bernie, the baby, Claire and Molly back to Oxbridge Street. When they finally arrived home he was washing the dust and sweat of a night spent digging in the rubble of bombed buildings for survivors from his face and hands.

'You got home safe then, thank God,' he said, hastily drying his hands before kissing Molly and then Bernie.

'Thanks to you. I would have had to bring her on the tram otherwise and I don't know just how we would all have managed. Now, let's get them upstairs and into bed and settled. The boys will have to come in with us, Joe. Bernie and Claire can have their room.'

'Would it not be best if I shared with Maria?' Claire asked, putting the two cases and a large brown paper parcel down on a chair. She wasn't going to work today. They would surely understand.

'If you like. Is she still upstairs? How is she, Joe?' Molly looked with concern at her husband.

'I haven't seen her, Moll, but I heard her sobbing still. It's a damned shame! Mam says Aunty Vi is devastated. He was such a nice lad but then I suppose they all are. Brave too.'

Bernie handed the sleeping Albie to Claire. 'Let me go and see her, Molly. Let me talk to her. I . . . I'm the only one who's been through what she's suffering now.'

'Oh, Bernie, I don't know if it's wise or not. You're hardly over having the baby and the horrors of last night and won't it be dragging it all up again and upsetting you?'

Bernie shook her head. Jimmy McCauley belonged in her past. His memory was beginning to fade even now. When she thought about him his features were no longer clear in her mind. 'Molly, I *do* know how she feels. I may be able to help her. You go and see to the twins and leave Maria to me.'

'Let me give you a hand to get upstairs, Bernie. Do you want me to carry you?' Joe offered. It was good of Bernie to try and help. Even though Maria hadn't been married or even engaged to George she'd obviously loved him. Bernie was the only person who could perhaps comfort the girl.

'I've only had a baby! Sure, my mam had twelve and wasn't she up and about the next day after all of us. I'll be grand,' Bernie replied determinedly. 'You stay down here and have a bit of a rest. You deserve it.'

Molly busied herself with getting the boys dressed and

getting something to eat while Claire began to unpack. Joe was brushing down his uniform for he had to be back on duty later that morning.

'But you've had no sleep!' Molly protested when he imparted this news to her.

'Oh, I'll catch up tonight. There's so much to do, Moll,' he answered.

Maria was lying on her crumpled bed clutching the small bundle of letters George had written her and the teddy bear he'd won for her at the amusements in New Brighton. She hadn't slept. Her head was aching and her eyes were sore and swollen from the hours spent crying. No one really knew just how much she had loved him and now she'd never see him again. She'd heard Joe come in, then Molly arrive and she'd realised that Claire and Bernie were with her. She thought she'd heard a baby cry but she just wasn't interested.

She heard the bedroom door open but she kept her face turned to the wall and her eyes closed. She didn't want to talk to anyone.

Bernie sat down on the edge of the bed, wincing a little. She was sore and it hadn't been easy to get upstairs either. She reached out and touched Maria's shoulder gently.

'Maria, it's Bernie. I'm sorry, so very sorry.'

Maria sniffed but didn't move.

'If anyone knows how you're feeing right now, it's me. You feel as if your life is over, that there's no point going on without him. You're wondering how you will face each long and miserable day. Then you begin to ask God, "Why him?" "Why did you have to take him from me? We had our lives ahead of us. Why? Why?" That's the way I felt the day a policeman came to tell me that my Jimmy had drowned.' Bernie's voice was low and steady but there was no mistaking the note of pain and regret.

Maria sat up and threw herself into Bernie's arms. 'Oh, Bernie! I miss him so much already!'

Bernie held her and stroked her tangled hair. 'I know you do and I'm not saying it's going to be easy. You've a long hard road ahead of you but you *will* get over it, I promise you. In time the pain will pass. You won't believe me now, but you'll find someone else and you'll be happy. You'll never forget him but you will find love again, Maria.'

Maria continued to sob and Bernie thought of Jimmy, dead these eleven years. Like George Jackson for Maria, he'd always be young and handsome in her memories. They would never grow old. Then she thought of Bertie whom she loved so much. Would they have the chance to grow old together? He faced death every hour of the day he was at sea. And he didn't even know he had a son.

When Molly opened the door half an hour later Maria was asleep and so was Bernie.

They were all a little cramped but they managed. There were no more raids until September and then there was just the one. Having been thwarted in their attempt to gain supremacy in the skies over Britain, the Luftwaffe had turned their attention and their wrath on London.

To Bernie's great relief Bertie had made it home safely again. He was delighted with his son but a little dismayed that he had been born in the middle of an air-raid. He worried about the effect it might have on Bernie. She was absolutely fine, she assured him, and she had managed to get a builder to start the repairs on the house, which was no mean feat.

'Won't we all be able to go home in a few weeks? Molly's been so good but it's not fair on her family, and Claire is always complaining that it's so much further for her to get to work.'

'I know but people are having to make all kinds of sacrifices these days, Bernie,' he'd answered, but just the same he acknowledged he'd be relieved when they could all move back to Arnot Street.

They moved the day before he was due to sail again. Molly had helped Bernie to clean up and Joe and Bertie between them moved Bernie's things.

'You did remember to pick up the ration books?' Molly asked as Bernie was wrapping Albie tightly in a shawl. The weather had turned much colder now November was almost upon them.

'I did so. Aren't they becoming more precious than gold? Bertie says this trip he's going to try to bring us some supplies. Nothing is on ration in Canada. Imagine not having to queue for hours for everything. I told him not to try and smuggle half a side of bacon in his kit-bag but I wouldn't mind some decent soap and some stockings.'

'If he can get stockings could he manage a few pairs for me? I'd be ever so grateful,' Molly asked, thinking of the days when you had just been able to walk into any shop and buy what you wanted, provided you had the money. Now, when there was plenty of work and people had the money, there was very little to buy. Everything had to be imported and the German U-boats were taking a terrible toll on shipping.

'Of course. He's going to look for some bits and pieces for Christmas too. Heaven knows what kind of a Christmas it will be this year. There'll be no turkey or goose or even a chicken!'

'Let's worry about that when Christmas is a bit nearer. Now, have we got everything?' Molly looked around the kitchen and then fastened the leading reins on to both her sons who wriggled with annoyance. Peter pulled off his navy-blue knitted balaclava.

'Now put that back on this minute! It's cold outside. I know you don't like having reins on but aren't you a pair of little devils? You'll be running away from me and putting the heart across me, like you did when I took you to the park.'

Bernie placed Albie in his pram and pulled the blankets up around him. 'Right. Let's be off then and don't go saying you're really sorry to see us go, Molly. You'll be relieved to get the house back to normal.'

'Ah, don't say that, Bernie. You know you're always welcome! And anyway, what's "normal" these days?'

Ita was asking herself the same question. Now there was rationing in Ireland too, although because they produced much of the food they needed they weren't too badly affected by the shortages. Coal was so scarce that the rail services were severely affected and there was talk of the trains being run on turf.

'Aren't we fortunate to have the bog on our doorstep?' Tess remarked as they walked back from visiting a neighbour who was sick.

It was a cold day with a raw easterly wind blowing the last remaining leaves from the trees and depositing them in the roadside ditch. The hedgerows were brown and bare too and the cattle no longer grazed in the fields.

'And fortunate to have a shed full of turf now winter is here,' Ita replied, wrapping her scarf more securely around her neck and jamming her woollen tam-o'-shanter more firmly on her head.

'I'm still worried sick about those girls and the little ones. I don't know how Bernie faces each day, what with worrying about Himself away on the high seas and whether she's going to have the house blown to bits around her again.'

Ita refrained from remarking that Molly had written to

say the damage to Bernie's house wasn't great compared to some. 'But isn't she settled back in the house now? Isn't it all repaired?'

'It is so, but look at the state of all those poor souls in London. It could happen to Liverpool. I don't know how they get through the day always listening for the siren to go and having to run for the shelter. Sure, my nerves would be shredded to bits, so they would.'

Ita nodded. They'd seen pictures of the terrible damage the 'Blitz', as it was being called, had inflicted on England's capital city. 'And haven't we had a taste of it too? Didn't they drop bombs on that carpet factory in Campile, in Wexford and that village in the Vale of Clara in Wicklow?'

'They did and haven't they attacked Irish ships too, and us supposed to be a neutral country? It makes you wonder.'

Ita sighed. 'Paddy keeps telling me not to worry but how can you not? At least we have to thank God that Joe isn't in the forces although Molly says he still wants to be.'

'Isn't he an eejit? Does he want to end up like that poor cousin of his? Does Molly say how Maria is? You know our Claire is Maria's best friend yet she won't put pen to paper to tell me how she's getting on.'

'She's worried about her and I am myself. Oh, doesn't she go to work every day in that fearful place but Molly says she's so listless and quiet and she's not eating properly. She has no interest in anything at all.'

Tess nodded. 'Ah, don't you remember how Bernie was after she lost poor Jimmy McCauley? When she came home here wasn't she just a shadow of herself? It took her a long time, Ita, to pull herself together. Maria will be the same. But she's young yet. She's time enough to meet someone else.'

Ita sighed. She took some comfort from Tess's words. After all, Bernie had married Bertie Hayes and she was happy.

They had reached the bend in the road where it forked. Tess would turn left and Ita would go to the right, along the canal towards the lock. 'I'm sure you're right, Tess, but isn't worrying over her just another cross I have to bear? I wish I had them all home here with me; at least I could do something to help Maria. Wouldn't I just love to see my two grandsons, but never mind. I can pray for them all and I'll try and send them a few things for Christmas. Sure, it won't be much of a Christmas with all that bombing and rationing. Well, I'll be seeing you, Tess. I've an afternoon's work ahead of me in that dairy. Mind yourself now.'

'And you mind yourself too, Ita. I'll remember you in my prayers tonight,' Tess replied, pulling her shawl more tightly around her and setting her face to the cold wind.

Chapter Eighteen

BERTIE WAS DELIGHTED THAT he'd managed to get the soap and the stockings Bernie had asked him for and he'd bought some tins of peaches, pears and stewing steak. For little Albie he'd got an all-in-one suit that the little Canadian children all wore in winter. It would be just the thing to keep him warm in his pram when Bernie was standing for hours in queues. He'd got him a few little toys too, even though he was as yet too young to play with them. For Bernie he had bought a pure silk underslip and matching camiknickers. Pure silk underwear was so hard to come by that women were using parachute silk, when they could get it, and making the things themselves. Everything was safely packed into his seabag, which was stowed under his bunk. Not that there was very much room under there. The *Southern Empress* was an old ship, a very old ship, and was coal-fired. That didn't bode well. It meant she just wasn't capable of any speed above six knots and a convoy travelled at the speed of the slowest ship. All the Navy could spare them as escorts were three old First World War destroyers and two Norwegian corvettes, which looked too small to brave the treacherous waters of the North Atlantic, especially in December. Still, it wasn't his job to question the Admiralty. He just wanted to get home.

The convoy was a large one of forty-six ships plus a rescue ship and the escorts, and, despite being delayed by fog on the Newfoundland Banks, it made it three-quarters of the way across the ocean before it ran into a German 'wolf pack', as the groups of U-boats had become known.

Bertie was on watch, muffled to the eyes in waterproofs. The weather had been atrocious for most of the way with howling storm-force winds and constant icy rain, sleet and snow. The old ship pitched and rolled heavily and men who had been at sea for years were seasick. You lived constantly with the fear of death but what you hated more than anything, he thought, was the bloody weather! He dug his hands more deeply into the pockets of his heavy coat as he scanned the heaving grey water. Every white-topped wave looked like a periscope: your eyes played tricks on you. The wind was blowing sleet across the deck and visibility was terrible to say the least. The convoy was strung out ahead and behind them, the destroyers almost out of sight. He stamped his feet to try to keep them warm; he could hardly feel them even though he wore thick woollen socks and heavy sea boots. Still, he only had another half an hour before he was relieved, he thought cheerfully.

As he scanned the line of ships a freighter suddenly heeled heavily to starboard, almost turning on her side.

'Christ! The *City of Dundee* has been hit, sir!' he yelled to the officer standing a few yards away from him.

They both watched in angry silence as the freighter's stern slid slowly beneath the cold, grey water.

'The *Mayfly* should be around to pick up survivors, if there are any in these waters,' the man said with a note of pity in his voice.

'Oh, God! There goes the *Brennan*, sir! Looks as though we've got a wolf pack in amongst us.'

They watched helplessly as three more ships were sunk, their crews clinging to liferafts or floundering in the icy waters until they could be picked up by the corvettes. The light was fading and the convoy began to scatter as the destroyers sailed in to drop depth charges.

'Hayes, aren't you off now?' Chief Petty Officer Jones shouted to Bertie above the wind.

'Yes, sir, but Metcalf hasn't come up to relieve me yet.'

'Bloody junior ratings!' Jones muttered, irritably.

'Too bloody right!' Bertie echoed, silently. He was frozen stiff.

They both heard the thud, followed closely by a second one. Bertie couldn't move. It was the moment he'd dreaded. He'd been so lucky so far. He'd never been on a ship that had been torpedoed but his luck had just run out. Over the howling wind he heard the sound of a whistle. Six long blasts followed by a short one. Every man on board knew what it meant but he was still paralysed with fear.

'For Christ's sake, Hayes! Move yourself! We've been hit! We're sinking! Abandon ship! Get to the bloody lifeboats!' CPO Jones roared at him, pushing him towards the stairwell.

Slipping and sliding on the wet deck as the ship listed heavily to port they ran. Bertie was assigned to boat number twelve but that was on this side of the ship and would be useless. They'd never be able to lower it with this list. He followed the chief to the starboard side where four boats were being lowered.

'Get in! Never mind if it's already overloaded, get yourself in!' Jones yelled, pushing him towards the boat that was swaying on its davits.

Bertie was in control of himself now: afraid, but the panic had gone. 'What about you, sir?'

'I'm right behind you, lad!'

He was half dragged, half pulled into the boat with the chief close behind him. The ship was sinking lower and lower into the water. He fell and landed awkwardly, screaming in pain as he felt the bone in his lower leg snap. He was foundering in cold water in the bottom of the lifeboat.

Jones pulled him up. 'You all right, Hayes? Sit there! I'll give them a hand with those ropes or we'll never get the damned thing down!'

With some difficulty the boat finally hit the top of a swell. Gasping and spluttering as they were all drenched, the crew pulled it clear of the hull of the doomed *Southern Empress*.

Bertie was white with pain and shock and cold. Someone wrapped a blanket around him but as the boat was tossed like a cork in the mountainous seas, he began to lose consciousness.

Jones shook him hard and waves of excruciating pain dragged him back to awareness.

'Don't let go, Hayes! Don't give in or you'll never wake up again!' The lad was seriously hurt and in these conditions hypothermia set in quickly. 'Are you married?'

'Yes. Yes, sir,' Bertie said through gritted teeth.

'Then think of your wife! Just keep thinking of her!'

Bertie nodded. Bernie! He had to keep thinking of Bernie and of little Albie. Then he remembered the things he'd bought them, still in his seabag, which was now at the bottom of the ocean. Regret at the waste washed over him before he slipped into unconsciousness.

Molly was freezing cold. She'd stood for hours and hours in queues. Thankfully she'd left the boys at home with Mrs Knight from next door looking after them. They just wouldn't stand for very long; they'd have been crying with boredom and the cold. All she'd managed to get was the butter and sugar ration for them all, some flour and four sausages and a very small end of a leg of lamb. The butcher had told her confidentially that he'd saved it for her. His daughter was married to an Irishman who had joined the Army and was fighting in North Africa. It would have to go a very long way indeed, she thought. It was very probably mutton and not lamb so she'd have to cook it slowly.

She hurried through the now dark streets towards the tram stop. It was four days to Christmas Eve and she was doing her best to make Christmas as enjoyable as it could be. They had a tree which she'd decorated with some small candles she'd saved from a long-eaten birthday cake. She'd spent hours making little ornaments from pipe cleaners and bits of material, braid and silver paper she'd begged from Mr Knight's cigarette packets. It looked really nice and the boys were delighted with it. She'd made paper chains from strips of newspaper she'd painted a variety of colours, which Joe had hung across the ceiling in the sitting room. She hadn't been able to get a single bit of holly though and she thought longingly of all the holly bushes at home: you could just go and cut great armfuls of it.

The food was proving very difficult. Raisins, sultanas, candied peel and glacé cherries were impossible to get hold of so there would be no cake and no pudding. Instead she had a small tin of pineapple and one of evaporated milk and she intended to try a recipe Bernie had given her called 'Pineapple Surprise'. Thinking about it, she would be the one who would get the 'surprise' if it turned out to be at all edible. Bernie was coming on Christmas Day with Claire and little Albie, as Bertie's convoy wasn't expected until after the holiday. She and Bernie were going to pool their coupons and she'd beg the butcher for a small chicken.

Clutching her purchases she boarded the tram and sank down thankfully on a seat. She was so tired with standing. She paid her fare and settled back. Joe would be working over the holiday, of course, but he would get some time off. She'd knitted the boys new jumpers out of an old one of Joe's: she'd painstakingly unpicked it and washed the wool. Out of a cardigan of hers and an old blouse, she'd made two toy rabbits, which she'd stuffed with rags, and Joe and his da had spent hours making the boys a wooden train, complete with wheels and a few carriages. She hoped to get them an orange each and a few penny bars of chocolate. She always saved her sweets for them but the oranges would prove hard to get. She sighed. So much planning, so much work and what was there to give them at the end of it? Not much at all. Still, it was more than a lot of children would be getting. She was determined that despite all the shortages Christmas was going to have some cheer in it.

As she got off the tram she realised that it was later than she had thought. People were coming home from work; it must be after six and Joe was due in at seven and she with no meal ready and the twins still next door . . .

She quickened her steps, her head bent against the cold wind. As she reached the top of Oxbridge Street the siren started to wail.

Molly broke into a run. 'God, let me get home. Please,

please, let me get home!' she prayed as she ran. Her house was in darkness. She burst into the kitchen.

'Andrew! Peter! It's Mammy! Are you here?' she shouted, dashing from room to room. She ran down the garden to the shelter. She could hear the drone of aircraft engines above the wailing notes of the siren.

'Molly! I was worried sick about you. Where have you been?' Maria cried as her sister fell into the small, low building.

Molly was out of breath but she was so relieved to see the twins sitting with Maria on the wooden bench. They had their coats on and mittens, scarves and woollen balaclava helmets.

'I've been standing in queues for hours and then just as I got to the top of the road the siren went.'

'I collected the boys from next door when I got in from work but when you didn't come home I was thinking of trying to get word to Joe. I was so worried about you, Molly!' Maria was near to tears. She'd been sick with anxiety, thinking that her sister had met with some kind of accident, and then when the siren had gone and there was still no sign of her she'd begun to panic.

'I'm really sorry. I didn't realise it was so late. It's starting early!'

Maria screamed as the first explosion shook the shelter. Molly put her arms around her sons and held them close, trying not to show her own fear. Maria sat huddled up against them, biting her lip to stifle a moan every time they heard the whistling, then the thud, followed by the roar of collapsing buildings.

Peter held on to his mother tightly. He didn't understand properly why they always had to come to this dark, musty shelter when all the big bangs started. He didn't like the noise and it scared Mummy, he could tell it did, even though her voice was always cheery. And he hated the fact that Daddy was never here with them when the big bangs started and that puzzled him too. He knew Mummy wouldn't be scared if Daddy were here but to all his questions about it she replied that Daddy had to go to work.

For hour after terrifying hour they sat there as wave after wave of bombers dropped hundreds of tons of incendiary and high-explosive bombs on the city. Soon fires were raging everywhere. Food warehouses in Dublin Street were ablaze as was the Waterloo Grain House. The docks were bearing the brunt of the raid and the Cunard Building and the Dock Board Offices at the Pier Head were hit.

Molly held her sons against her and prayed that they would all come through this terrible night safely. She knew Joe was out there somewhere, doing anything at all he could to help both injured civilians and the fire-fighters. And she prayed for Bernie, too. She and Albie and Claire would be sitting in their shelter, as terrified as she was but trying not to show it.

At four o'clock the following morning the all-clear finally sounded.

Maria began to sob quietly. She was tired and cold and frightened and she had to go to work today. But at least they had survived.

'Thank God! I never thought it would end. I'm so cold and I feel utterly exhausted. Will you help me with the boys? Let's get inside and have a cup of tea.' Molly eased her stiff limbs and gently picked up Andrew who was asleep.

Maria lifted Peter, who whimpered but didn't wake. She wondered how they could sleep through such noise.

When the boys were in bed, still fully dressed, Molly went to the front door and looked out. 'Oh, Lord!' she gasped. The sky was bright orange with the glow from the hundreds of fires that were raging across the battered city. The air was full of the smell of burning, of dust and smoke. Further down a pile of rubble completely blocked the road and she saw gaps in the houses and realised that until eight hours ago that rubble had been someone's home.

She went back inside to find Maria sitting miserably by the cold range.

'It's shocking, it really is. It looks as if the whole city is in ruins.'

'Oh, Molly! How are we going to manage? The electric is out, and the gas, the water and the phone . . .'

Molly put her arms around her sister. 'We'll just manage. We've got a roof over our heads and we're not hurt. There's food in the press and I'll get the fire going in no time. We'll have something hot, I promise. I'll cook it over the fire. We'll all feel better then. We've got to be thankful for what we've got. Sure, there'll be hundreds tonight who have lost their homes, who'll have nothing left, and those who'll be hurt and have lost loved ones. Think of all that and be thankful, Maria. Now, light that hurricane lamp while I get this fire started.'

As she raked out the embers and relaid the fire she was shaking, partly with cold and partly with anxiety about Joe and Bernie. She didn't know if they were alive or dead.

When the siren had gone Joe had immediately dashed back to the station. The police were the first in the chain of command. From all parts of the district men and boys began to arrive. Joe and two other constables and the sergeant issued orders that sent the wardens out to evacuate shelters in immediate danger, direct the fire crews to buildings already on fire and send the vital messages to other police stations. Joe was always concerned about Molly but tonight he worried more than ever, as he knew the raid was heaviest near his own home.

After an hour he went out into the street. Above him the sky was lurid with flames and the air was thick with smoke and dust and soot. At the far end of the street he could see figures running back towards a burning building. He broke into a run himself, sweating from the intense heat. The noise of battle beat against his ears: the droning of the planes; the firing of the anti-aircraft guns; the explosions; and the crash of falling masonry.

'Stay back! Stay back! Don't go in there!' he yelled as he made out the figure of a young lad, edging his way towards the burning building. The heat beat them both back.

'It's me dog! It's Blackie! He was dead scared of the bombs and he wouldn't come ter the shelter with us!' The lad's face was blackened with soot but white rivulets showed on his cheeks: the pathways of his tears. 'I've got ter get him out, mister!'

Joe looked towards the house. Nothing could survive those flames. He put his arm around the boy.

'We can't do anything for him, son. But he won't have felt anything; the smoke would overcome him before the fire took hold. I'm sorry. Where's your mam and dad?'

'In the shelter.' The boy dashed away his tears with the back of his hand. 'Are yer sure poor Blackie wouldn't have been in pain?'

'I'm sure. Now, come on. Let's get you back to your parents; they must be worried sick.' Joe put his arm around the lad's shoulder to comfort him. He'd get over it; maybe he'd even get another dog. It was the lad's parents he was worried about. They couldn't get another son quite as easily. The sooner he reunited them the better.

An hour later Joe came home – a flying visit to check on his family. He was still on duty. He was covered in dust and his face was streaked with sweat and dirt. Molly threw herself into his arms. 'Oh, Joe! I was so worried!'

'I'm all right and when I had time to think I was worried

about you too. There's been a lot of damage, Moll. I've never seen anything like it. It's pitiful to see people standing on the street, dazed and bewildered, having lost everything. Not knowing what to do, where to go . . .'

Molly nodded. 'We won't be complaining that there's no water or gas. We've a roof over our heads – thanks be to God! You . . . you couldn't find out how Bernie is?'

'I'll try, Moll, but the phone lines are down everywhere. We're having to send messages from station to station by any means we can, usually young lads on bicycles! I will try, I promise.'

She managed a smile. 'The boys are in bed. They slept through most of it. How, I don't know. I was terrified.'

Joe grinned through the grime on his face. 'So was I, Moll. So was I.'

Chapter Nineteen

RELUCTANTLY MARIA HAD GONE to work. Molly had tried to clean and go about her usual daily tasks as best she could. Joe had finally got off duty at midday and had fallen asleep in the easy chair Molly had set beside the kitchen range. It was so cold and grey and miserable, she thought. It was impossible to heat the house; coal was scarce. The boys were playing together in the front room so as not to wake Joe.

At a quarter to one Bernie arrived with Albie. Molly hugged her tightly.

'I was worried about you even though Joe said you were safe. You shouldn't have come trailing all the way up here. It's bitterly cold out.'

'I couldn't stay in that house by myself, Moll! Claire has gone to work though what time she'll get there is anyone's guess. Sure, the place is in a terrible mess! I had to walk most of the way: there are no trams. All the lines are twisted and there are great holes in some roads. I thought they'd never go and leave us alone!'

'Come here to the fire and get warm. Give Albie to me; you must be worn out!' Molly gave her friend a gentle push towards the small fire that was struggling to heat the room and took the baby who was well wrapped up and sleeping peacefully. She noticed for the first time that Bernie had brought a bag with her.

'Are you intending to stay?'

Bernie was holding her hands out to the flames. 'I am so – if you don't mind. I told Claire to come here tonight. If they come back again, Moll, I'm not staying there. I'd sooner be with you. At least that way we'll all be terrified together.'

'Do you think they'll be back?' Molly asked fearfully.

'Everyone seems to think so. Would you look at the way they bombed London night after night? And Coventry? I won't hear anything from Bertie; they're not due until the day after St Stephen's Day at least.'

'I hope they leave us alone for Christmas!'

'So do I. How were the boys?'

'They slept but Joe was out in it. He didn't get off duty until three-quarters of an hour ago. He's asleep in the kitchen, still in his filthy uniform and without even a wash. There's no water yet although he said they're trying to get it on this afternoon.'

'How was Maria? Our Claire surprised me. I thought

she'd be reduced to a wreck but she wasn't. She kept my spirits up.'

'She was terrified and she didn't want to go to work this morning.'

'Sure, she'll be all right once she gets there. All the other women will cheer her up. Right, now that I'm a bit warmer will we sit down and work out just what we can have for our Christmas dinner? Didn't I manage to get a large tin of apricots in syrup? They'll be just gorgeous!'

Molly was astonished. 'Where did you get them?'

'From a lad who sometimes sells stuff,' Bernie answered evasively.

Molly gaped at her. 'You bought them on the black market? Bernie Hayes! And me married to a policeman!'

Bernie grinned at her. 'Sure, where's the harm in one tin of apricots? You don't have to tell him where they came from.'

'Bernie, he's not a fool! How much did you give for them?'

'I'm not telling you – you'd have ten blue fits. But don't I get Bertie's money and Claire pays me something for her keep and there's nothing to buy!'

Molly laughed. 'You are desperate, do you know that?'

Bernie rummaged in her bag and brought out the tin. 'Here, put them in the pantry and say nothing.'

They managed to scratch a meal together for Joe, and for Maria and Claire when they returned from work. Molly had to admit that she felt better having Bernie here with her.

Tonight she was prepared. She had a large square biscuit tin in which she'd put tea and sugar and a piece of soda bread. She had also filled a thermos flask with hot water, the water supply having been reinstated. Bernie had both the hurricane lamp and candles, matches and the game of Ludo that she and Bertie sometimes played when there was nothing on the wireless worth listening to.

'What are you bringing that for? Sure, I couldn't concentrate,' Maria said.

'It might help to take our minds off things. Claire and I played it last night – after we'd calmed down a bit.'

'We might not need it,' Molly said, seeing the fear in her sister's eyes.

'We will so! Grab your coat and those blankets, Maria. Here we go again,' Bernie said grimly as the piercing notes of the siren split the frosty evening air.

Joe dragged on his boots, grabbed his helmet and his heavy overcoat, hastily kissed Molly and his sons, hugged Bernie, Maria and Claire and dashed out of the front door.

Molly and Bernie shepherded them all into the shelter. They lit the hurricane lamp and a few candles, safely stuck into small empty tins that had once contained bicarbonate of soda, and settled themselves as comfortably as they could.

'Planes, Mammy! Aeroplanes!' Andrew cried as the siren fell silent.

'Yes, I can hear them. Now, sit close to Mammy and try and go to sleep, like you did last night.' Molly tried to keep her voice calm.

Maria clutched Claire's hand. 'Oh, Mary, Mother of God!'

'Hush now, don't frighten the boys. It will be all right. It might not be as bad as last night,' Claire soothed.

After an hour and a half they knew it was just as bad. Explosion after explosion rocked them. The candles blew out and Bernie's hand was shaking so much that she couldn't relight them. Every minute they expected to be blown to bits. Both boys were crying and Molly was holding them tightly, her thoughts on Joe who was without even the protection of a flimsy shelter. How could they go on like this? How could the city take such a beating?

Bernie was holding a sleeping Albie in her arms, her body bent over him to shield him as much as she could. Her nerves were stretched to breaking point. They had never expected to have to suffer such terror. How did Bertie live with it, when for him the terror came not only from the skies but from under the waves too?

At eleven o'clock, when it seemed as if the raid was getting lighter, Joe appeared. 'I can't stay; I just dashed up here to make sure you were all coping. It's worse tonight but it seems to have got lighter now.' His voice was hoarse from shouting to make himself heard above the noise.

'Are they going home? Will they leave us in peace now?' Molly pleaded.

'I don't know, Moll, and that's the truth. There seem to be hundreds of them and there are so many fires that it's like daylight, which helps their aim. The docks are taking the worst of it again. Just try and stay as calm as you can.' He kissed her and then he was gone.

'Calm? Sure, I'll never be calm again,' Maria said with a sob in her voice. She wanted to go home. She wanted her mam. She wanted to live in a country where there was no risk of death raining out of the skies and where young lads like George Jackson didn't get shot to pieces.

By midnight it had got worse again. They could hear the planes and, as Joe had said, there were apparently hundreds of them. The drone of their engines was loud even over the explosions. Thankfully both the boys had cried themselves to sleep; they were worn out. Molly was so afraid that she couldn't even think straight. Maria was almost hysterical and Claire was still trying to calm her down.

'In the name of God, pull yourself together, Maria. You're a grown woman. Won't you wake the boys and terrify them with the antics out of you?' Bernie snapped. 'Aren't we all petrified? Screaming like that won't help anyone!'

Maria calmed down a little and just sobbed quietly on Claire's shoulder.

'Will we have a cup of tea? It might help,' Molly suggested. 'Claire, get that thermos flask and the biscuit tin. There's a bit of soda bread too.' The last thing Bernie felt like doing was eating but it would help to try to bring some sense of normality to the situation. She grimaced. Normality! This was about as far from 'normality' as you could possibly get.

Claire was carefully pouring the hot water into the small teapot. It wasn't easy as, like Bernie's, her hands were shaking so much. Molly had settled the boys on the bench beside her and was tucking a blanket around them. The force of the blast knocked them all off balance. Claire screamed as the hot water scalded her arm. Maria shrieked in pure terror. Dust and debris rained down on them; the hurricane lamp smashed on the floor; and if Molly hadn't snatched the blanket from around the boys and smothered the flames, the place would have caught fire.

Bernie recovered herself first. They were in pitch darkness. 'Is everyone all right?'

'I've scalded my arm but apart from that I'm in one piece,' Claire answered.

'I'm all right. Shaken, but not hurt.' Molly coughed and tried to reassure her frightened sons. The air was thick with dust. 'Maria? Maria, are you hurt?'

'N— No,' Maria answered tremulously.

Bernie somehow managed to find a candle and the matches. It helped to have even that flicker of light. 'Claire, will you and Maria see to the children? I think Molly and I had better go and see what that was.'

'Bernie, you can't go out there!' Claire protested. She didn't want to be left here to look after the children and Maria.

'Just a quick look. Come on, Moll,' Bernie urged.

'Mammy! Mammy, don't go away!' Peter sobbed.

'It's all right. Mammy will only be a few seconds, I promise,' Molly soothed. The poor child was white and shaking with fear but she had to see what had happened out there.

They emerged from the shelter to a scene from what Bernie could only think of as hell. The sky was a lurid orange and above them the dark sinister shapes of the bombers were clearly visible. The sound of the anti-aircraft guns at their battery in Prince's Park was loud in their ears.

'Jesus . . . Bernie . . .' Molly clutched her friend's arm tightly.

Not a single house in the street was left standing. Everything had been reduced to a mountain of smouldering rubble. Fractured gas pipes were filling the air with fumes and many were burning fiercely.

'Oh, Moll. It was such a lovely house. All your things!'

'Everything . . . everything's gone. Sure, we haven't a single thing left, except what we stand up in.'

Bernie put her arm around her friend. 'But we're alive, Moll. We're alive and none of us is hurt.'

'So far, Bernie. It's not over yet and Joe . . . Joe is out there!'

'He'll be fine. He'll look in to see us when he realises that . . . that the house has taken a direct hit. Come on, Molly, we'd better get back.'

They went back inside the shelter and Molly sank down beside her sons.

'A direct hit. The house has gone. All the houses in the street have gone,' Bernie informed the two girls.

'All we have is what we've got here with us.' Molly felt dazed. The home she loved was in ruins. Every single possession she had had been destroyed.

'If I've still got a home left you'll all have to come and live with me. We'll manage. Sure, didn't you take us in when I had that hole in the roof? We've just got to be thankful that we're alive and well.' Bernie tried to cheer them up a little.

'What kind of a Christmas will it be now?' Claire said miserably.

'Oh, Bernie, all the things I'd made and queued hours for,' Molly wailed, feeling close to tears.

'And that lovely tin of apricots! Ah, well, serves me right for buying it on the black market.'

Molly managed a wry smile. Bernie was doing her best to make light of everything.

Joe had watched in horror as the bombs had fallen on Oxbridge Street. He'd been scribbling a message for one of the lads who cycled from police station to police station with directions for fire crews and ambulances, Civil Defence workers and volunteers who dug into the rubble to rescue trapped and injured civilians. The heat from the burning buildings was intense and he was sweating profusely. He was almost oblivious now to the explosions all around him but for a moment he'd looked up.

'Take that to the sergeant at Parliament Street!' he yelled, thrusting the piece of paper into the lad's hand, and then he was running. It wasn't easy to negotiate the rubble and the electricity and phone wires that lay twisted on the ground. Broken water mains made the ground slippery and there was the constant danger from crumbling masonry, fires and the bombs that still rained down.

He uttered a cry of disbelief as he reached Oxbridge Street. No! Not Molly and his boys! It took him a while to scramble over the remains of his home and reach the battered shelter. At least it was still standing. It had withstood the blast.

'*Joe!* Oh, Joe.' Molly burst into tears as he almost fell in.

'It's all right, luv, it's all right! Oh, thank God, you're not hurt. I've seen the house.' He held her tightly, tears of relief pricking his eyes.

'You can all come and live with me,' Bernie said. She was very relieved to see him too. 'Now that you're here shall we have that cup of tea we were going to have before we were all blown off our feet?'

Molly brushed away her tears. 'Sure, isn't the hot water all spilled? We'll have to wait until it's all over. We'll get a cup from the WVS. Those women are always out with tea after a raid.'

Joe picked up his sons. 'How are my boys? Being big brave soldiers and looking after Mammy?'

They nodded silently, then buried their heads against his shoulders.

'Ah, Joe, aren't they only babies, still? They're not even four yet,' Bernie reminded him.

Molly looked at her two little boys. No child should have to endure what they'd endured this night. Children should grow up not in terror but in peace. Suddenly she knew what she was going to do. She was going to take them home. Home to the safety and peace of the countryside. Home to her mam who would be delighted to have them.

Chapter Twenty

When it was all over at five o'clock next morning after ten hours of constant bombardment, the work of clearing up began. Joe returned but after a few minutes told them he had to get back.

'I've managed to find out that your house is still standing, Bernie, but a landmine came down two streets away and there's a lot of damage. I'm afraid you haven't a window left in the place.'

'Even though I put tape across them all? Ah, sure, never mind. It's better than having nothing.'

'It will take you a while to get there, I'm afraid.'

Bernie nodded. 'Aren't we getting used to walking?'

Claire and Molly had made an effort to pick through the rubble to see if there was anything to be salvaged. There was very little but Molly managed to find a few bits of clothing for the boys and in the wreckage of her front room, under the charred remains of the Christmas tree, she found one of the knitted rabbits. It was grubby and one ear was singed but it was *something*. She stuffed it inside her coat.

'I can't find anything else at all, Molly. Everything is destroyed entirely,' Claire said wearily.

'I know. Well, we'd better start out for Arnot Street if we want to get there before dinnertime.'

Dust and a sea of broken glass met them when they finally reached Bernie's home.

'We'll have it cleaned up in no time and then we'll get ourselves organised,' Bernie said firmly.

They worked steadily although they were all exhausted and no one dared to contemplate what would happen if the Luftwaffe returned again that night.

By evening they'd managed to get most of the windows boarded up with plywood or cardboard. Bernie had lit a fire in the kitchen range, dusted off what groceries she had in the pantry and made a scratch meal for them all. Claire was sorting out some clothes for Maria and all the children were asleep.

'Well, it's after six and there's no sign of them, thanks be to God!' Bernie remarked. They were both tense, waiting for the dreaded sound of the siren.

'Not yet!' Molly said.

'Drink up your tea, Moll, and try not to think about it. Joe should be here soon.'

Molly nodded. 'I want to talk to him when he does get

here and before he collapses from exhaustion. I . . . I've decided to take the boys home to Mam. I'll take Albie too, if you'll let me?'

Bernie stared at her and then shook her head. 'He's too young, Moll. I'm still feeding him myself, but thanks. Will you . . . will you come back?'

Molly nodded. 'I will so. I couldn't leave Joe here alone. The boys will be fine with Mam. I can't see them terrified like this, Bernie!'

'It could be years before you see them again, Molly.'

'I know. I've thought about that. I'll miss them terribly but they'll be safe there.'

'Do you think Joe will object?'

'I don't know.'

Bernie didn't say any more. She could see why Molly thought it a good idea; after all, thousands of children had been evacuated from the cities to the countryside, and thousands more had gone to Canada.

Molly waited until Joe had had his meal. Everyone was relieved that it seemed that tonight the battered city was being left in peace. Bernie tactfully took Albie and went upstairs.

'What's on your mind, Moll? I know you well enough to know that it's more than losing our home,' Joe asked, wearily. He could hardly keep his eyes open.

'I . . . I can put up with everything, Joe, if I have to, and we've not much choice in the matter, but I'm not having the boys terrified. It's not fair on them and I'm so afraid that something will happen to them. I want to take them to Ireland, to Mam. It will be good for them. Peace and quiet, and clean fresh air that's not full of dust and soot and the smell of burning. They'll have decent food too. Mam says the rationing isn't affecting them too badly.'

Joe could see she was determined. 'You really mean it, Moll? You'd send them away?'

She nodded vehemently. 'I'll miss them terribly, I will, but, Joe, you should have seen them last night. Oh, it broke my heart far more than losing everything. If I lost them, it would kill me!'

He took her in his arms. 'Then take them, Moll. But it won't be an easy journey.'

'I know but I won't mind.'

'You will come back, Moll, though? I couldn't face the future without you. It's terrible being out there. Dragging people – women, children – from under the rubble. Seeing babies killed in their cots. Finding poor old women wandering around looking for their loved ones, totally bewildered, and the family all dead. Families with no homes, no belongings!'

'Like us,' she reminded him. 'We've only the clothes on our backs.'

'Like us. But at least we've got good friends like Bernie who make it more bearable.'

'Of course I'll come back, Joe. I love you. I'll just get the boys settled and then I'll be back. I couldn't let you face this on your own.'

'Then you'd better write and let your parents know. I'll try and sort out the ferry tickets.'

She nodded. 'I'll go after the holiday. At least there isn't much to pack. In fact there's hardly anything at all!' She sighed. 'It's not going to be much of a Christmas now, I'm afraid. Everything we had is in bits.'

'But we'll be together and we've a roof over our heads. I know Mam has got a few bits and pieces for the boys,' he added. He didn't blame Molly for wanting the boys to be safe and well looked after; he'd miss them but he could face anything as long as he had her to come home to. Even if the 'home' in question happened to be Bernie's.

Ita and Tess had been worried to death when they'd heard of the bombardment of Liverpool: Tess in particular as she'd lived in a state of constant fear ever since Bernie had had such a near miss the night Albie had been born.

Ita had wrapped up well and had walked the short distance to Tess's home after she'd received Molly's short letter.

'Ita, come on in with ye out of the cold! I've a good fire put down and I'll put on the kettle,' Tess instructed, ushering Ita to the blazing turf fire and filling the heavy iron kettle from the big enamel jug. They still had to draw their water from the spring.

'I've had a letter from Molly,' Ita informed her.

'Thanks be to God! Are they all all right? I've had no word from either Bernie or Claire.'

'She says it's been bad, very bad. The house was bombed. It's destroyed entirely. They've nothing at all left.'

Tess crossed herself. 'Ah, God help her! And didn't she have such a lovely home? The best of everything and all the conveniences, so Bernie told me. But I suppose we should be down on our knees thanking God and His Holy Mother that they weren't all blown to bits with it.'

'We should, Tess. Bernie and the baby and Claire were in the shelter with them and now they're all living with Bernie. But she says the boys are so terrified that she can't stand to see their little faces and she's bringing them home.'

Tess shook her head, busying herself with making the tea. 'Ah, God love them!'

'She said she offered to bring Albie too but Bernie says he's too young to leave her: she's still feeding him.'

'I wish Bernie would come home too,' Tess said with feeling.

'Molly's not staying, Tess. No, isn't she going to see the boys settled and then she's going back.'

'Is Joe coming too? Seeing as it's only going to be a visit?'

'No. He can't be spared. But she's bringing Maria. Maria is in a shocking state of nerves, she says, and she's not got over the death of George Jackson. And the boys are fond of Maria and used to her being around, so it will help them settle. I'm relieved, Tess, I am.'

Tess set the cups down on the table and sat down. 'Wouldn't anyone be in a shocking state of nerves having to put up with all that? I don't suppose she said anything about Bertie and when he'll be home?'

'No. You know all the letters are censored.'

'So when do you expect them?'

'After the holiday – not that there will be much to celebrate in that city by the sound of it.'

'It will be dangerous for her, Ita. Haven't there been bombs dropped above on Sandycove and wasn't the mail boat bombed and fired on just after it left Dun Laoghaire?'

Ita nodded. She knew all that. 'I suppose she thinks it's worth the risk and she's not coming into Dun Laoghaire, she's coming into Dublin.'

Due in the main to the generosity of Bernie's neighbours and Joe's family, Christmas wasn't as grim as Molly thought it would be. There were a few little toys for Andrew and Peter and Effie shared her meagre Christmas dinner with them. She was having Joe's sister Annie for the day, who had brought her rations with her.

There had been no further raids on Liverpool; Manchester had been the target on December 23 and Christmas itself had seen a lull. On the morning of the twenty-seventh Bernie wrapped up warmly and prepared to go down to the Pier Head. She was leaving Albie with Molly for it was far too cold to be taking him out.

'How can you be so calm?' Molly asked.

'I'm not really, Molly. I might look it but inside . . . Ah, sometimes I feel so sick with nerves.'

Molly settled Albie in his crib. 'Do you ever think back to when we had just arrived here? We were so young, so carefree. We had such high hopes for the future. Now look at us. Wives, mothers and with nothing but a heap of worries on our shoulders and terrified of what the future will bring – and me with not even a roof over my head that I can call my own.'

Bernie nodded. 'But would we really change things, Moll? Would we swap the fine men we have and the gorgeous children? I know I wouldn't.'

'I suppose you're right. I expect that's Mrs Harper; she said she had a few things that might fit me or that I could alter to fit, if I wanted them. As if I'd turn anything down . . .' Molly went to answer the front door but thought it strange that Bernie's neighbour hadn't come around the back; she usually did.

'Mrs Hayes?'

Molly eyed the man standing on the doorstep with suspicion. 'No. I'm Mrs Jackson. I'm staying with her; we were bombed out. Who are you?'

'Chief Petty Officer Jones, Royal Navy.'

'Oh, God! What's wrong? Is it Bertie?'

'I'm sorry to have alarmed you, Mrs Jackson. The convoy got in around first light this morning – what's left of it. Able Seaman Hayes was injured when we were torpedoed. Well, when we were getting into the lifeboat, more like.'

Molly pulled herself together. 'Come on inside, Mr Jones. It's freezing.'

He followed Molly into the house. Bertie had begged him to come and see Bernie. He didn't want her to worry.

'It's a Mr Jones. He's got some news for you, Bernie,' Molly announced.

Bernie stared at the him. Once before a man in uniform had arrived with news of her husband. Bad news. All those years ago a policeman had arrived to tell her that Jimmy was dead. Her hand went to her mouth to stifle the cry of fear. She recalled so vividly the way she had felt then. Oh, dear God, please don't let it happen again! she prayed.

'It's Chief Petty Officer Jones, Mrs Hayes. Your husband was with me on watch when we were torpedoed. We managed to get into a lifeboat but the sea was very rough and the boat was all over the place and he . . . he's broken his leg. Rather badly, I'm afraid. Conditions aren't the best on any ship; we were lucky enough to be picked up by a corvette fairly quickly, though. They've taken him straight to hospital. In himself he's bright enough.'

Bernie sat down. Now that her worst fear hadn't materialised she felt a little light-headed with relief.

'You've gone as white as a ghost! Are you feeling faint?' Molly asked.

Bernie shook her head. 'No! No, I'm grand! When did you get in?'

'At first light.' He made no mention of the shock they had all felt when they'd seen the state of the battered city, or that he knew of men who had survived this convoy who were now faced with hearing that their loved ones had been killed. 'He asked me to come and tell you what had happened.'

'Which hospital have they taken him to?' Bernie asked, getting to her feet.

'Walton. It's not far from here, is it?'

'No. I can walk there. Thank you, it's good of you to come. Will you stay and have something to drink? There's only tea, I'm afraid. I wish I had something stronger I could offer you.'

'No, thank you, Mrs Hayes. I've to find my way to West Derby. My wife will be expecting me and, like you, she's a bundle of nerves until I get home. It's a pity we didn't make it for Christmas.'

'Sure, it wasn't much of a Christmas, I can tell you. Have you seen the state of the place? We had some heavy raids.'

'I know. It seems as though no place is safe these days. Well, I'd best be off.'

'Do you want me to come with you?' Molly asked Bernie after he'd left.

'No. I wouldn't be dragging you out on a freezing morning like this when there's no need. Aren't I well able for any starched apron I might come across!' Bernie answered with determination. After what they had all come through no officious matron or sister was going to stop her from seeing her husband, even if it wasn't visiting time. There was a war on, for heaven's sake!

It didn't take her long to walk the distance to Walton

Hospital and, after asking various people where she would find an injured survivor of the convoy, she was finally taken to a ward just under the clock tower.

'I'm looking for my husband, Able Seaman Albert Hayes. He was brought in this morning from the convoy that's just arrived,' she informed the sister sitting at her desk.

'Ah, yes. He has a fractured leg, a badly sprained wrist and some cuts and bruises, and he's suffering from exhaustion, but I'm sure he'll be delighted to see you, Mrs Hayes,' Sister finished with a smile, having read Bertie's list of injuries from her record card. 'He won't be going anywhere for quite a while.'

Bernie could have hugged her. She followed the nurse to where Bertie was lying in a bed at the end of the ward. His wrist was bandaged, his leg was in a plaster cast and a cut over his left eye had been stitched. His eyes were closed and he looked so much older than his thirty-six years.

'You've a visitor,' Sister announced before leaving them.

Bertie opened his eyes, but remained speechless.

Bernie sat down in the chair beside the bed and took his unbandaged hand. 'Aren't you in a fine mess, but it's so glad I am to see you!' She smiled, her eyes bright with unshed tears.

'*Bernie!* I'm so glad to be home,' he whispered, almost overcome with emotion.

'And you won't be going anywhere for quite a long time.'

He managed a grin. 'They've told me there may be some permanent damage as nothing much could be done about the leg for some time.'

'Was it very bad? That nice Mr Jones said you were sunk and you ended up in a lifeboat and the sea was very rough.'

'I was paralysed with fear, Bernie. That "nice Mr Jones" as you call him saved my life. He got me into a lifeboat; the ship was sinking under us. He helped get me up the scrambling nets into the corvette that picked us up. We lost so many ships. All I wanted was to get home. My seafaring days may well be over at last. If this doesn't heal well I'll be no use on a ship.'

Bernie squeezed his hand. She knew she shouldn't be thankful that he was injured but if that injury kept him at home then she would be so grateful. She wanted him to see his son grow up. She wanted him by her side to help her face whatever dangers might lie ahead. Her nerves were strung out like piano wires as it was; it would be a relief not to have him leave her and face again the treacherous ocean and the wolf packs.

'Don't worry about that now. You just get well. You look exhausted.'

'I'll be able to sleep easy now I've seen you, Bernie, and I'm safely home.'

Chapter Twenty-One

THREE DAYS LATER JOE accompanied Molly, the boys and Maria to the ferry. He had managed to get the necessary permits for them all. Before they boarded he bent down and put an arm around each of his sons.

'Now, I want you two to be very good and you're to look after Mammy and Aunty Maria for me. Will you promise me that?'

Andrew nodded solemnly but Peter looked a little mutinous.

'I want you to come to Granny's too, Daddy.'

'I've told you why I can't come. I'd like to. I'd like to see Granny Ita again and Granda Paddy and all the farm animals and have lots of lovely things to eat, but I have to stay here and look after all the people who haven't got nice houses any more.'

'And you have to send the fire engines to the right places,' Andrew added.

'I do, and the ambulances, and I have to make sure that all the traffic keeps moving. Now, off you go on the big ship. Isn't it a big adventure?' He kissed them both and stood up.

Molly put her arms around him. She knew how hard it was for him to be parted from his sons. 'They'll be fine and I'll be back as soon as I've seen them settled. I'll miss you, Joe. Please take care of yourself.'

He kissed her. 'I will and Bernie will look after me, see that I eat and have a clean shirt to put on. But don't be away too long, Moll. I need you.'

'I love you, Joe.'

'We'd better be going, Molly, or we'll not get a seat. I didn't think it would be so crowded but I suppose people are . . .' Maria chose her words carefully so as not to upset the boys. '. . . going for the same reason as us.'

Molly took Peter's hand and Maria took Andrew's and when they got to the gangway the two boys waved to their father.

Joe watched them go. They were so young to be left in another country without a mother or father but Molly was right. They would sleep peacefully in their beds at night. They would never have to be dragged terrified to sit in a cold, damp shelter while death rained down on them. Ita and Paddy would spoil them. They'd be fine, as long as the U-boats were kept at bay as they travelled. But as he walked away he couldn't shake off his sadness, for he had no idea when he'd see them again.

Molly thought they would never get to Tullamore. The ferry crossing hadn't been too bad. It was bitterly cold but calm. Ice glistened on the ship's deck and superstructure and the bright moonlight made a silver path across the calm black water. She'd been afraid once the ferry was out of the estuary, knowing that the U-boats lurked not far away in the Western Approaches, but they'd reached Dublin safely.

It was the train journey that had been so desperately slow. All the trains were delayed, so they'd been told on reaching Kingsbridge Station, which was now called Heuston Station. No, the station master had no idea what time they could expect to arrive at Tullamore. Hadn't the Cork to Skibbereen train taken fourteen hours to cover the fifty-three miles because the firebox kept going out with the shockingly inferior coal they were having to use and it taking hours and hours to relight it? And indeed there was worse to come, he'd assured them woefully, weren't the trains going to have to be run on turf and the Holy Virgin Herself couldn't keep the firebox lit on that!

When the train had finally left it seemed to stop and start the whole way through County Kildare and after that it had hardly moved at all for hours on end. The boys were tired, bored and hungry and Molly's nerves were getting very frayed by the time they finally arrived at Tullamore at almost eight o'clock that evening.

'Oh, I hope Da is here to meet us. Pray God he hasn't given up and gone home,' Maria said anxiously, peering into the gloom of the station yard.

'If he has, God knows what we'll do. Give me your hand, Peter, and I'm afraid you'll have to carry your own bag for a little while. Just until Granda arrives,' Molly added seeing the little lip begin to tremble. Oh, the last thing she needed now was a tantrum.

'Molly! Maria! Sure, I thought the blasted train was never going to arrive! I've been sitting in O'Neill's Bar this last two hours with a hot toddy waiting on his lad to come and fetch me.' Paddy hugged both his daughters in turn.

'Oh, Da, it would drive you mad! Stopping and starting – something to do with the firebox and inferior coal.'

'So, you're my two fine grandsons? Come on now and we'll get you into the trap and home to your granny and a roaring fire and a hot supper!' Paddy scooped up the two tired and bewildered little boys and deposited them in the trap. The two girls followed with the luggage.

The boys brightened up at the novelty of riding in a pony and trap as Paddy set the animal at a brisk trot out on to the Charleville Road.

It was still very cold, Molly thought as she tucked the rug more firmly around them all. Frost was sparkling in the moonlight as it etched a delicate tracery on the hedgerows.

The sky was almost black and the stars were very bright. There was no light except that of the stars and the carriage lamps and no sound except that of the pony's iron-shod hooves on the road surface. She'd almost forgotten how peaceful it was here at night. She closed her eyes. At least the stillness would never be shattered by the mournful wailing of the siren, the terrifying drone of aircraft engines and the sound of anti-aircraft guns.

The waters of the canal were dark and the dead reeds at the edges were ramrod-stiff with frost but, despite the cold, when they turned into the yard Ita was waiting with the half-door open.

Maria was near to tears. Exhausted after the tribulations of the journey, the sight of home with lights blazing in every window and her mother waiting at the door was almost too much for her.

'Thanks be to God! I expected you hours and hours ago!' Ita came out to meet them and lifted down one of her grandsons and hugged him. 'And would you be Andrew or is it Peter?'

'That's Andrew,' Molly informed her.

'Ah, child, it's good to have you home!' Ita hugged her daughters, noting the strain and tiredness in both their faces and the fact that Maria had lost a great deal of weight.

'Peter, would you like to see me put the pony to bed?' Paddy had lifted the child down and the little boy was clinging to his hand.

'Ah, would you have some sense, Paddy. Isn't the child frozen and he must be starving too,' Ita protested.

'Let him go with Da if he wants to. They won't be long,' Molly said.

'I want to go with Granda,' Peter said firmly. He had always been the more adventurous of the two and he had instantly liked the big man who had swept him up in his arms at the station.

'Don't you be long, so!' Ita called after them, ushering the rest of her family into the kitchen.

'Oh, Mam, it's so good to be home!' Maria said, sinking down into her da's easy chair by the range and pulling off her scarf and hat.

'Now, Tom, Aiden, make yourselves useful and take up their things,' Ita instructed her younger sons. 'I've the beds aired and beds made up for the little ones in your old room, Molly. And there's hot-water bottles in the beds, too. Aiden, before you go put down some more turf on that fire.' Ita was like a small whirlwind, setting the table, stirring pans on the range, taking the girls' coats and pausing to give her grandson a hug.

Molly got to her feet. 'Mam, let me give you a hand.'

'Sit down, Molly. Aren't the pair of you worn out?'

'No. Come on, Maria. Here's Da and Peter now. Ah, this smells so good!' She sniffed appreciatively at the aroma coming from one of the pans.

'I've a piece of bacon boiled and there's fresh cabbage and potatoes, a blackberry pie and soda bread and butter.'

The abundance of food almost brought tears to Molly's eyes. 'Won't you have us as fat as pigs in no time?'

They all ate well and while Maria helped her mother with the dishes, Molly and Paddy took the boys up to bed. When they were fast asleep, she looked down at them fondly and with a feeling of intense relief.

She glanced around the familiar bedroom with its well-polished furniture that smelled of beeswax. The quilts on the beds were of bright patchwork; the linen was clean and crisp. On the washstand was the china jug and bowl with the pattern of pink roses; on the walls the pictures she remembered so well from her childhood. On the windowsill stood the statue of the Child of Prague. This was where her boys would sleep each night after a day spent in the fresh air and after, no doubt, some adventures and scrapes. 'Oh, Da, it's such a relief to know they'll be safe,' she said quietly, making sure the little nightlight was burning.

'You did the right thing, Moll. Won't they be grand here with your ma and me and the two boys and Maria,' Paddy assured her as he closed the door.

Maria had gone to bed, so Ita informed them. 'Sure, isn't she dead on her feet and so thin!'

'She'll soon put back the weight, Mam. She's been a nervous wreck since the first raid and after losing George.'

'She needs time to recover but she's young, she'll get over him. And there're a few decent lads in the parish.'

Molly smiled. 'Have you someone picked out for her already then?'

'I have not. I was only saying there're plenty more fish in the sea. I'm glad to have her home. She can help me in the house and in the dairy; that's heavy enough work for her. I wasn't at all happy about her working with explosives.'

Molly sighed. 'It's like a different world here, Mam.'

'It will do you good too, Molly. How long do you think you'll be staying yourself?'

Molly shook her head. 'I don't know. I don't want to leave Joe for too long. Maybe two weeks. It depends on how the boys settle. They're nervous and Andrew tends to be clingy.'

'And who could blame them at all! Isn't the world in a desperate state when little children have to be dragged from their beds and subjected to all that?'

'It is, Mam. You'll never know just how bad things are, but I suppose they could be worse. At least we've not been invaded and we've a roof over our heads – even if it is Bernie's roof.'

'Thanks be to God none of you were hurt.'

'I know, but it's so hard, Mam, to see everything you've worked for reduced to a pile of smouldering rubble. Bernie and Effie and even the neighbours have been so good, but we've *nothing* – and it's not as if you can even go out and buy more clothes and things. Everything is on ration: you'd be at your wits' end trying to put a decent meal on the table and that's after you've spent hours and hours standing in queues. I seem to spend my entire day standing in them.'

'Ah, well, you're home now. We're not too badly off at all. We've plenty of turf and all the things we produce ourselves. I hear they're desperately short of coal in Dublin. Isn't it a terrible thing to have no heat in the depths of winter?'

'It is, Mam. Believe me, it is.'

'Well, you'd get off to bed yourself now or that hot-water bottle won't be hot at all,' Ita urged. 'And tomorrow the first thing we've to do is go and see Tess. She's fit to be tied that Bernie and Claire didn't come with you.'

'Claire won't come and Bernie won't leave Bertie. I told you he's injured his leg very badly. But she's very relieved that his seafaring days are over.'

'She's had a lot of tragedy in her young life, so she has, but please God she'll have no more. 'Twas a blessing in disguise that his ship was sunk and wasn't the good Lord looking out for him? Will he be able to get some class of a job when he's able?'

'I should imagine so. There's plenty of work,' Molly answered, getting to her feet. She was utterly exhausted. She seemed to have been on her feet for almost two days.

As she slid under the bedcovers and felt the warmth of the stone hot-water bottle at her feet, she smiled. The boys were fast asleep; they hadn't even moved. She thought of Joe who would at least be getting some much-needed sleep, providing there hadn't been another raid, and she said a quick prayer that he'd be safe. She missed him already. Yet despite her exhaustion she was looking forward to the days ahead.

The sound of the cattle shuffling and lowing in the byres came to her ears, and the rushing of the water through the lock gates. She smiled again, sleepily. The lock-keeper had opened the racks. It was a sound she remembered from her childhood, safe and reassuring.

Chapter Twenty-Two

TESS WAS SO PLEASED to see them when they called to see her the following morning. Maria had said she would do the housework and the boys had gone off with their grandfather and Dessie.

'I'll put on the kettle. Sit down, so.'

'We didn't get here until late last night. It was a desperate journey and your man above at the station in Dublin was telling me they'll be running the trains on turf soon. Heaven knows how long the journey will take then,' Molly informed Bernie's mother.

'Ah, things are getting in a shocking state in this country, so they are. We have the rationing and bombs dropped on us too, and the mail boat was bombed and fired on. Ah, 'tis a terrible state the world is in!'

Ita glared at her. She had refrained from telling Molly about the incident with the mail boat and as Molly hadn't mentioned it she'd been sure her daughter hadn't known.

Molly looked at Tess in alarm. 'I never heard about that!'

'Ah, 'twas a mistake and hasn't Mr de Valera complained bitterly to the German ambassador about it,' Ita replied. 'The boys are just gorgeous, Tess. They've Molly's hair and eyes but they look just like Joe and they're tall for their age too. I couldn't tempt them to come with us, not with Paddy taking them to see the new calves and the ducks and the geese and giving them rides on the cart.'

'Ah, I wish Bernie would have brought *my* grandson to see me, and that bold strap, Claire.'

'Claire has been a big help to Bernie. She didn't go to pieces during the raids, and she's been company while Bertie was away.'

Tess set the teapot down on the table. 'Thanks be to God he came through all that with no more than a broken leg. Isn't it a blessing in many ways that the old lady died? Sure, she couldn't have stood all that bombing.'

Molly sipped her tea and thought that Augusta Hayes might well have stood 'all that bombing' far better than Maria had, while Ita wondered how *anyone* stood it at all.

After two weeks of peace and quiet and being able to run around the farmyard and the fields the boys had settled down well enough for Molly to consider going home. She felt better herself: rested, more relaxed and well fed. The weather had continued cold but bright and so she'd wrapped up well and gone for long walks, sometimes with Maria and very occasionally with the boys – when she'd been able to prise them away from her father's side. It delighted her to see them rosy-cheeked and laughing as they rode up beside her father or Dessie on the farm cart.

She had written to Joe and to Bernie and had received the welcome news that there had been a few further raids but nothing serious and that they were all managing. She dreaded the return journey, wondering how long it would take to get from Tullamore to Dublin by train and apprehensive of the ferry crossing and its dangers.

She had managed to get all kinds of things in Tullamore that it was impossible to get in Liverpool. She'd bought dress materials and knitting wool, clothes for herself and the boys and a good winter overcoat for Joe.

'Don't forget you've to carry them home,' Ita had reminded her. 'And you've to leave room in the bag for the rashers, butter, cheese, eggs and flour.'

Molly had laughed. 'Mam, I'm very grateful for all the food but there's only so much I *can* carry.'

'I was going to give you a good bit of the pork too. It will keep in this weather,' Ita said, Paddy having killed a pig especially.

'Mam, won't she be destroyed altogether with the weight of everything!' Maria had giggled and Ita had smiled. It was good to hear her daughter's laughter once more.

Molly had broached the subject of her return with the

boys and had been very relieved that there had been no tears or tantrums; in fact they seemed quite happy with the arrangement, which Molly put down to the fact that her father had come home yesterday with two black and white puppies.

She was sitting in the kitchen with Ita before a roaring turf fire. Maria and her da had gone to bed. She had just finished sewing a piece of velvet to the collar of her mother's winter coat to 'smarten it up a bit'.

'I remember when you came home with Joe, the November before you were married. You had that lovely grey coat with a velvet collar and a matching beret.'

Molly sighed. She remembered it too. She had unpicked it and made two little matching coats for the boys from the material. 'Do you still have the outfit you had for my wedding, Mam?'

'I do so. Didn't it cost a small fortune? Sure, there's plenty of wear in it yet. I wear it for Mass on Holy Days in the summer. Do you still have your wedding dress?'

Molly shook her head. 'It went the way of everything else in the house, Mam.'

'Ah, isn't that a terrible shame. It was beautiful and you could have made all kinds of things out of that satin.'

'I know, but never mind. I think I'll go home on Saturday, Mam. The boys seem to be fine and I do miss Joe and worry about him.'

Ita nodded. 'It's your place to be with him, Molly. The boys will be fine. They're grand little lads and don't they love it here? Sure, your da has them spoiled entirely.'

'And so do you.'

'Ah, I never had the time to spoil all of you and I doubt I'll ever get to see the grandchildren I have in Boston. No, you've nothing to worry about. We'll make sure they have the best of everything and if they have to go to school here, well, it's no bad thing. You know you can trust us to make sure they go to Mass and get their first Confession and Communion.'

'Mam, I hope it will all be over long before they're seven.'

'So do I, Molly, but, sure, you never know. Joe's very good with them, isn't he? He'll miss them.'

Molly nodded. 'He idolises them.'

'Was it a difficult birth, Molly? I mean going through all that with one child is bad enough, but then to have to go through it all again . . . sure, you must have been worn out entirely.'

'I was, but it wasn't too bad, Mam. I didn't know there were two babies. I suppose if I had I might have been a bit more apprehensive.'

'You must have been scared; everyone is with their first. You never know what to expect. No matter what anyone tells you the first time is always the worst.'

Molly gazed into the flames, thinking of Billy Marshall. When she'd had the twins she had known what to expect: it wasn't her first pregnancy.

'What is it, Molly? What's troubling you?' Ita probed.

She could tell by Molly's face that there was something wrong.

Molly knew the time had come to confide in her mother, to reveal the secret she'd carried all these years. She sighed heavily. 'I let you down badly, Mam.'

'How? Aren't you a respectable wife and mother? I couldn't wish for more,' Ita protested.

'I . . . I disgraced you and myself when I was eighteen. You remember I was seeing a lad called Billy Marshall? When Bernie was getting married to Jimmy McCauley. I wanted him to come over and meet you but he . . . he wouldn't and now I realise why. I . . . I believed everything he told me, Mam. Oh, I was such a little eejit!'

It was beginning to dawn on Ita just what Molly was trying to tell her. 'Molly, you didn't . . . ?'

Molly nodded. Her cheeks were burning with shame but she couldn't go back now. 'I . . . I was pregnant and he refused to marry me. I'd believed he would, that everything would be just fine in the end but . . .'

Ita reached for her hand. 'Oh, Molly! Why didn't you tell me?'

'How could I, Mam? Da would have gone mad; you both would. He would have disowned me and you remember what happened to Maggie O'Dwyer? Is she still in the Laundry with the nuns, after all these years?'

Ita nodded, but no matter what Paddy would have said she would never have condemned Molly to that fate. 'We would never have done that to you.'

'I wasn't to know that and I was in a desperate state.'

Ita looked alarmed. 'Molly, you didn't . . . ?'

'No, Mam. I didn't even contemplate having an abortion but I did try to kill myself.'

Ita was appalled. 'Holy Mother of God! Molly!'

'That's how I met Joe. He dragged me out of the river. He saved my life. Bernie came home and we decided we'd move away from Liverpool. That I'd have the baby and keep it, but Aunt Augusta let us stay. She was very good to me.'

'Oh, Molly! A stranger knew and she helped you and you couldn't confide in me, your own mother!' Ita was reeling from the shock of learning that Molly had been prepared to take her own life, to die in mortal sin with no chance at all of redemption. To consign her soul to the flames of hell for eternity. Beside all that the shame of an illegitimate child paled almost into insignificance. But somehow Molly had been saved from both death and eternal damnation and for this she silently thanked God and His Holy Mother. 'What . . . what happened?' she managed to ask, pushing the thought of Molly lying dead to the back of her mind.

'I lost it. I miscarried. I suppose it was a blessing really; it would have had to carry the stigma of being illegitimate for the whole of its life and now that I have the twins I can see how awful that would have been.'

'It would. So, Joe knows all this? And he still married you?'

'Yes. We have no secrets.'

'He's a fine man, Molly. A fine man indeed.'

'He is and I love him very much. Oh, I had a patch of hating Billy Marshall but I was to blame too. I should have had more respect for myself. I don't know what happened to him and I don't care. I never think about him. I do know that Bernie's cousin Matty O'Sullivan and some of the other men from around there beat him up badly. I think Bernie instigated that. She'll never admit to it though.'

'She cares about you, Molly. She's been a good friend to you.'

'She has, Mam. The best friend I could ever have and she always will be. But things worked out for the best. I should have told you.'

'You *should*! But it's in the past now. You have a good husband and two lovely sons.'

'And if this terrible war was over things would be perfect.'

Ita sighed heavily. 'Ah, Molly, don't I pray every night that it soon will be.'

'It doesn't look like it, Mam. I hate to say it but I think it's really only just begun.'

It was raining heavily on Saturday morning when Molly left Tullamore. Ita had insisted that the boys stay with her while Paddy took Molly to the station.

'Sure, they'll be soaked to the skin and get a chill and that's the last thing we want. Leave them here with me in the warm; they can help me with the baking and then, if it clears up at all, we can take those two little dogs for a walk. It's about time they started to learn some manners. They're working dogs, or they will be when they've grown, and it doesn't do to spoil them too much. We'll have a grand day,' she'd finished firmly.

Molly and Paddy were swathed in mackintoshes and Molly had the big umbrella. Molly also had a case and two big bags that contained all the things she'd bought plus the food Ita had packed for her.

'Will you be able to manage all this stuff?' Paddy asked as he helped her into a carriage. To their surprise the train was already in. When exactly it would leave, however, was anyone's guess, so they'd been informed.

'I'll have to. You've no idea of the reception I'll get from Bernie if I tell her I've left half of it behind.'

'Well, if you're sure. Joe is meeting you, isn't he?'

'He is, Da. Getting from the train to the ferry is going to be the hard part. That's if I get to Dublin in time to catch the ferry.'

Paddy delved into his pocket and handed her some money. 'If you get stuck in Dublin get yourself lodgings in a decent boarding house or hotel for the night.'

'Thanks, Da. I will. If I'm not on the ferry Joe will know what's happened and meet the next one but I'm hoping I'll be in time.'

'You mind yourself, Molly. There's no need for you to worry about the boys. They'll be grand.'

'I know they will, Da. And there's no need for you to wait with me until they decide to get this train moving. You've work to do.'

Paddy nodded and hugged her.

Molly sat back in the seat and closed her eyes. She wished the journey was over and she was in Liverpool.

An hour later, to everyone's relief, the train finally pulled out of the station. She was going home but a part of her would remain here, with her sons, she thought. Still, she was cheered by the thought of how delighted everyone would be when they saw the food she had brought with her.

Chapter Twenty-Three

JOE WAS WAITING FOR her at the Pier Head. The rain hadn't ceased and she was tired, cold and very damp.

He hugged her. 'Molly! You look terrible, luv! Oh, I've missed you!'

'I've missed you too, but isn't that a terrible poor way to greet anyone! I got soaked going from the station to the ferry and I've had to sit for hours in damp clothes.'

'Here, give me those bags. What in the name of God have you got in them?' Joe took them all from her and they made their way towards the trams.

'I managed to get all kinds of things in Tullamore and Mam has packed me up with so much food I'm like a walking pantry!'

'Bernie will be glad to hear that.'

'It will save us time queuing and it will save our coupons. How is Bertie?'

Joe dumped all the bags down on the long seat near the door of the tram and they both sat down. 'He's coming out next week. We're not sure exactly which day yet.'

'Can he walk?'

'The plaster won't come off for a while yet but he can get around with a stick, so Bernie says. She says he's in fine form.'

Molly smiled. She was glad he was on the road to recovery. 'I just want to get home, Joe. It's been a long, long journey.'

Bernie was delighted to see her and even more delighted when Joe began to empty the contents of the bags on to the kitchen table.

'Oh, Moll! Rashers! Eggs! Butter! Won't we have a *feast* tonight?'

'And cheese! Oh, I love a nice wedge of cheese with some bread and pickles,' Joe added.

'There's a jar of pickles in there somewhere. Mam knows how you like her pickled shallots. I'm sure there's a hunk of pork too. We'll have to cook that today or it will be spoiled.'

'Oh, can you imagine the smell of roasting pork?' Bernie went into transports of delight. 'And real eggs. No messing about with that dried egg powder, which tastes like sawdust mixed with water! Bread spread thick with butter! Real meat! Do you know what the butcher told me yesterday? He'll be having whale meat in next week. *Whale meat!*

I told him I'd sooner do without than be eating that.'

'And I managed to get some dress lengths so we can all have something new. You too, Claire.'

Joe laughed. 'I don't somehow think I'd suit a dress.'

'Didn't I get the most gorgeous Donegal tweed overcoat for you?'

'Ah, you spoil me!'

Molly looked at him fondly. 'Don't you deserve to be spoiled? Aren't you the best husband in the world?'

Bernie was businesslike. 'Right, Claire, put most of this stuff in the pantry while I get this grand piece of pork ready for the oven. I managed to get some carrots and a swede and there's potatoes. So it will be roast pork, carrot and turnip and roast potatoes for dinner. And I'll plate up a dinner for Bertie.'

'Are you allowed to take his dinner in to him?' Molly asked in surprise.

'No, but the food isn't up to much and I'm sure they won't mind this once. Someone else can have his rations.'

Joe grinned at her. 'You're the only person I know who can get round all the rules they have in that place.'

'Ah, it's the way you talk to Sister.'

'You mean it's the way you bribe her shamelessly with fresh soda bread.'

Bernie laughed. 'Sure, she loves it! Her mother was Irish, from Mayo. I'll take her some in today, spread with butter. Won't that be a treat for her?'

*

Both Joe and Molly found the place didn't seem the same without the boys. 'But I've had a bit longer to get used to them not being here,' Joe said wistfully.

Now that she no longer had the responsibility of the twins Molly knew she would have to go out to work.

'I suppose it will have to be the munitions factory with Claire,' she said to Bernie. 'I feel awful every time Joe goes out to work, knowing he has so much to do and I'm here doing nothing.'

'Do you really want to go and work there?' Bernie asked.

'The money is good. Five pounds a week for nights and three pounds a week for days.'

Bernie nodded. Claire often said she'd never earned so much money in her life. She was saving most of it to spend when the war was over.

'What else can I do?' Molly asked.

'I'd like to do something too. I've Albie of course during the day but I could work in the evenings.'

'You'll have Bertie home soon; he'll need looking after too.'

'But not to the same extent as Albie and once Albie's asleep he usually doesn't wake.'

'So what can we do?'

'Why don't we ask Norman Clarke? He's the warden. He's bound to know *everything* that's going on around here. Isn't that what being a warden is all about?'

Molly nodded. It would be great if they could do

something together. In all the time they'd been friends the only time they'd worked together was for a short time at Frisby Dyke's.

Bernie went to see the ARP warden for the area and came back looking delighted with herself.

'What did he say that's got you looking so excited?' Molly demanded, her mouth full of pins. She was cutting out a skirt from a length of black and white dogtooth check.

'He said they are *desperate* for ambulance crews. We're to go down to Walton Hospital; there's a depot there.'

Molly stared at her with something akin to horror. 'Are you mad? Have you lost the run of yourself entirely? Neither of us can drive and neither of us know anything about . . . casualties!'

'We can learn. Someone will teach us; sure, it can't be *that* hard. And we'll get some training. There are no men to do it, Moll. They're all either fighting or in the Civil Defence or the Home Guard or the Auxiliary Fire Service. We'll be on duty mainly in the evenings, but could be called out any time we're needed.' She became more serious. 'He said it can be dangerous. We'd have to go out in a raid, so we'd better have a word with the lads, but if we explain that they're doing their bit and we want to do ours it should be all right. Joe's been out in the thick of all the raids we've had and Bertie, well, he's done his fair share.'

Molly sat back on her heels. 'I suppose we can try to make some kind of a fist of it, if the lads agree.'

Bertie wasn't too happy about it and neither was Joe but their wives argued so successfully that there wasn't much they could say. Ambulance crews *were* desperately needed. Two evenings later both girls went down to the depot at the hospital.

'So you're my two new recruits? You're a sight for sore eyes, both of you, and not only because I need every pair of hands!' Charlie Dixon welcomed them. He was in charge of the depot and the Control Centre, which directed not only the ambulances, but also the rescue parties, and the first-aid parties. He worked closely with the police who were in overall charge of everything.

'We are indeed,' Bernie answered.

'Can either of you drive?'

They shook their heads.

'Any first-aid experience?'

'Not really. Just the usual things with a young family,' Molly replied, thinking they really weren't much use at all.

'Never mind. We'll soon remedy that.'

'We're fast learners,' Bernie promised.

They spent a hair-raising hour learning the controls and gears on an ambulance and Molly thought frantically that she'd never be able to get the vehicle to go in a straight line, never mind around corners. Bernie seemed to pick it up very quickly and it was decided that she would be the driver. Molly was quite thankful and as they went off to start a crash course in first aid she whispered to Bernie that she would be more than happy to be classed as 'crew'.

'Sure, you've more control over the damned thing than I'll ever have, even if they give me a hundred lessons!'

'How did you get on?' Joe asked when they returned.

'I was useless. Utterly useless,' Molly replied, taking off her heavy coat.

'You were just great at the first aid though. They said she was very calm and competent,' Bernie informed him. 'And isn't that what's needed with injured people?'

'Bernie was just as great at the driving. Isn't she to be the driver and I'm to be the crew. They gave us armbands and tin hats. I'll have to have a few more lessons though before I can go out.'

'Imagine you being able to drive, Bernie! Wait until Mam hears that. Sure, there's hardly a woman in the parish that can drive,' Claire marvelled. 'Maybe one day you'll have a car of your own.'

'And maybe one day you'll have washed up the dishes for me,' came the tart reply.

'I'll do them, Bernie, you get off to see Bertie. You should have gone when we were at the hospital.'

'It wasn't visiting time and you know what they're like. At least he's coming home tomorrow.'

After Bernie had gone, Molly and Claire washed up and then Claire got herself ready to go to the pictures with a friend from work. Molly got out her sewing and Joe sat listening to the wireless.

Molly's thought turned to her sons. She wondered what

they would be doing now. More than likely they would be ready for bed, and maybe playing with the puppies in the warm kitchen. Her mam would be finishing off the dishes and her da would be sitting by the fire, reading his newspaper or his *Farmer's Journal*. The kitchen would be bathed in the soft glow of the oil lamps and the flames of the turf fire. She looked around at Bernie's kitchen. It had modern conveniences, electricity and gas, but the shortage of coal meant that the fire was a very poor one. There wasn't the food in the pantry that there was at home. Her mam's windows weren't criss-crossed with sticky tape or covered in the heavy blackout curtains. She shook herself mentally. The boys were safe and, thanks to Ita's generosity, she and Bernie had more food in their pantry than hundreds of people had.

'A penny for them, Moll?' Joe asked, seeing the expression in her eyes.

'Oh, I was just thinking of the boys.'

'They'll be fine. Do you really want to go on with this ambulance crew thing? You could find other work. It can be dangerous, Moll. I've seen them in action.'

'Bernie's set on it and I don't mind, just as long as I don't have to drive the damned thing! I just know I could never get the hang of it.'

Joe laughed. 'I'm sure you could, Moll, given time and the right circumstances.'

She shook her head. 'Give me a pony and trap any time!'

Next morning she gave the place a good clean and built

up the fire. The kitchen looked warm and welcoming, but Bernie asked if she intended to use the entire week's coal ration in one day.

'What about Bertie? Sure, you can't have the poor man coming home to a miserable-looking place,' she replied.

'Ah, wouldn't it be just great if we had the bog on our doorstep like we used to have,' Bernie had sighed.

'And spend hours breaking our backs footing it and drawing it down to the yard?' Molly reminded her laughingly.

Bertie was very appreciative of the warmth when they got him settled in an armchair. 'It's freezing in that hospital. Those wards are so big that you can't feel the bit of warmth there is in the pipes. They gave us extra blankets but it was still bitter.'

'Never mind, aren't you home now and don't we have the best of everything here, compared to most people? There's some rashers and a real egg for your dinner, followed by a slice of cherry cake,' Bernie informed him. She was so glad to have him home. She was going to spoil him and at last he could really get to know his son.

'Cherry cake! Where did you get the cherries?' he asked.

She laughed and then grimaced. 'They're not cherries. It's bits of carrot. Mrs Harper next door gave me the recipe. Here, will you mind your son while I go and see who is at the door?' She placed a sleeping Albie in his arms and went to the front door.

'Mrs Hayes?' A small man in a pinstripe suit, a heavy

dark overcoat and a bowler hat stood on the doorstep, a clipboard in his hand.

'Yes,' Bernie answered a little suspiciously.

'I'm the Billeting Officer for the area. Now, how many rooms do you have in this house?'

Bernie glared at him. Of all times to come annoying her about billeting with Bertie only this minute home from hospital and the 'cherry' cake in the oven. 'Six, if you include the scullery and the bathroom and there's already myself, my husband, the baby, my sister and my friend and her husband living here. They were bombed out and doesn't my poor sister have to sleep on the sofa and she has to work twelve hours in the munitions factory,' she snapped.

'At a push you could take another four, in the parlour?' He was busy writing on the sheet of paper attached to the clipboard.

'I could not! Isn't it a desperate crush now in the kitchen and the bathroom when we have to cook and eat and when people want to get washed and shaved?'

'At least you do *have* a bathroom. You also have a scullery; I presume there is a sink and running water in there? And you have an Anderson shelter.'

'And aren't we crowded in that too!' Bernie was determined that he wasn't going to foist complete strangers on her.

'I'll put you down for two more people then. Good day.'

'You can write it down on your list but that still doesn't

mean I'll have them! Good day to you!' she replied before slamming the door.

'Who was it?' Molly asked, seeing the look of acute annoyance on her friend's face.

'The damned billeting officer. Didn't he want me to have four strangers living in the parlour? *Four!* Sure, you never know who you'd get!'

'Bernie, there's a war on and people have no homes,' Bertie reminded her, looking at Molly.

'I know that and I don't mind having Molly and Joe – didn't we go and live with them?'

'Ah, it might not come to that. We might not have any more raids. There've only been a couple of light ones recently,' Molly said to pacify her.

Bernie suddenly sniffed. 'Oh, Mary Mother of God! The cherry cake!' She grabbed the oven cloth and pulled the now decidedly overdone cake from the oven. 'Oh, damn him to hell and back! Isn't it destroyed altogether?'

'Never mind, Bernie. We'll cut off the burned bits. There's some custard powder left: we'll have it with that. We won't notice the taste much then,' Molly suggested.

'It was meant to be a celebration cake,' Bernie wailed.

Bertie laughed. 'Aren't I home, luv? Isn't that enough of a celebration?'

Chapter Twenty-Four

BERTIE PROGRESSED WELL AND by the end of March he was able to get around without the aid of a stick. He had begun to get restless and Bernie was afraid that he wanted to go back to sea but he assured her that he just wanted to get work. He signed on at the Labour Exchange and was sent out to a munitions factory at Long Lane in Aintree, which, as Claire remarked, was far better than having to drag all the way out to Kirkby. She was slightly annoyed to find that he was earning more than she was but he was a foreman, Bernie impressed upon her.

Although there were many women and girls already doing the jobs the men had done, in March the Minister of Labour, Ernest Bevin, called for one hundred thousand women to volunteer for work.

Molly read out his words from the newspaper. "'I cannot offer them a delightful life. They will have to suffer some inconveniences. But I want them to come forward in the spirit of determination to help us through."'

'Aren't we suffering inconvenience already and doing our bit to "help us through"?' Bernie remarked. She was now quite competent at driving an ambulance and both she and Molly were trained in the care of casualties. So far they had only been called out twice but they had both found it quite nerve-racking. 'Sure, we'll get used to it,' she'd assured Molly.

Claire, too, was 'doing her bit'. She was assigned fire-watching duties in the street. One of the worst dangers to property was the incendiary bombs. Bertie, too, was fire-watching and he had said he would be happy to join the Civil Defence as a rescue worker.

'Will you just wait until you're properly better?' Bernie had urged.

'If I'm well enough to work during the day, I'm well enough to help dig people out of the rubble,' he'd replied and Joe had agreed with him, much to Bernie's annoyance. Still, between them all they made sure the baby was looked after.

On Thursday May 1, Molly and Bernie returned from their evening stint at the hospital depot to find Bertie listening to the wireless and Claire, who had just got in, making a cup of tea.

'Will Joe be in soon or will I just make enough for the four of us?' Claire asked. Tea was so scarce that people were now reduced to reusing the leaves. The supplies Ita had sent were long since gone.

'He'll be about five minutes, I think,' Molly replied.

'Has Albie been all right?' Bernie asked of her husband.

'Not a murmur, luv. I looked in on him half an hour ago. Snug as a bug in a rug, he was.'

Claire handed round the cups. 'I sometimes wonder if all this fire-watching is necessary? Wasn't I bored stiff tonight and I could have been after having an early night.'

'If you hadn't been out on the tiles with that Donald Whitworth all last weekend you wouldn't be so tired. It catches up with you, even when you're young! Sure, working twelve hours a day and all that travelling is bound to wear you out,' Bernie chided.

'Have I walked into an argument?' Joe asked as he entered the kitchen.

'Not at all. Just a few words of advice for your one there. I'll put more water in the pot,' Bernie replied breezily.

'Don't bother, Bernie. Here we go again!' Joe said as the warning notes of the siren sounded.

'Oh, hell and damnation! Claire, get yourself back out there! Bertie, I'll go and get Albie. You collect the blankets and the other stuff and then get down to the shelter,' Bernie instructed, flying out of the room and up the stairs to snatch the baby from his cot.

Molly dragged on her coat and grabbed both her own and Bernie's tin hats.

Joe kissed her. 'Take care, luv! See she drives carefully. Let's hope it won't be too bad.'

'You take care too! Don't go taking unnecessary risks,' she urged.

They were in luck, Bernie thought as they both ran towards County Road. There was a tram coming towards them.

'We're not going far, girls! Just to the nearest shelter,' the conductor informed them.

'Then we'll hitch a ride that far!' Bernie replied as they both jumped on to the platform.

Seeing the armbands on their sleeves he didn't press them but when the tram stopped at the top of Breeze Hill they had to jump off and start running again.

Incendiaries had already started to fall as they ran down towards the hospital and their depot and they were both out of breath when they finally reached it.

'Get revved up, girls, you have to be ready for when the first incidents start to come in.'

Bernie jumped in and switched on the engine and then they sat waiting. For Molly that was the hardest part.

Before long they heard the thud of explosions and could see the flames from several fires. The sky above them was filled with bursting anti-aircraft shells and the powerful, glaring beams of the searchlights.

'Oh, I hope it won't be a long one,' Molly said, wincing as another bomb found its target not too far away.

Charlie Dixon started to wave them forward, poking his

head through the side window. 'Get out to Nixon Street, top of Bedford Road; two houses had a direct hit. The rescue party and first-aid party are on their way.'

Bernie nodded and shoved the gearstick into first, then she slammed her foot down on the accelerator pedal. 'What's the quickest way, Moll?'

Molly acted as navigator, having studied the street maps. 'Straight down the main road until you get to the swimming baths, past the church then turn right.'

Bernie drove on, peering intently ahead of her into the blacked-out roadway. Ahead of them two fire engines were hurtling along, their bells clanging loudly.

They came to a halt at the top of the street. A pile of rubble blocked the way.

'We'll have to wait here until the rescue party brings us the poor souls who were in that, if they're alive at all,' Bernie said with a note of resignation in her voice.

Before long, men covered in dust and soot brought them three stretchers.

'Two women with broken bones; the doc has splinted them up. The other's dead. You'll have to take him too, to the mortuary.'

Molly jumped out and helped them get the casualties into the back of the ambulance.

'Don't worry now. We'll have you to the hospital in no time at all,' she assured a young woman of about her own age who was crying and holding her shattered arm. There was blood on her cheeks, her hair was tangled and her clothes were torn and dirty. Molly pushed back a few strands of the girl's red-gold hair. 'I know it's hard but you're going to feel much better when they've set your arm.' You couldn't help but feel pity for them, she thought.

They worked steadily on as the hours passed, Bernie grim-faced and determined as she drove through streets where tram lines were buckled and twisted and fractured mains poured gallons of water on to the cobbles. Above them the sky was bright with the deadly fireworks of battle but neither of them seemed to notice.

At last at one o'clock the all-clear sounded and they climbed wearily out of the vehicle and turned for home.

When they arrived back Claire was slumped exhausted in a chair and Bertie was making tea. Albie, as usual, was asleep. He was rolled up in a blanket and lay in the big deep drawer that served as a makeshift cot.

'Oh, that's great. Tea!' Bernie cried, thankful that everyone was safe.

'I'm destroyed altogether. Evelyn Caldwell and meself have spent hours running up and down the street putting out fires! Only small ones but I never thought they'd stop dropping the blasted incendiaries,' Claire wailed. She was dropping with exhaustion.

'Then get yourself to bed. You'll get a few hours' sleep before you have to go to work,' Bernie instructed.

'Isn't it well for you, you don't have to get up,' Claire moaned.

'Don't I have to get up to see to himself there? He

might have slept all night but he's still awake just after six and wants feeding,' Bernie answered tartly.

'I hope Joe is all right. I don't expect I'll see him for a good while yet. I sometimes think he wouldn't be so hard worked if he was in the Army and he stands just as much chance of being killed as any soldier does,' Molly said wearily.

'Are you going to wait up for him?' Bernie asked. Sometimes Molly did.

Molly shook her head. 'I don't think so. It didn't look as if there was much damage where he is. At least the sky over that part of the city wasn't lit up with the fires.'

It was three o'clock before Joe arrived home. Everyone was in bed and he didn't blame them. They'd all be as exhausted as he was. He seemed to be able to exist on very little sleep these days, he thought, which was just as well because he didn't get much. He eased off his boots and unbuttoned his tunic. He'd have to give it a good brushing – again. The kettle was still warm and he boiled it up again.

When he'd joined up he'd never thought that he'd be burdened with so much responsibility. Now, as well as keeping law and order, it was his job to report 'incidents', as bombs were called, to the Control Centre and then get the emergency services into action. He had to move people from shelters if they were considered unsafe. If there was an unexploded bomb he had to evacuate everyone from nearby buildings and divert traffic. If people were trapped he had to try to dig them out until the rescue party arrived.

If people were injured he had to give first aid. If incendiaries fell he had to try to deal with the fire until the Fire Brigade arrived. If shops were damaged he had to find someone to see that their contents weren't looted or do that job himself. All this when bombs were dropping all around him. When the raid was over he had to make a count of the dead and injured in his area for the official records and it was his job to inform the relatives. He hated that most. Of course the Specials helped out and the men of the Auxiliary Police War Rescue but there was still a heavy burden placed on all their shoulders.

He'd just finished his tea and was preparing to go up when the front-door knocker sounded loudly through the silent house. Oh, God! Now what? he thought irritably. He knew his parents were safe; it was something he always checked on before he came off duty after a raid.

He went quickly down the lobby, fearing that the whole house would be roused.

On the doorstep stood Nellie O'Sullivan and her six tired and frightened kids.

'Oh, Joe! Thanks be ter God! I never thought we'd get here! I've had ter drag this lot all the way. There's no trams or nothin'!'

'Nellie! What happened?'

'We was bombed out, Joe! We got out of the shelter an' when I got ter the end of the street I could see me house was gone! God help us, we never had much but we've got nothin' now!'

'Come on in. Where's Matty?' He ushered them all into the lobby and closed the door.

Nellie wiped the sleeve of her cardigan across her eyes. 'He's followin' on. He stayed ter help out. There's people still buried down our end of the city.'

'I want me da!' the youngest of her brood started to wail.

Nellie gave him a push. 'Shurrup, youse! I've told yer he's followin' us on!'

'Joe? Is that you? Is everything all right?' Molly had appeared at the top of the stairs.

'It's Nellie. They've been bombed out.'

Molly quickly came down followed by Bernie and then Bertie. The parlour door opened and Claire stuck her head out sleepily.

'I'm so sorry!' Molly said sincerely. She knew how it felt.

'There's norra brick left standin'. All we've got is the clothes on our backs.'

'Come on into the kitchen. I'll put the kettle on,' Bernie instructed.

'Them fellers wanted ter send us ter one of them rest centres but they're nothin' but the street with a roof on, so I said no, I've got family out here; we'd come ter youse.'

Claire cast her eyes to the ceiling and went back to bed. She'd leave Bernie to deal with Nellie.

Bernie became businesslike as she made tea. Claire would just have to move in with either themselves or Molly and Joe. How she was going to fit Nellie, Matty and six kids into the parlour she didn't know but she couldn't turn them out. With any luck, they'd be rehoused, but until then she'd have to put them up. They were family, after all.

'Molly, will you go and tell Madam in there in the parlour that she'll have to sleep on the floor in our room.'

'You've got the baby. She can come in with Joe and me,' Molly offered. It was going to be very cramped but there was no choice. Nellie and Matty had given them a home when they'd first come to Liverpool and they were Bernie's cousins.

'I don't care iffen we all has ter sleep on the floor, luv, just as long as we've somewhere decent ter lay our heads.'

'You drink this up, Nellie. You must be destroyed,' Bernie soothed.

'In the morning we'll sort out some proper beds. It might only be mattresses on the floor but it will be better than just the floor,' Molly said, handing cups to the kids who were all clustered around their distraught mother. 'And we'll sort out clothes and new ration books and identity cards.'

'I've got them in me handbag. I always take them ter the shelter cos it's murder gettin' sorted out with new ones, so I heard.' Nellie indicated the large and very battered handbag on her arm, which she guarded with her life.

'Well, that's something. Are you lot hungry?' Molly asked.

Nellie's brood all nodded and looked at her expectantly. They were always hungry.

Bernie brought a cake of soda bread from the pantry and began to cut it up. It was going to be a dreadful crush and by the looks of them Nellie's kids all needed a good bath. They probably all had nits and lice too, despite Nellie's constant war on the vermin that infested those houses. Feeding them all would be no easy matter either.

'Ah, well, Nellie, look on the bright side. Those houses should have been demolished years ago,' Molly said, smiling and trying to lift the atmosphere.

'Yer're right there, Molly. Well, I suppose I've somethin' ter thank the bloody Nazis fer.'

'And I can tell the flaming billeting officer that I've more than got a house full now!' Bernie grinned. 'He won't be after trying to fill the place with strangers – haven't I got my own relations to look after first?'

Chapter Twenty-Five

CLAIRE WASN'T IN THE least bit amused by the arrival of her cousins. She had been dragged from a warm, comfortable bed and had had to try to sleep for the few remaining hours on the floor in Molly and Joe's room, even though Joe had said she should sleep in the bed with Molly. He'd been so exhausted that she had vehemently refused. It had been crowded enough before but she didn't mind Molly and Joe; at least they were what she called 'civilised'. Her relatives were, in her opinion, far from that. And, unlike Bernie, she owed them no debt of gratitude. The kids were noisy and unruly; Nellie she thought was lazy and slovenly; and Bernie had warned her that they probably all had nits and worse. And added to that, all the kids stank! She didn't know how Molly, Bernie, Joe or Bertie seemed able to ignore all this. They'd all come from homes that were clean. She was quite thankful to escape to her work but she certainly wasn't looking forward to returning home that evening.

Bernie was very thankful that both the water and the electricity supply had been reconnected, thanks to the heroic efforts of the engineers of both departments.

'If we're not to have everyone scratching themselves to bits we've to get those kids deloused as soon as possible. Sure, Nellie does make an effort but half the time I think she cuts corners, and who can blame her?' she whispered to Molly after they had got everyone fed. Both Bertie and Joe had gone to work, as had Matty, after he'd thanked her profusely for taking them all in.

'Sure, didn't you take Molly and meself in when we first came here and aren't you all family?' Bernie had replied.

'I'll go up to the chemist and see what I can get,' Molly hissed back now.

'I'll make sure there's plenty of hot water.'

'I'd better go along to the Relief Office too, and see what I can get in the way of clothes for them. There's no use in getting them all scrubbed clean if they've only the rags to put back on them,' Molly said practically.

'Will you see what you can get for Nellie herself? There's nothing you or I have that will fit her.'

'I will and I'll see what can be done in the way of bedding for them.'

'And will you ask if they have any rubber sheets? At least two of them wet the bed and the place will stink to high heaven in no time,' Bernie said grimly.

Molly raised her eyes to the ceiling and grimaced. 'Let's hope they can rehouse them soon or they'll have your home destroyed altogether.'

'Sure, they're not used to a decent home and what with bombs falling on them is it any wonder they wet the bed – or my parlour carpet in this case. I'll have to get Bertie to throw it in the yard this evening and give it a good wash down with Jeyes Fluid.'

'I'd get Matty to give him a hand. They're his kids!' Molly advised.

Nellie decided to accompany Molly for, as she said, she'd have to give her former address to the people in the Relief Office before they'd get anything.

'Right then, you lot, if you're going to stay with me while your mam goes and sorts things out you can give me a hand with the chores,' Bernie informed Nellie's kids, who looked at her with something akin to horror.

'Me mam never has me scrubbin' an' cleanin'!' Lizzie complained.

'Well, maybe she should and then she wouldn't be so tired! Aren't you a fine strong girl and won't you have a home of your own one day and you'll need to know how to keep it,' Bernie replied determinedly, handing the girl a bar of carbolic soap, a scrubbing brush and a bucket.

When Molly and Nellie returned, weighed down with brown paper bags and parcels, the place looked decidedly cleaner and tidier than it had when they'd left.

'Right, before we sort out these clothes for you, you're

all to have a bath and your hair washed,' Bernie announced.

There were cries of dismay and outrage but she ignored them all. 'There's no point at all putting these clean things on you and you all still covered in the dust and dirt of last night's trek down here. Nellie, will you give me a hand?' she finished pointedly. Nellie was intent on trying on the clothes she had been given, which, as she'd said to Molly on the way home, were far better than anything she'd had before she was bombed out.

'And I'll take charge of the hair washing and the Derbac combing,' Molly said, just as determinedly.

Nellie reluctantly put down the dress she had been holding up to herself with admiration and helped Bernie shepherd the two youngest of her brood to the bathroom.

'Holy Mother of God! What have you on them at all, Nellie?' Bernie asked in astonishment as she stripped off Maureen's faded and dirty cotton dress, revealing an unbelievably filthy liberty bodice.

'We always sew them inter what underclothes they have, fer the winter, like,' Nellie answered matter-of-factly.

Bernie was horrified. 'You never take them off them for the whole winter? And isn't it now nearly summer?'

'It's that cold in them houses that yer'd freeze ter death in winter an' I was goin' ter take them offen them but what with all this bombin' I fergot. We always did that with the kids' clothes in winter.'

'Well, now the weather is much warmer they can all have a bath on a Saturday night.'

'Every Saturday night?' Nellie asked in amazement.

'Every Saturday and then won't they all be nice and fresh for Mass on Sunday,' Bernie answered brightly.

When Bertie, Joe and Claire arrived home that evening they were all greatly relieved to see six extremely clean and tidy children seated around the kitchen table. Even Nellie looked much smarter than Claire had ever seen her look before. What Matty's views on the matter were were anyone's guess as, apart from 'Well, isn't that a grand sight!' uttered as he'd come in the door, there had been no comment on the transformation of his wife and family.

'We've managed to get some mattresses. A man from the Relief Office brought them this afternoon, and we've made them up with the bedding so everyone should get a better night's sleep tonight,' Bernie informed Bertie.

'Did you get anything for me? I'm worn out and don't forget I have to go fire-watching,' Claire asked pointedly.

'I did so and I've made it up in Molly's room,' Bernie answered. 'And let's hope we won't be called out again tonight.'

Molly looked anxiously at Joe. 'Do you think we will?'

'The sky's clear, there's no cloud at all and there'll be a full moon later.'

'Perfect! Just bloody perfect for them!' Bertie said bitterly.

Joe nodded. He'd thought the same thing himself but hadn't voiced his fear.

'Then we'd better get all the stuff ready that we'll need in the shelter,' Bernie said, her mind on the meal she was preparing for the adults. There were just too many of them to sit down at the table together.

'You mean "they'll" need. We'll be called out,' Molly reminded her.

'I'll go fire-watching with Claire. I'm sure Nellie won't mind keeping her eye on Albie, will you? You've more than enough experience in that field, Nellie.' Bertie laughed.

'I'll come with yer,' Matty stated.

'Wouldn't we all be better off goin' ter the public shelter? Them Anderson shelters don't look very safe ter me,' Nellie said, looking rather anxious.

'You will not! Aren't they just as safe? Won't you all be grand,' Bernie said emphatically. She wasn't having Albie dragged all the way to the nearest public shelter and passed from pillar to post, not when they had a perfectly safe shelter in their own back yard. 'But please God no one will have to go to *any* kind of shelter tonight,' she added fervently.

Nellie, with Bernie's help, had got the kids to bed at half past eight. Bernie had marched them all to the toilet and had instructed them that if they needed to go again they were to do so. They were beginning to view her with a mixture of fear, rebellion and some respect.

'Yer won't have no trouble with that lad of yours when he gets older, Bernie,' Nellie said with some admiration after Bernie had successfully dealt with a fight between Lizzie and Franny.

'I wouldn't be too sure of that, Nellie. Isn't it always easier to sort out other people's kids than your own? And won't it be a while yet before I have any "sorting out" to do?' Bernie replied.

After Matty, Bertie and Claire had gone out Molly urged Joe to go and try to get an hour's rest.

'There's a bit of peace in the house now and we're going to take up the hems of some of the clothes we got today. They're a bit too long for Maureen and Patricia but it was the best they could do.'

'An' beggars can't be choosers,' Nellie added. 'I was never much of a one with the sewin' meself,' she finished ruefully. She'd always admired Molly's ability to make and alter clothes, let alone her skill at making curtains and things. 'Ah, God! I was just thinkin' of them lovely curtains yer made me, Molly. I was the envy of the entire neighbourhood and I was always bein' asked ter loan them out when anyone had a daughter gettin' married. I'll never have another pair like them,' she finished sadly.

Molly smiled at her. 'You will, Nellie. When this is all over and they give us both new houses, I'll make you another pair, I promise.'

Nellie smiled back. 'I'll hold yer ter that, Molly.'

Bernie, who could manage hems and buttons and straight seams, helped Molly out. They had decided to try to 'dress up' one of the outfits that Nellie had been given with a new collar and cuffs, made from some white piqué that had come from an old blouse of Bernie's that had been unpicked and made into a romper suit for Albie.

'It will really make that navy two-piece look smart, Nellie. You can wear it for Mass,' Molly enthused.

'And Claire was showing me how to tie a broad strip of material into a turban. Sure, she has to wear one in the factory but she says the women are making them out of any kind of fancy bit of material they can get hold of, and sewing sequins and all kind of things on them and using them for going out,' Bernie added.

'I had some lovely hats,' Molly said wistfully.

'I did myself and now look what we're reduced to,' Bernie added.

'The only decent hat I ever had was the one I was married in so I'll be dead glad ter wear a fancy turban,' Nellie remarked.

'I wish Bertie would take things a bit easier. His leg is still giving him trouble and he's on his feet all day.' Bernie was anxious about her husband, who, although he said little about it, she knew was often in a lot of pain.

'I suppose he feels as though he's not doing enough if he's sitting at home when Claire is out fire-watching after she's been working all day,' Molly said sympathetically.

'That lad has done his fair share, Bernie. All them months on them convoys. Out in all weathers an' then bein' torpedoed an' in an open boat fer all them hours,' Nellie reminded her.

'I know but try and tell him that.'

'I've never known Matty work so hard! Iffen he'd have had this much work on the docks years ago we'd have been out of Hopwood Street an' in a decent house an' I'd have been able ter put a decent meal on the table every day an' have a home like this yer've got here, Bernie. *Iffen* he'd have stayed out of the pub! Well, now he's got money in his pocket an' the pubs have no ale!' Nellie finished, laughing. 'Have yer heard from yer mam, Molly?' she asked to change the subject.

'She writes regularly. The boys are just grand. She says they've grown so much I'd hardly recognise them.'

'That'll be because they're getting good food an' plenty of it an' all that good clean country air,' Nellie said.

'They'll be four this month and God knows what I'll find to send them for their birthday. It won't look anything beside what she says Da is going to get for them.'

'What's that, luv?' Nellie asked.

'A pony of their own, no less! Sure, he was always the one giving out about animals having to earn their keep and now he's after buying them a pony that will spend its days doing nothing but getting fat! They have them spoiled. Mam is always taking them on outings to Tullamore and Birr and even Athlone. She never took us, unless it was to visit family.'

'Grannies always spoil kids,' Nellie agreed.

'When all this is over I intend to take Albie to see his granny. Sure, he's the only grandchild she'll see, God help her. The rest of them are half a world away and isn't Katie in Australia,' Bernie said.

'Isn't she the one that went to be a nun?' Nellie asked.

'She is so. I can hardly remember what she looks like. Sister Assumpta she is now. Mam is so proud of her even though she hardly ever hears from her.'

Nellie shook her head. 'Isn't it shockin' how they all had ter leave.'

'It is. Well, thanks be to God, I won't have to wave Albie off one day,' Bernie said.

'Nellie, you remember the Great War, don't you? How long did it go on for?' Molly asked, tacking the new collar to the navy jacket.

'Four years, Molly, an' I lost me eldest brother. He lied about his age. Sixteen he was an' he was killed on the Somme. Me poor mam never got over it. They gave her a fancy brass plate, all engraved, like, with his name. She polished it every week until she died. She gave it ter our Eddie an' he went an' lost it! I'll never fergive him fer that!' Nellie finished venomously.

Bernie and Molly exchanged glances. This war had been going on for more than a year and a half already. How many more long, arduous, terrifying years had they yet to face?

Chapter Twenty-Six

THE SEWING HAD BEEN put away and Bernie had made them all a cup of cocoa.

'Claire and Bertie should be in soon and then I'll . . .' Bernie's words died.

'Oh, Mary, Mother of God! Just when we was gettin' settled!' Nellie cried heatedly as the so-familiar sound came to their ears.

Molly went to wake Joe while Bernie ran to get Albie from his cot. Nellie had already started to wake her kids.

'Take good care of him and stay in the shelter until it's all over!' Bernie instructed Nellie as she shoved her baby into the older woman's arms.

By the time they reached the depot they could see the glow in the sky.

'It's the city centre. Joe's patch,' Molly said.

'And Nellie's old neighbourhood,' Bernie added.

'You're to go and help out downtown,' Charlie Dixon informed them.

'But we don't really know that area well, not in a blackout.' Bernie was perturbed.

'You'll manage. There are enough bloody searchlights and fires and ack-ack shells exploding to help you! Off you go! Report to the Royal in Pembroke Place.'

The nearer to the city centre they drew, the worse it became. Molly stared straight ahead of her, her eyes fixed on the road. She somehow managed to blot out the chaos and destruction that surrounded them. She had to concentrate hard; she *had* to, she told herself.

Bernie swerved sharply as the side of a burning building began to collapse into the road and Molly was flung hard against the door of the vehicle.

'Sorry, Moll!' Bernie yelled over the cacophony of noise.

'I'm just fine, Bernie,' Molly assured her.

'Oh, Jesus!' Bernie's voice was shrill with fear as she dragged the wheel as hard as she could to the left. A row of shops to their right suddenly exploded into a shower of bricks, cement particles and thousands of shards of glass. The blast almost overturned the vehicle and Bernie fought hard to keep control while Molly, white-faced, hung on for dear life.

'That was a close one, Bernie,' Molly cried as the ambulance came to a halt.

Bernie was trembling with shock and the sheer physical

effort of controlling the vehicle. 'Do we go on or do we go back, Moll?'

'We'd better go on. If . . . if it's this bad here, what is it going to be like in town?'

Bernie nodded. If they'd been just a few feet further ahead they would have caught the full force of the explosion. You couldn't think about it. You just *couldn't*! She put the vehicle into gear and they moved off slowly.

It was hard to know just exactly where they were, Molly thought. Streets and roads that had been so familiar were now transformed. Nothing looked the same at all. Bernie had to make a detour around a burning tram that was lying on its side, blocking almost the entire roadway. The tram lines in front of it were twisted up like a giant corkscrew. Molly began to pray, not just for Joe but also for everyone she knew. She was certain that only with the help of God would they survive this night.

When they reached the hospital there was no time to think, no time to pray. For four hours they worked frantically, ferrying casualties, the living and the dead, from the mountains of rubble to the hospitals. Around them thousands of incendiaries and high-explosive bombs fell, demolishing the city centre landmarks. There was no time even for fear.

They were both exhausted to the point of collapse as they finally drove back to Walton in silence. Beneath their tin hats their hair was stuck to their scalps with sweat. Their faces were streaked with dirt and tears for the sights they'd witnessed. Their cheeks were seared from the heat and flames of burning buildings. Their coats were caked in dust and soot and blood.

As they reached the top of Breeze Hill Molly screamed and she wrenched the steering wheel away from her friend, dragging on it with all her strength. 'STOP! BERNIE, STOP!'

Bernie slammed her foot on the brake pedal and they were both thrown forward as the ambulance swerved and slid to a halt.

'Jesus, Mary and Joseph! What's the matter with you, Moll?' Bernie yelled, peered ahead of her into the blacked-out roadway.

'We'd . . . we'd better get out, Bernie,' Molly replied, shakily.

Gingerly they both climbed out and Bernie's eyes widened in horror and she grabbed Molly and clung to her. A mere foot away from them was a gaping crater sixty feet wide.

'A parachute mine! Only one of those things makes a hole this big! Oh, Moll! If . . . if . . . we'd driven into *that* . . .' Bernie couldn't go on. She was transfixed by the yawning chasm of black charred earth at their feet.

Molly was shaking. All the night's experiences were as nothing compared to this. 'We'd have been killed, Bernie. We wouldn't have stood a chance.' Suddenly she felt angry and terrified at the same time. 'How did we end up in the middle of all this, Bernie? They're not going to stop until they've bombed every building to bits and killed everyone – one way or another!'

Bernie was trying to pull herself together. 'It can't go on, Molly. It just can't. They'll have to send us help. They'll have to send every plane they've got to destroy those . . . those . . . fiends from hell! How many dead children – babies – did we take to the mortuary tonight? What kind of people kill helpless children in their own homes? But sure, wasn't the Blessed Virgin watching over us tonight? Didn't she let you see *this* in time? Come on, Molly, let's get home. They're bound to be worried about us. The all-clear went ages ago.'

Molly nodded. She didn't know where Bernie got her strength from but she was glad her friend could keep calm and rational. She knew that she herself wasn't far from the brink of what her mam called a nervous collapse.

They were too exhausted to do little more than drink the tea Nellie made for them and wash off the worst of the dirt.

'Dear God, the last war was bad enough but at least we wasn't killed in our own homes an' girls an' women didn't have ter go out an' risk getting blown ter bits or have their necks broke drivin' inter bomb craters!' Nellie said, shaking her head. She'd spent a terrifying night, the only adult in the shelter with all the kids. There had been no one else to try to keep her spirits up or share her fears and no way of knowing if any of them would come back to her.

Bertie and Joe exchanged worried glances but there was

nothing they could say. Ambulance crews were vital if they were all going to survive this terror that flew by night.

They were all heavy-eyed and weary next morning but Matty tried to look on the bright side.

'Sure, isn't it Saturday? Claire has the afternoon off and it's fine and dry: will we all go off to the park for an hour or two?'

'Yer can take the kids out from under our feet fer an hour or two, Matty. We'll try an' get some washin' done, when the water's back on. Everythin' is flamin' filthy an' a fine mess we'll look at Mass in the mornin',' Nellie replied, grimly holding her wriggling daughter while she plaited the child's hair.

'And I'm going to try to summon up enough energy to do a bit of baking. There's flour and dried egg powder and some lard,' Bernie added.

'Any carrots?' Bertie asked.

'Carrots?'

He grinned. 'Cherry cake!'

She managed a tired smile. 'Sorry, no cherry cake today.'

'Da, can we take the cassie ter the park?' Franny asked hopefully. His prize possession was an old and battered football which he'd clung to and carted everywhere with him, despite protests from his long-suffering mother.

'Ah, go on with you. Kick the ball around. Have a bit of fun, there's not been much of that lately,' Bernie urged.

'At least there's no flamin' windows ter break these days.

The bloody bombs have seen ter that,' Nellie commented acerbically.

Bertie entered into the spirit of things. 'Put Albie in his pram and I'll go with them. The fresh air will do us all good. Do you feel up to a bit of a game of footie, Joe?'

Joe laughed but shook his head. 'I'd like to but I've got to get back. There's still so much to do.'

'But aren't you dead on your feet? You haven't even had a change of clothes!' Molly protested.

'Maybe I'll get a few hours tomorrow.'

She nodded. No one wanted to voice the fear that was in all their minds. That the Luftwaffe would come again tonight.

Peter tugged petulantly at Ita's skirt. 'Granny, when will Granda be back? He's been gone a long, long time.'

She sighed. He was an impatient child. 'Ah, he'll be along any minute now. Why don't the pair of you go down to the yard gate and wait for him there. But don't be going beyond the gate now,' she warned. She was always fearful of the close proximity of the canal lock and its dangers.

Reluctantly the boys went out into the yard and Ita resumed her baking.

'Sure, I wish your da hadn't told them he was going to Ballycumber Fair today to see your man about a pony for them. I warned him we'd have no peace at all.'

'Is he bringing it home with him?' Maria enquired, smiling as the two little figures disappeared from sight.

'Sure, there'll be tantrums if he doesn't.'

'Well, then there will have to be tantrums and he can deal with them, for he said he'd have Himself drive it over in time for the birthday.'

Maria sighed. 'Sure, I know it's not for another ten days, but there was never all this fuss over birthdays when we were young. A cake, no less, and with candles!' She picked up the little packet of coloured wax candles that her mother had somehow managed to wheedle out of Mrs Flannagan in the stationery shop in town. They were almost as precious as tea and sugar and had come from America. How much her mother had paid for them, she didn't know.

'Ah, you have to make a bit of a fuss of them. No mammy or da here to mark the day that's in it, bless them!'

Maria nodded. 'Did you see what Mr O'Sullivan has for them?'

'I did so. Tess showed it to me last week. Didn't she say he never made such a fuss of his own? Hours and hours, she said he's spent whittling away. And would you ever have believed that he could make anything like that?' Ita had been astounded when Tess had shown her the model of a tractor Dessie had made from a solid block of wood he'd picked up. It was perfect in every way and really much too good to have to withstand the treatment her grandsons would subject it to.

Maria sighed. 'Joe made them a train for Christmas. He spent hours on it too but wasn't it lost when the house was bombed?'

They both looked up on hearing a slight commotion in the yard.

'There's your da home now. Put on the kettle, Maria.'

Paddy came in, a grandson perched on each shoulder. 'Now, I've told them that "Catch" Wheelan will be over with the little pony first thing on Monday morning so there's to be no tears and no pusses! Won't they both be busy getting a stable ready for it in that little shed at the back of the dairy.'

Ita was thankful that Paddy had managed to divert their attention. 'Now, let your granda have his tea in peace.'

Maria furnished them with brushes and they went off to sweep out the shed.

Paddy watched them go in sombre silence.

'What is it? Did you not get the pony?' Ita asked, perturbed by his change of mood.

'I did so but I heard some news too and it's not good.'

'What?' Ita demanded.

'Liverpool has been bombed hard these past two nights. There's terrible damage and awful casualties. I heard there were three hundred planes and didn't it go on for hours and hours?'

Ita crossed herself. 'Maria, get your coat and hat. We're going up to the church. Oh, I pray to God those two little boys still have a mammy and a da! When will we know, Paddy? When will we know they're safe?'

He shook his head. 'Who knows, Ita? Who knows?'

Chapter Twenty-Seven

FOR THE BATTERED AND weary city there was to be no respite. From half past ten on Saturday night to five o'clock on Sunday morning five hundred Nazi bombers reduced it to a wasteland of rubble.

Lewis's, Kelly's and Blackler's were destroyed, along with their entire contents, due to fractured water mains, which rendered the fire crews helpless to do anything but stand and watch them burn. The Central Lending Library, the Music Library, the Reference Library, the Museum, the Walker Art Gallery and the Technical College were destroyed. Wool and tobacco warehouses in Pall Mall, oil and fat works in Cheapside, the Salvage Headquarters, the General Post Office, the Bank and Telephone Exchanges: all were casualties. The Law Society lost its entire 35,000-volume library with the burning of the Cook Street Arcade. In a swath of destruction that encompassed

Paradise Street, Lord Street, South John Street, South Castle Street, Canning Place and Hanover Street not a building remained standing. Mill Road Infirmary received a direct hit, killing fourteen ambulance drivers and thirty patients outright. The city's schools and churches had been decimated and after a night of unmitigated terror the citizens emerged on Sunday morning to view the carnage.

Everyone in Arnot Street had come through the ordeal. Nellie was badly shaken and unusually quiet. The kids were cowed and weepy. The men were grey-faced and haggard with exhaustion and Joe hadn't come home at all. He'd got word to them that he was safe, as were his parents. For as long as they lived Bernie and Molly vowed they would never forget that night. Molly thanked God on her knees at Mass that morning that she had sent her boys to her parents.

It was four o'clock in the afternoon when Joe finally arrived home. He was so filthy that Molly hardly recognised him.

'Take off that uniform and I'll try and get some of the dirt out of it. Have you had anything to eat or drink at all?'

'I had a cup of tea and a sandwich from the WVS canteen wagon about half an hour after the *Malakand* blew up,' he replied, stripping off his tunic.

'I thought the end of the world had come when she went up,' Nellie said quietly.

Joe nodded. The ship had been loaded with a thousand tons of ammunition. Despite frantic efforts to put out the fire, she'd blown up, taking the whole of the No. 2 Huskisson Dock with her and causing the biggest explosion of the entire night.

'They're sending fire brigades from thirty towns in Lancashire, Cheshire and North Wales to help out. Troops are being drafted in to help clear the rubble and demolish unsafe buildings. We just can't cope on our own. Sixteen planes were shot down but if it had been sixty it wouldn't have helped much. Nearly every road is blocked with rubble and covered with broken glass. There's a pall of smoke hanging over the whole place and there's millions of bits of charred paper blowing everywhere. It's like a black blizzard.'

'And they'll come back again tonight, to try to finish us off,' Bertie said grimly.

Joe nodded. It was useless to try to pretend it wouldn't happen and he was too tired, too heart-sore even to try.

Molly leaned her head against his shoulder. How much more could they take? Even now explosions were still rocking the city as the *Malakand* blew herself out.

As midnight approached they all dared to hope that the ordeal was over but at a minute to the hour the dreaded moaning of the siren shattered that hope. For another four and a half hours they endured the raid but by the time dawn came they were all just too tired to care that it was the start of another week.

Ita and Paddy heard the news with dread and Tess wrote to Bernie imploring her to come home and bring both her child and her sister with her. They were all relieved when brief telegrams arrived, assuring them everyone was safe, but their relief was short lived when they heard that for the fifth consecutive night the city was bombed.

It was more and more difficult for both Claire and Bertie to get to work but it became a matter of honour to make that effort. During the day the three women tried as best they could to carry on the routine chores but with supplies of everything severely disrupted, to say nothing of shops that were now reduced to rubble, it was almost impossible. Claire was one of hundreds of women who mourned the loss of a consignment of silk stockings that had gone up in flames when Blackler's had been burned out.

'Wait until I write and tell Mam that Lewis's is destroyed entirely. She always said it was a lovely shop and she still has that lilac outfit,' Molly said to Bernie.

'Ah, sure, won't the censor cut out all those bits,' Bernie answered wearily. 'Oh, what are we going to give everyone for their tea, Molly? Aren't I sick and tired of there being nothing decent to put on the table.'

'Will I try and ask Mam to send us a bit of something, if I can word it so the fecking censor doesn't cut it out?'

'I just daren't *think* of that piece of pork! I'd break down and cry, so I would!'

'I don't think I'll ever get Joe's shirts clean again. He's not had this one off his back for days, and there's no water to wash it in!'

'We none of us have had the clothes off our back for days, Moll! Now it's just a matter of "getting through the next night". I've even stopped asking when it will end. Most of the time I'm just too tired to care.'

'I know and they'll be back again tonight. It's just a matter of what time and will we get the meal over first? At least Joe's getting a change of scenery: they've moved him to the Brunswick Dock area. Not that it's any easier, or so he tells me, and it's even further for him to get home. Wouldn't you think they'd have a bit more consideration? But no, aren't they desperate for someone with more experience down that end of the docks.'

Bernie nodded. Who could fathom the workings of the minds of the powers that be? Who could fathom the workings of anyone's mind these days?

Again it was midnight when the siren went and they all dragged themselves once more to the shelter, to their fire-watching duties, to the ambulance depot. Joe had already gone on duty at ten.

Cooper's Building in Church Street was hit. High-explosive bombs fell on Moorfields, Seel Street, St James's Street, George's Pier Head and the Landing Stage.

Joe was new to the Brunswick Dock area although he was familiar with its layout, having been seconded to the docks police before the war. When the rain of high-explosive bombs, followed by the inevitable incendiaries, started to fall he worked alongside the fire-watchers until the brigade arrived.

'Jackson, will you get down to the North-East Brunswick? The yard down there has received two direct hits and there's barges on fire that could cause serious problems for other vessels,' the superintendent in charge instructed.

Joe nodded and left, running quickly down the dockside between the cargo sheds. It wasn't too bad as yet down here, he thought, but if those fires couldn't be brought under control quickly it would be. Any fire acted as a beacon for the planes that were droning overhead. At least the anti-aircraft gunners were getting far better in their aim, but then he supposed they'd had plenty of practice these last five nights.

When he reached the barges he could see they were well alight. Damn! He'd need more than the puny stirrup pump he'd snatched up before he'd left. There were emergency hoses situated in the cargo sheds, which in happier times had contained grain, which was always prone to combustion. An older police constable joined him together with four other men who'd been assigned fire-watching duties at the dock.

'Give me a hand to unroll this hose and hook it up to the hydrant. The brigade will be on its way but if we don't get this lot under control they'll blow the whole damn dock up!' he warned.

The small party divided into two and tackled both fires until, almost half an hour later, the brigade arrived.

'What kept you?' the older policeman asked irritably. Like everyone else he was almost out on his feet.

'What do you think? What usually keeps us? Miles of bloody tangled-up wires and pipes and tram lines and bloody great craters in the road!' snapped an equally exhausted fireman who the night before had seen a blazing warehouse roof collapse on three of his colleagues.

'Let's save our energies for the fire and our tempers for the bloody Nazis!' Joe intervened.

'Come on with me, Sarge. The police hut is just across the road; these lads should be able to deal with this now. I've a drop of something that will put a bit of heart into us.'

'Drinking on duty? You know damn well you'll get kicked out,' Joe warned, but his grin belied his words.

'What harm is there in a nip? Don't we need it after what we've all been through? And they call this a Reserved Occupation? There's nothing bloody "reserved" about it and I've only got two years to do before I go on pension. I was looking forward to putting my feet up!'

'You haven't got a bit of tea over there by any chance?' Joe asked. It was one thing for him to turn a blind eye to 'a nip', quite another to partake of the same himself.

'Might have,' came the guarded reply.

The police hut was just that: a small brick building containing a single room that served as an office.

'I take it this is your usual haunt?' Joe stated, looking around.

Tom Hudson lit a cigarette and offered Joe one. Joe shook his head. 'Never use them, thanks.'

'A feller I know slips me the odd packet.'

It had always been one of the perks of the dock police so Joe just nodded and busied himself with searching the various tins on a shelf on one wall for the tea. After a few minutes he gave up.

'Ah, well, there's no time to try to boil up that kettle, even if by a miracle there's gas for the ring. Come on, we'd better get back to it.'

'There's no rush, Sarge!' Hudson protested.

'There is. The super will have my guts for garters if he finds out I've been idling down here while pandemonium reigns back there.'

Reluctantly the older man shoved the small bottle back in the desk drawer and locked it, pocketing the key.

Outside the raid was still raging and the sky was criss-crossed with the beams of searchlights and bright with bursting shells.

'I wish the buggers would pack it in!' Hudson said with venom as he hastened his steps.

Joe looked up as he heard the eerie whistling and saw what he knew to be an oil bomb descending rapidly. He shoved Hudson hard and heard him yell out in surprise and pain. He looked up again and his cry came from a throat constricted with terror. 'Oh, God! Molly!'

Hudson was dazed and bruised and he knew his arm was shattered, but he managed to crawl back to where the police hut had been. Beside a few fragments of wood from its door lay Joe's helmet.

*

It was almost dawn before Molly and Bernie got home. Nellie was waiting in the lobby for them.

'I thought you'd have been trying to get the kids back down to sleep,' Bernie said wearily.

Nellie jerked her head in the direction of the kitchen and looked fearfully at Bernie.

'What's wrong?' Bernie demanded.

'There's . . . there's a police superintendent here ter see . . . Molly.'

Bernie stared at her hard and then she heard Molly's scream and, turning, she flung her arms around her friend.

'He . . . he's . . . dead, Bernie!' Nellie sobbed, unable to contain her shock and grief any longer.

Molly crumpled in Bernie's arms. 'NO! Oh, Bernie! No! Not my Joe! Not my Joe!'

Chapter Twenty-Eight

SUPERINTENDENT MITFORD WAS JUST as exhausted as all his men but he tried his best to be alert and sympathetic as he described to an ashen and shaking Molly just how Joe had been killed.

It was Bertie who showed him out.

'A damn shame! He was a fine man and a fine officer. It's thanks to him that Constable Hudson is still alive.'

Bertie nodded. 'He'll be missed by a lot of people.'

When he went back inside he found Nellie and Claire sitting at the kitchen table. Nellie had her head in her hands, the tears trickling through her fingers. Claire was shaking her head in disbelief; she couldn't take it in. She had seen death all around her for days, but this was different. This was *Joe*!

Molly and Bernie sat on the edge of the bed in Molly's room. A room and a bed she would never again share with her husband. Bernie had her arms around her friend and her cheeks were wet with tears. She would miss him terribly. She knew exactly how Molly felt at this moment. It was the way she had felt twelve years ago. She searched her memory for something, anything that she could say or do that would help Molly. She had gone to Nellie's the day Jimmy had drowned and someone had gone to the dispensary for something to calm her down but she couldn't even do that for Molly. The dispensary was a burned-out shell; there was no laudanum to give her. Molly was shaking and Bernie pulled the blanket around her shoulders.

'Cry, Molly, cry. It will help, a bit.'

Molly shook her head. She couldn't cry. Her heart felt as though it was bursting with shock and grief but tears wouldn't come.

'Everything is going to be . . . unreal for a while, Moll, believe me. You'll feel that it's all a bad dream, that you'll wake up and he'll be here. I'm not going to say anything about "time". It's not what you want to hear right now. Later . . . maybe.'

'I . . . I . . . never even kissed him goodbye last night. Oh, Bernie, was it only *last night*? It . . . it feels like *for ever*!'

'It's the shock.' Bernie raged inwardly that she couldn't even give her friend a cup of hot sweet tea. There was no water and no gas or electricity.

'When . . . will they bring him . . . home?' Molly's mind was numb.

'I don't know. Bertie will see to all the arrangements. You're not even to try to think about anything like that.' Bernie knew she had to prevent Molly from seeing Joe. His superior had told them he'd been badly mutilated but obviously that hadn't registered in Molly's dazed mind yet. Bernie was glad. She'd make sure the coffin was closed.

Molly was trying to think straight but her mind was playing tricks on her. He'd have to have a decent funeral but where was she to get flowers and a headstone? Did his mother know? Had someone told Effie and Fred yet? What was happening to her? She was cold, so very cold. Icy fingers were clutching at her heart and yet warm sunlight streamed in through the window. Why weren't the blackout curtains pulled across? But no, it was daylight. It was a new day but there was the clearing up to be done. Joe always said it was the aftermath that wore you down but Joe always did his share of the clearing up. Suddenly and with a terrible clarity she realised that he wasn't coming home today. He was never coming home again. She would never see him or hear his voice again. He was dead!

Great gulping sobs shook her as she clung to her friend. 'Bernie? Oh, Bernie, he's dead! He's DEAD!'

'I know, Moll. God help us, I know,' Bernie choked.

It was an hour later when Bernie came downstairs. She'd left Molly sobbing quietly but she was calmer. The hysteria had gone and she was lying down. There was nothing Bernie could do for her now; Molly had to cry. Later there would be time to talk, to soothe, and to try to sow the seeds of hope.

'How is she, luv?' Nellie asked, wiping her eyes with the corner of her apron.

'Just as you would expect her to be. She's crying but that's good and she's so exhausted that maybe she'll sleep.'

Nellie nodded. She, too, was remembering the day Bernie had come to her in a similar state to poor Molly. 'It'll be hard fer her but in time, well . . . just look at yerself.'

'I know, but I was so much younger and Jimmy and I had been married for such a short time.'

'I've managed ter get a decent bit of fire goin'. Will I boil the kettle on it?'

Bernie nodded. 'Has Bertie gone to work?'

'Aye, and Claire. They're both shook up but, well, yer know how it is. They've got ter keep goin' fer the war effort. Yer won't be goin' down ter the depot later, will yer?' Nellie didn't feel up to dealing with the kids and a devastated Molly on her own.

'No. They'll have to do without us for a while. They'll understand. I'll get word to them.'

'How are we goin' ter cope ternight if those buggers come again?'

'We'll just have to sit it out in the shelter, Nellie. There's nothing else we can do.'

'Maybe, just maybe they'll give us a rest,' Nellie said hopefully.

But they didn't. The siren sounded at midnight and only seconds later the distinct sound of the first wave of bombers could be clearly heard.

Bernie hugged her husband tightly before he left and then, passing Albie to Nellie, she guided a still-dazed Molly to the shelter.

Soon the fires blazed from Seaforth to the Huskisson Dock. It was the seventh consecutive night the city had been bombed.

Nellie sat on the wooden bench with her kids clustered around her, her rosary beads clenched tightly in her hand. Bernie held a quietly sobbing Molly and prayed that both her husband and her sister would come through this night safely. She was beset with worry for them all and for Molly. If this continued how would Molly cope? It was bad enough to have to grieve when there was calm and quiet in which to do so, but to have to try and pick up the pieces of your life in *this* . . .

Molly's thoughts were running on the same lines. Her heart ached for him. So many memories came crowding into her mind only to be obliterated by the explosions that shook the shelter and the terrified cries of Nellie's kids. She wanted her own children. She wanted to see them, hold them. Oh, they were so like Joe. And she wanted some peace. She wanted a place where she could cry out her anguish without the sounds of hell battering her ears. She wanted to go home, to Ita and to her sons.

*

Two weeks later Bernie stood with her on the bomb-scarred Landing Stage. Behind them was a backdrop of a city in ruins but the last heavy raid had been on the eighth of May and the clear-up had begun.

Bertie guided them towards the ferry. He was sorry to see Molly go but he could understand. She needed time and peace and her sons. Bernie was going with her, just for a few days: the journey would be long and arduous and Molly just wasn't up to it on her own. Besides, it would do Bernie good to get away and it would do Tess as much good to see her grandson. Claire was remaining with them in Arnot Street.

'You've got everything you need for Albie?' he asked.

Bernie nodded. 'Everything I could think of. We'll be just grand, don't worry.'

He kissed his wife and then kissed Molly's cheek.

She managed a weak smile. 'Goodbye. Thanks . . . for everything you've done.'

'Take care, both of you. You'll write, Molly?'

'Soon, I promise.'

She looked for the last time at the city that had been her home for thirteen years. Where she had been married; where she'd had her sons; where she'd been so happy. But it was no longer the city she knew so well. It had been changed beyond recognition – and so had she. Her home had gone; her husband and her heart lay buried in the churchyard of St Francis de Salles and she was going back to Ireland, to her sons – forever.

Bernie put her arm around her friend. 'Come on, Moll, let's go and get a seat,' she urged. She was torn with emotions. She wanted so much to see her parents and she too needed a bit of tranquillity, but Molly wasn't coming back and it was the first time they would really be parted since childhood. Molly was her dearest friend and they had been through so much together. It would break her heart to leave Molly behind when the time came for her to return, but as her friend had said there was nothing left for Molly here. No husband, no family, no home, no children. Whatever kind of a future lay ahead, it was in Ireland. She had been adamant that Joe's sons would grow up never knowing the terrors of a war that had robbed them of a father.

Bernie turned and waved to Bertie who was still standing watching them and she smiled bravely. She would be back. She would stick out the dark days ahead at her husband's side. This was her home and, after all, only a strip of water would separate her from Molly. One day, when the world had come to its senses, she'd see her friend again. It was a promise she made to herself and it was a promise she was determined to keep. After all, they were friends forever.

Epilogue

1949

MOLLY WALKED IMPATIENTLY UP and down the station platform. It was almost midday and the sun was hot on her back. The trains hadn't got back to normal yet, or that was the excuse the station master had given her as to why the Dublin to Galway 'express' was an hour late. She'd left the trap in the station yard and the pony making inroads into the ornamental shrubs: no doubt Himself back there in the office would be giving out to her about that. She didn't care. Nothing could mar the day for her. Today Bernie, along with Bertie and Albie and Claire and her new husband, was coming for two weeks.

She peered once more along the empty track and then sat down on the little bench in the shade. They'd written once a week, exchanging news and gossip and the occasional snapshot taken on special occasions. Peter and Andrew's First Communion; Albie's second birthday; the celebrations for VE Day and then VJ Day; Claire's engagement; Maria's engagement; and finally Claire's wedding. Maria was due to marry Kevin Corrigan in September but Bernie had said she couldn't wait for that and Claire's honeymoon trip was just the excuse she needed to pay a visit to her parents and her dear friend. Claire and David were going on to Salthill in Galway after a two-day visit to Rahan.

'Would ye restrain that animal? Isn't it destroying the place entirely!' came the annoyed tones of the station master from the office window.

'And what am I supposed to do with the creature? If the trains can't run to time isn't it only to be expected that people and animals get bored and hungry?' she replied.

'It will be here in a few minutes now, Mrs Jackson, so it will. I'm just after hearing that it's left Clara Station,' he announced in more conciliatory tones. After all, hadn't she just opened that fine shop in William Street where you could get curtains and cushions and all manner of fancy things just as good if not better than anything to be got above in Dublin, or so his wife had told him.

Molly pulled her hat further down to keep the sun off her face and peered down the track. Yes, she could just make out a few puffs of smoke on the horizon. They wouldn't all fit into the trap so she'd arranged for Claire and David to be driven out in the town's taxi. Claire at least was coming home in style. Of course both the boys and

Maria had wanted to come to the station but there just hadn't been room.

At last the train pulled slowly alongside the platform and she walked quickly along the line of carriages but there wasn't any need to go too far. Bernie was leaning out of the door waving madly. Molly broke into a run.

'Bernie! Bernie! I've been waiting for hours!'

'And haven't we been delayed for hours? Ah, sure, nothing changes!' Bernie almost fell out of the carriage and the two women hugged each other.

'You haven't changed a bit! Your hair is shorter, that's all!' Molly exclaimed.

'Neither have you and don't you look smart? Where did you get the material for that dress? Don't tell me Cleary's are selling stuff like that now – it's better than anything I can get my hands on.' Bernie was openly envious of Molly's jade-green silk two-piece.

'From Boston. Didn't I write and tell you that June, Denis's wife, is proving to be just great at supplying me with all kinds of things? And she's got wonderful taste too.'

'Would she have anything that would suit me?' Claire asked, giving Molly a hug and eyeing Molly's outfit with admiration.

Bernie laughed. 'Isn't she the bold one!'

'Molly, you do look really well!' Bertie greeted her, kissing her on the cheek.

He looked tired and hot and there were strands of grey in his hair, Molly noticed.

'And this is Albie! Haven't you grown into a grand big lad!' Molly bent down and ruffled the child's dark curly hair. He took after Bernie: he had her eyes and her smile too.

'And this is my husband, David,' Claire said proudly.

Molly shook his hand warmly. 'You're very welcome. Right, now I'd better get you all home or Mam, Maria and Tess will eat me, to say nothing of Peter and Andrew and Da and Dessie.'

Claire and David were duly ushered to the taxi and Molly escorted Bernie and her family to the trap.

'You should see the spread Mam has laid on. They've been baking and preparing for days.'

'Ah, real food!' Bernie said dreamily. Things had eased a lot in England but certain things were still on ration.

'And we're all going to the Thatch tonight for a celebration,' Molly added.

Bertie laughed. 'Ah, a drop of decent whiskey!'

Molly joined in. 'Tullamore Dew! Nothing but the best!'

There was a great reunion when they had all arrived back. Tess and Dessie and their remaining children had joined Ita and her family and after much exclaiming over how good it was to be reunited and introduced to new family members, they had all sat down to what Bernie and Claire said was an 'absolute feast' of roast goose with the trimmings, fresh vegetables and home-grown potatoes, followed by apple and blackcurrant pies with cream, and barmbrack and fresh soda bread spread thickly with butter.

Everyone then went out to sit in the side garden in which Ita and Molly had planted not only herbs but also roses, and the twins took Albie to see the two sturdy ponies that had replaced the original occupant of the stable, which they had outgrown.

Molly watched them go with pride. Peter and Andrew were twelve years old now and tall and wiry. Their hair gleamed like burnished copper in the afternoon sun, a contrast to the dark curls of Bernie's son.

'Will he be all right? He won't be falling off and breaking something? I'd hate to come all this way and end up in Tullamore General Hospital having his arm put in plaster the first day we're here.' Bernie sounded anxious.

Molly laughed. 'He'll be just grand: they'll mind him. Won't he be more likely to hurt himself playing on one of those bomb sites you write and tell me you're always dragging him away from?'

Bernie sighed. 'I suppose so.'

'Will we leave them to it and go for a walk?' Molly suggested, jerking her head in the direction of the main party.

'Let me get my hat. That sun is strong.'

They both put on wide-brimmed straw hats before walking out on to the road that ran beside the canal. They crossed the bridge at the lock and walked down in the direction of Pollagh, the next village.

'Oh, I'd forgotten just how quiet and peaceful it is, Moll,' Bernie said a little wistfully.

'I know. I'm always glad to get back after the hustle and bustle of town and now I spend nearly every day in the shop.'

'Is it doing well?'

'It is indeed. I can hardly keep up with demand. Most of my material comes from Boston. Some things I can get in Dublin but not all. The shortages hit us hard here too. I'm having to work to an appointments system and I've had to employ two girls to help me.'

'I'm so glad, Molly. You've worked hard and you've overcome so much.'

Molly nodded. 'It's not been easy. When I first came home it was terrible. Mam helped me so much with the boys. I couldn't have got through it without her. I still miss him, I suppose I always will.' There were still nights when she cried herself to sleep, but not as many now.

Bernie nodded her understanding. 'Then there isn't the chance of anyone else?'

'No. I know everyone in the parish and a lot of people in the area but, well, I don't think anyone can ever take Joe's place. The boys are quite happy; they look on Da as not just their grandfather but as a bit more than that. They don't remember Joe very clearly; they were not even four the last time they saw him.'

'They look like him.'

'They do and sometimes that's a comfort. And Albie looks like you.'

Bernie laughed. 'Poor child!'

'Ah, give over with the "poor child"! You're a very attractive woman.'

'Bertie seems to think so and I suppose that's all that matters.'

'You are happy, Bernie?'

'I am so. I don't even mind that we haven't been blessed with any more children. Oh, the city is still in a mess and things are rather austere but I know they will improve. Even the ferry boat is a bit more comfortable now with decent seats and a bit of a café. I was so glad to see the back of Nellie and the kids. I thought they'd never get rehoused. Three months of Nellie O'Sullivan and her tribe is enough to send any sane person mad! Still, at least she's finally got a decent house in Norris Green and she's delighted with herself.'

'How is Bertie getting on at Jacob's?'

'Just grand. He's a foreman in the warehouse and don't we get free biscuits? Mis-shapes of course but biscuits just the same.'

They'd reached the next lock and Bernie hoisted herself up on the wall that bounded the ruin of a small cabin and farmyard. Molly pulled herself up beside her.

'You'll ruin that dress,' Bernie warned.

'I won't. We've had no rain for over a week now. It's nice and cool here.'

Patches of shade from the trees overhead extended out over the waters of the canal, whose banks were thick with yellow bog iris and water buttercup and tall green rushes.

'Do you remember we sat here all those years ago the day your mam and da agreed to let you come to Liverpool with me?'

Molly laughed. 'And we were so excited thinking we were going to stay with Nellie and Matty in their grand house.'

'We've come a long way from those two excited kids who were going out into the wide world looking for adventure.'

'We found that and we found love and happiness and tragedy and loss.'

'But we stuck together, Moll, through it all.'

Molly reached for her hand. 'We did and no matter that we live in different countries and have different priorities, we'll go on "sticking together" for the rest of our lives.'

'And maybe our sons will grow up in a world without war. Hasn't every mother's son the right to expect that?'

'They have, Bernie, they surely have,' Molly replied.